"Okay, everyone. Time to light the candles."

Ben and Jill joined in as everyone crowded around the menorah. From the candle holder, Jill's father lifted the middle candle, which he would use to light the others. His voice resonant, he recited the traditional blessing. Then he lit four candles, for the fourth night of the festival.

Ben stood watching, his arm around Jill. When the candles were lit, they looked at each other. "I see the glow of the candles in your eyes," he murmured.

Her smile was radiant. "That's how I feel," she said. "Warm and bright."

He wanted to ask her if he'd put those feelings there, or if she always felt that way during Chanukah. He wanted to kiss her right now, here with all the people around them. He wanted to take her home and make love to her....

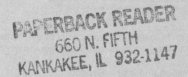

ABOUT THE AUTHOR

"I was delighted to have a chance to share the beauty, symbolism and history of the Chanukah holiday and what it means to a Jewish family," writes Lorna Michaels of *Season of Light,* her third Super-romance novel. "I wanted family relationships to be an important part of the story, and I wanted to use Chanukah, the Festival of Lights, as a backdrop to show how, over the eight-day holiday, the heroine's life becomes brighter as she confronts her past. By the time the eighth candle is lit, Jill is ready to embrace the future." Lorna lives in Texas, but she set her novel in Cincinnati, because "I wanted a setting where the weather would be cold and snowy in December."

Books by Lorna Michaels

HARLEQUIN SUPERROMANCE
412—BLESSING IN DISGUISE
503—A MATTER OF PRIVILEGE

SEASON of LIGHT

Lorna Michaels

Harlequin Books

TORONTO • NEW YORK • LONDON
AMSTERDAM • PARIS • SYDNEY • HAMBURG
STOCKHOLM • ATHENS • TOKYO • MILAN
MADRID • WARSAW • BUDAPEST • AUCKLAND

Published December 1992

ISBN 0-373-70528-X

SEASON OF LIGHT

To my children, Lori and Michael,
who have given me joy and laughter . . .
and a pen name

ACKNOWLEDGMENTS

My special thanks to Michael Krieger, who provided background on advertising, Patty Towbin, who gave me information about Cincinnati, and Heather MacAllister, aka Heather Allison, who served as my earring consultant.

CHAPTER ONE

OF ALL MORNINGS to be late! Jill Levin pulled her coat tighter around her as she hurried through the parking garage. Her hair, always flyaway, whipped around her shoulders in the brisk December wind that whistled through the open building.

Checking her watch, she quickened her steps. Anything that could possibly go wrong this morning, had. The wake-up call to her hotel room had been half an hour late, she'd found a run in her panty hose and service in the coffee shop had been slow enough to set her teeth on edge.

Why today? Her first day in Cincinnati. Her first time to be involved in pitching a new account for her ad agency. Her chance for a major promotion. She couldn't be late; yet here she was, tearing through the garage with only minutes to spare.

Her colleague Hope Wilson was doubtless already upstairs in the headquarters of the Wellner Corporation, calm and poised, waiting for Jill to arrive with the videocassette showing the agency's top commercials—

"Oh, my God! The agency reel!" She'd left it in the car.

Skidding to a halt, Jill spun around...and collided with a solid wall of humanity. She heard a masculine "Oomph" and felt hands grasp her shoulders, but she was so stunned from the unexpected impact that all she could see were black specks dancing before her eyes.

When her vision cleared, her first view was of a paisley silk tie precisely knotted over a pale blue shirt. She raised her eyes and met a liquid brown gaze filled with concern.

"Are you all right?" the man asked, his breath tickling her forehead.

"I'm . . . fine. How about you?"

"No injuries."

Simultaneously, Jill became aware of his gentle grip on her shoulders and of the passing of time. The reel! Shifting away from the man, she murmured, "Sorry about that," and slipped around him.

"Say, aren't you—" he began, but she didn't take the time to listen to any more as she dashed toward her car.

Five minutes later, after a brief stop to repair her windblown hair, she stepped off the elevator on the sixth floor, directly across from a door that said Wellner Corporation: Steak Expectations.

Her heart speeded up. Here she was. Beyond that door lay her future. If she and her creative team could formulate a dynamite ad campaign for Wellner's newest restaurant chain, she had nowhere to go but up. She opened the door.

Hope was waiting inside. Jill handed her the cassette and announced herself to the receptionist, whose desk was flanked by a majestic Christmas tree decorated in red and silver. "Jill Levin with Carnaby and Ross."

"Have a seat. Mr. McMinn just called to say he's running a few minutes late. Can I get you some coffee?"

Jill shook her head. She didn't need caffeine to give her a lift this morning. The excitement of being here, of being involved in negotiations for a new account, was heady enough. In fact, she could use some calming down. Envying her friend's cool, confident demeanor, Jill sat beside Hope, who was leafing through a magazine. Of course, Hope, an account director, was an old hand at this kind of situation, whereas Jill was a novice at dealing with a potential new client.

She glanced surreptitiously at her jacket, searching for lint, then smoothed a hand over her skirt. Hope looked up, noticed and gave her a knowing smile.

Okay, Jill thought, *so I'm not comfortable in a suit, even one that's fire-engine red.* She wished she could have worn her usual pants and baggy sweater. She'd even packed her "lucky" sweater, a diamond-patterned V neck of fuchsia, teal and purple trimmed with black braid, but she'd bowed to convention and left it in the hotel-room closet.

The receptionist smiled at Jill. "Is this your first trip to Cincinnati, Ms. Levin?"

"No, I grew up here."

"Does your family still live in town?" When Jill nodded, she said, "How nice for you to have a trip home during the holidays."

Jill forced a smile. A trip home was not high on her list of nice things. In fact, she'd rather be anywhere but Cincinnati. Especially now, during the week of Chanukah. Family parties, her sister arriving with her kids, too much food and, most of all, too many memories. Even though Jill was staying at the Hyatt instead of her parents' house, she was bound to see more of her family during the eight days of Chanukah than she had in years. But when her job was involved, she'd go anywhere, Cincinnati included.

Jill picked up a magazine and tried to read. While pretending to be engrossed in an article, she gave herself a stern lecture. *Relax,* she ordered and took a deep breath. She held it to a count of three, then let it out slowly. Another breath, and—

"Welcome to Steak Expectations."

She'd heard the voice before; in fact, only moments before. In the parking garage.

She looked up from the magazine and stared into dark eyes alight with deviltry. The man stepped close as she rose. "How nice to run into you again," he murmured.

In spite of herself, Jill laughed as she held out her hand. "I'm Jill Levin, the creative director."

"I know." He took her hand and smiled, revealing deep dimples at the corners of his mouth. "I've been looking forward to seeing you again." He waited an instant as if expecting a response, then added, "I'm Ben Abrams."

She recognized the name from Hope's briefings. "The advertising manager," she said, then glanced pointedly at the hand he still held. He uncurled his fingers...slowly. Instead of stepping back after their handshake, he remained close. Too close; he was invading her space.

Jill gave him a cool glance, then deliberately turned her attention to Abrams's companion, who was talking with Hope.

He must be Frank McMinn, the advertising director. An intense, harried man, Jill decided. She'd bet he had a packet of antacids in the pocket of his immaculately tailored suit. Hope had said he didn't like dealing with women, that he thought them scatterbrained and irresponsible. That was why she'd instructed Jill to pack conservative suits. Jill grinned to herself. Her red jacket could hardly be called conservative. And this morning, in a further gesture of defiance, she'd accented her out-

fit with her favorite pair of oversize earrings—gold star-
bursts with dangly red balls. After all, as an assistant
creative director she was allowed, even expected, to look
a tad unconventional. As McMinn greeted her, his eyes
flicked over her critically. Jill smiled and offered her
hand, then clasped his in a firm handshake.

"I'd like to discuss our preliminary ideas for strategy," Hope said when McMinn turned back to her.

"Fine. We'll go over them in my office."

Hope and McMinn led the way. Jill fell into step behind them, and Ben Abrams strolled along beside her.
She recognized the scent of Drakkar cologne; he was still
much too close.

When they reached McMinn's office Hope said, "We
brought the agency reel to show you first." She set her
briefcase by a straight-backed chair and reached inside.
McMinn nodded to the VCR and sat behind his desk.
That left the love seat for Jill to share with Abrams. With
an inward sigh she sat down, unobtrusively positioning
herself as far from him as she could.

Hope flipped on the monitor, and the Carnaby and
Ross logo appeared. Jill had seen the agency's tape of its
best commercials on hundreds of occasions, but she
watched intently as ads for automobiles, a soft drink,
toothpaste—she'd worked on that one—and fabric soft-
ener played across the screen. She noticed that Hope had
added the series the agency had done for an Italian restaurant chain in Boston, and silently applauded.

"Impressive," McMinn said when the tape ended, but
he didn't sound sincere. There'd been rumors that he favored another ad agency. *Too bad,* Jill thought. She and
Hope were going to snare this account for Carnaby and
Ross. They would come up with a campaign that would

make Steak Expectations a household word...and put Jill Levin on the fast track.

Throughout the strategy discussion Jill concentrated on the interaction between Hope and McMinn, admiring Hope's ease and diplomacy in handling the man and filing away her methods for future reference.

When their meeting ended, McMinn rose. "Thank you for your ideas, Ms. Wilson. Mr. Abrams and I will take some time to study them, and we'll want to see the preliminary ads by next Monday morning." He glanced at his watch. "If you'll come with us, I'd like you to meet some of our marketing staff." He turned to Jill. "Ms. Levin?"

"My art director will be here tomorrow. Meanwhile, I'd like to spend some time looking over the ads you've used before."

"I'll have my secretary find you a quiet spot." He buzzed her, then told Jill, "She'll be right in."

Abrams turned at the doorway. "Let me know if you need anything."

She smiled politely and nodded. *Not likely*.

A few minutes later, ensconced in a small, bare office with a file of newspaper clippings and a box filled with tapes of radio spots, she again felt the keen edge of excitement. She was in familiar territory now, doing what she excelled at, what she loved.

She spent an hour reviewing the company's previous ads but didn't find them particularly appealing. Steak Expectations was a restaurant where customers cooked their own steaks. The idea seemed ludicrous to Jill. "Out to eat" did not equal "cooking" in her book. Nevertheless, she guessed the Wellner Corporation knew what they were doing. The company had both chicken and hamburger chains, two of the most successful in the fast-food business. Now they'd stepped up to a sit-down restaurant.

Chewing on her pencil, she wondered what would attract people to a place like Steak Expectations. She'd always thrived on challenges; this campaign should provide her with plenty.

She looked up as the door opened and Hope came in. "How's it going?" Hope asked.

"Fine."

"No first-day-of-the-first-pitch butterflies?"

"Uh-uh. I'm saving my nerves for tonight at my parents'."

"Tough evening, huh?" Hope's look was sympathetic.

"It will be." Jill sighed. "Visiting them is always difficult. We're not alienated, nothing like that, but there are…tensions between us. Especially between me and my sister."

"Your sister? The cute kid who visited you last summer? Is this something new?"

"No, not Sherry. My older sister, Lisa."

"You've never mentioned her."

"I try not to. But I can't avoid seeing her this week. She's home for Chanukah, kids and all."

"Do you have to go over there tonight?"

"'Fraid so. My parents are miffed enough that I'm staying at a hotel while I'm here. I can't miss their annual Chanukah party. God, I wish you could go with me. Having a guest would make the evening a lot easier."

"I wish I could, too, but this is the only night my friend Diane and I could get together. I'd enjoy a Chanukah celebration. You light candles, don't you?"

"For eight nights."

"And don't you exchange presents every night?"

Jill smiled. "The children usually get eight presents, grown-ups only one."

Hope leaned over the desk and eyed the notes Jill had made on a yellow legal pad. "I see you're getting started on the ads."

"Trying to. Would *you* go to a restaurant where you had to cook?"

"Maybe. Convince me."

"How about 'cook-it-yourself restaurant—an oxy-moron'?"

"Somehow I don't think that'll fly."

"Me, either." Jill chuckled. "I think I'll visit Steak Expectations this afternoon. Maybe that'll inspire me."

"Don't forget, we're taking McMinn to lunch," Hope said, and lowered her voice. "Honestly, I think that man has a terminal case of sourness."

"He does lack charm," Jill agreed.

"You got his attention, though," Hope told her. "Every time you turned your head and those darn red earrings jiggled, his eyes went right to them."

Jill laughed, then, lowering her voice, she asked, "What do you think of Abrams?"

"Nice guy. Maybe Wellner has a charm quota, and he filled it."

"He was a little too charming for my taste."

"What do you mean?"

Jill fiddled with her pencil. "It could have been my imagination, but I felt like he was coming on to me."

"Jill," her friend said with a sigh, "you're too edgy with men. I didn't notice anything inappropriate about Abrams's behavior. What did he do?"

"He . . . he stood too close."

Hope laughed and shook her head. "You never let any man get close. Literally or figuratively."

"I go out with men," Jill protested.

"Yes, but you don't develop any serious relationships."

Jill shrugged. "Maybe I'll change if I find someone who'll take me to Steak Expectations *and* cook the steaks. Hey, how's that for an angle? 'He cooked my steak. That's how I knew our love was real.' What do you think?"

"You don't want to know." Hope leaned back in her chair and stretched. "I should find a phone book and call in lunch reservations. Where do you recommend? We need a place classy enough to turn McMinn's head."

"Maisonette, Cincinnati's own five-star restaurant. Of course, I haven't been there in a couple of years."

"I'll take a chance." Hope rose and glanced at her watch. "Be ready in an hour. Oh, and don't worry about the charming Mr. Abrams. He has an appointment, so he won't be joining us for lunch." With a grin over her shoulder, she left the room.

Worry about Abrams? Jill stared at the closed door. *No way.* She had other, more important things, to think about. She picked up her notepad and put Ben Abrams and his charm out of her mind.

JILL LEVIN DIDN'T remember him, Ben thought as he sat behind his desk. Not great for his ego, he admitted. In fact, downright deflating.

He remembered her, though, very well, even though he hadn't seen her in nearly nine years. The clear, honey gold skin that could grace an ad for beauty cream. The wide hazel eyes. The long ash-blond hair, still curly, still worn in the same carefree style. The generous mouth with the pouting lower lip that looked so kissable.

As a teenager she'd been cute and lively, and he'd immediately picked her out of the crowd of eager high school girls attending their first Ohio State frat party. With the lofty sophistication of a college junior, he'd sauntered over and asked her to dance. She fit perfectly in his arms, and he liked talking to her. He wanted to go on dancing with her, but his date was looking daggers at him, and he had to let Jill go. When he spotted her again, she was dancing with one of his fraternity brothers, Mickey Zimmerman. She'd danced with Mickey all evening, and by the time Ben had another chance to talk to her he couldn't keep her attention because her eyes were following Zimmerman's every move.

She'd come to Columbus many times that semester, always as Zimmerman's date, and although Ben had had a couple of enjoyable conversations with her, he was a practical guy, so he'd put her out of his mind. In fact, he hadn't thought of her again until he'd seen her name in a letter from Carnaby and Ross and had wondered if she was the same Jill Levin. As soon as he'd spotted her in the garage this morning, he'd known she was.

Not just cute now, she'd matured into the kind of woman a man would immediately notice. She had an intriguing air of the offbeat about her, enhanced by the vivid colors and funky jewelry she wore. Even if he hadn't already been curious about her, she would have attracted him. And this time, he resolved, he'd make damn sure she didn't forget him.

The phone interrupted his thoughts. "Ben Abrams," he said, tucking the receiver on his shoulder and picking up a pen.

"How about dinner Wednesday?" His friend Alan Jeffreys rarely wasted time on preliminaries.

Ben hesitated, thinking of Jill. She'd only be here a week.... "Let's make it a drink after work," he suggested, reaching for his appointment book and turning to Wednesday's date.

"Better, actually. The kids will probably want to make another 'last-minute' visit to Santa."

"Okay. I've penciled you in."

"Good. I have projected figures to show you. Looks like this business idea we've been playing around with could really take off."

Ben could hear the excitement in Alan's voice, and his own pulse picked up. "Yeah?"

"Yeah. It's decision time, buddy. See you Wednesday."

Ben put the phone down and took a deep breath. Between Alan's figures and Jill Levin's stay, this could prove to be a very interesting week.

JILL FROWNED at the slogans she'd scribbled on the paper. "Steak Expectations. Let us meet your great expectations." She marked that one out. "Great expectations? Try Steak Expectations." No better. "Lousy," she muttered and shut her eyes, willing the ideas to flow.

A sharp knock at the door almost had her jumping out of her chair. Had she been concentrating so hard she'd forgotten the luncheon? No, her watch showed plenty of time left. The knock sounded again. "Come in," she called and wasn't surprised at all when Ben Abrams entered the office. She tensed.

"Finding everything you need?" he inquired.

"Yes."

"Good." He crossed the room and sat on the corner of the desk she was using. Again he was too close, his presence dominating. Jill squelched the urge to scoot her chair away.

He glanced at the array of ads she'd spread across the desk. "What do you think?"

A safe, familiar topic. A *professional* topic. Jill's confidence returned. "See this one?" She lifted a sheet out of the pile. "You have nothing here to catch the reader's eye, to make him pay attention. He'd read this ad and yawn and say, 'Okay. Another steak restaurant.' But you're not just another steak restaurant, and that's what you have to get across. I think you can do better," she said.

He grinned. "You think *you* can do better."

"Right."

"I'm sure you can."

He stared down at her. Silence stretched between them, and Jill fumbled for something to say to break the tension. Something tactful. Something businesslike.

She was still struggling to come up with the right words when he said, "You don't remember me, do you?"

Startled, she looked up at him. "Of course I do. We met in the parking garage."

His dimples appeared. "Uh-uh. Long before that."

Jill felt her cheeks redden. She'd always had a poor memory for faces, but how could she have forgotten this one? Below wavy brown hair were eyes like melted chocolate, a Roman nose and a pair of frankly sensual lips. And, of course, those incredible dimples.

She hadn't been home in two years, and she was certain she hadn't met him in New York. Or had she? She searched her mind for a time and place where they might have met but came up with a blank. She saw his eyes crinkle. Damn him. He was enjoying her embarrassment.

Despite her irritation, she was relieved. Now she could relax in his presence. As she frequently did with men, she'd overreacted earlier. What she'd interpreted as a line had been simple friendliness because he recognized her from somewhere. But where?

"I'll refresh your memory," he said. "You were in high school, and you came down to Ohio State for fraternity parties."

Jill's muscles tightened. No wonder she didn't recognize him. She'd blocked out everything about that period in her life. And now, when she was home again, was a poor time to revive those memories. Still, for the sake of business, she should at least let Abrams think she knew who he was. "Of course," she said brightly. "Now I remember."

His expression gave her no clue as to whether he believed her. He simply smiled and said, "Since we're old friends, can I help you with anything?"

"You can give me directions to one of your restaurants. Ads are a good introduction, but I need to see the real thing."

"I'll drive you."

Maybe they were "old friends," but she wasn't sure she wanted to spend the afternoon in his company. He was, as Hope had said, charming, and the last thing she wanted was to be charmed by a man.

"No, thanks," she said. "I'd rather not take the grand tour. I can get a better feel for the restaurant if I roam around on my own." Hoping she was being properly diplomatic, she added, "Besides, I'll probably take up plenty of your time later in the week."

"No problem," he said. "I have to talk to one of our managers today. I'll drive you over, introduce you and turn you loose." Before she had a chance to come up with another excuse he got up and headed for the door. "I'll see you after lunch. We'll talk about old times."

Jill stared at the door after he'd gone. He had an engaging smile, with white, even teeth. She wondered if he used Dazzle toothpaste, the product she'd just finished writing an ad for. *Dazzle them with your smile.* Yes, he could definitely do that.

Steak ads forgotten, she doodled on her notepad, drawing a smiling mouth and teeth with little sparkles, and wondered which party she'd met him at. She could only recall a crowd of fraternity men, all reduced to a blur in her memory. Finally she gave up. She didn't remember Ben at all.

BEN LED THE WAY to a shiny silver car, the sleek, sporty type that appealed to young, on-the-way-up executives. Jill's eyes zeroed in on the logo. Unlike faces, trademarks stuck in her memory.

When their seat belts were fastened, Ben drove smoothly out of the parking garage and headed down a busy street. He glanced sideways at Jill. "You really don't remember me, do you?"

"Of course I . . . no, actually, I don't," she admitted, aware that her cheeks were flushing. But why pretend? He'd be sure to trip her up eventually.

Ben chuckled. "I didn't think so. You had other interests at the time. Mickey Zimmerman, right?"

She nodded and eyed Ben warily. Had he and Mickey been friends? Was that why he remembered her so well? And how much did he know about her?

He went on, his tone casual. "I remember the fraternity had a Disney party that year, and you two came as Mickey and Minnie Mouse."

Though she hadn't thought of it in years, she recalled that party very well—her thigh-skimming red-and-white-polka-dot dress with the big sash, the black leotards and the mouse ears, and how she and Mickey had doubled over with laughter as they painted on mouse faces.

But her memories didn't include Ben. Maybe if he told her what character he'd been . . . "Who were you?"

"Prince Charming."

She began to laugh. *Figures.* When he glanced at her questioningly, she shook her head. "Private joke," she muttered. And she still didn't remember him.

"I didn't see much of you after that party," he remarked.

"No, Mickey and I—we broke up soon after." A facile term for what had been the disaster of her life, she thought with the old bitterness.

"I heard he married a girl from Cincinnati. Someone named Ruth, I think. . . ."

"Roz," she said sharply. "Roz Kaplan."

"Friend of yours?"

"My cousin." Why did saying that still hurt, even after all these years? She didn't want to rehash that, especially not now.

"I heard they had a baby recently."

"Adopted," she corrected him. "A little girl." Since Ben hadn't been sure of Roz's name, he and Mickey couldn't have been close friends, she thought, with some measure of relief. "Tell me about Steak Expectations," she said abruptly.

Without questioning her sudden change of subject, he did. "Thomas Wellner, our illustrious founder, always had a weakness for good red meat. According to company lore he wanted to open a steak restaurant, but when he first started out he lacked the capital and he couldn't get anyone to back him. So he bought a quarter share in a fried-chicken franchise.''

''Wellner's Chicken?''

''At the time, it was called Pik-a-Chik.'' He held up a hand to forestall her laughter. ''No kidding, that was the name. But within five years it was Wellner's. Old Tom bought the chain. And the rest is history.''

''And now he's going to realize his dream.''

''Yeah. He opened three Steak Expectations here a couple of years ago, and now he's ready to expand throughout the Midwest. If that goes as well as we expect, we'll go national. Hence, a national ad agency.''

He'd given her the perfect opening. ''Hence, Carnaby and Ross,'' she said and crossed her fingers.

''Could be,'' he said. His vague response, she decided, was designed not to get her hopes up.

He pulled into the parking lot of a small shopping center. ''Here we are.''

Jill got out of the car and scrutinized the Steak Expectations sign. *Nothing to grab your attention,* she thought. Too bad, because the logo would have to go in the ads. Well, she'd let her art director, Dan Givens, worry about that when he arrived tomorrow.

Next she surveyed the building. Plain, unpretentious. Not much on the outside to recommend the restaurant. Knowing Dan, he'd want to redesign the logo *and* the building.

Ben opened the shiny black door, and she stepped inside. The interior was a surprise. ''The restaurant of the future,'' she murmured with delight, looking around. The words *glossy, high tech, functional* came to mind. She saw crisp white cloths on black acrylic tables surrounded by gleaming black chairs. Busboys in white shirts and trousers and long, black aprons. In the center of the room, up two steps, long black grills and above them, glossy chrome hoods. In keeping with the season, a huge Christmas tree that matched the one she'd seen earlier in the chain's headquarters stood in one corner.

Ben introduced her to the manager, who offered to show her around.

Jill thanked him but declined. "I'd rather wander, if you don't mind."

For the next hour and a half she ambled through the dining room, toured the spotless kitchen, glanced at menus and chatted with employees, jotting down their comments about their customers' and their own reactions to Steak Expectations.

From a busboy: "Customers love this place, and I do, too. With my discount, I eat here every chance I get. The food's awesome."

From a waitress: "Eat here? Are you kidding? Honey, when I get off, I wanna sit down, put my feet up and have somebody wait on me."

She cornered one of the cooks, who was preparing vegetables for the salad bar. "Why does a cook-it-yourself restaurant need a cook?"

"Most customers broil their own, but a few want service, so we give it to them."

"Is the meat good?"

"The best. Top grade beef, prime cuts."

"Do you eat here?"

The man laughed and patted his ample stomach. "Nah. I'm watching my fat and cholesterol, and this isn't the place to do it. But don't put that in your ad."

"Don't worry. The word *cholesterol* is definitely out."

The man had a valid point, though, she thought as she strolled on. In these diet-conscious times, how would you lure customers to an eating place that practically guar-

anteed their cholesterol would skyrocket? Though the
menu listed chicken and fish, the name emphasized
steaks, and she doubted Wellner would go for a recom-
mendation that they change the name.

She continued to ponder that as she went back to the
office for Ben. When she reached the door she heard the
sound of laughter. His. She didn't question how she
knew; she simply did. And she liked the sound.

She heard it again as they drove back to the Wellner
building, filling the car with warmth and camaraderie.
She was enjoying herself, thanks to Ben. By the time they
reached their destination she felt they actually were old
friends.

When they pulled up next to her rental car, she smiled
at him. "Thanks."

"My pleasure." He looked at her for a moment, his
dark eyes gleaming. "Since we've renewed our friendship," he said, "how about dinner?"

To her surprise, she regretted having to say no. "Sorry,
but I can't. My parents are having their annual Chanukah party tonight." She hesitated a moment. Why not
ask him to come along? He could take Hope's place as
her buffer on an evening when she badly needed one.
"Why don't you come?"

His eyes lit up. "Thanks. I'd like that."

She gave him her parents' address and the time of the
party and he wrote the information down. Jill opened the
door, but before she could get out he reached over and
touched her hand. "I'm looking forward to the evening," he murmured.

The contact was light, fingertips only, but she felt as if
he'd seared her skin. Carefully she moved her arm away.
"So am I," she said in the tone she'd use with any acquaintance, "since we're...old friends." She slipped out

of the car and turned away, still feeling the imprint of his fingers on her hand.

Berating herself, she fumbled for her car keys. She shouldn't have issued that impulsive invitation. She didn't want to get mixed up with any man, especially someone even vaguely connected with her past. "Idiot," she muttered to herself. She had a sinking feeling that having asked Ben over tonight, even as a friend, was a serious and irrevocable mistake.

Ben watched her walk away. He hadn't missed the subtle emphasis she'd placed on the word *friend,* nor the glint of fear in her eyes. He wanted to be her friend, but from the moment he'd recognized her this morning, he'd wanted more.

She'd set the limits on their relationship just now, drawn her line in the sand. What she didn't know was that he didn't take kindly to ultimatums, not when he wanted something as badly as he wanted Jill Levin. When she'd hurtled into his arms this morning, he'd experienced a jolt far stronger than the impact warranted. The feel of her shoulders under his hands, the sight of her wide, startled eyes had awakened the kind of instantaneous desire he'd thought only happened in mushy movies. Maybe his feelings didn't make sense, perhaps they were happening too fast, but they were real. And whether Jill realized it or not, he intended to act on them.

CHAPTER TWO

As SHE NEARED the Amberley area, where her parents lived, Jill slowed the car. In a few minutes she'd have to face her entire family. She felt the muscles in her chest and stomach tense and wondered if she'd be able to choke down her dinner.

She turned the corner and inched down the block. In the early dusk she could see Christmas-tree lights winking in some of the windows, a star of David on a front door. A Santa Claus drove his sleigh across the snow-covered yard on the corner. Christmas and Chanukah. For Christians and Jews, this season was a time for families. And Jill felt like an outsider.

There was her parents' home, *her* home for most of her childhood years. She stopped, let the engine idle and gazed at the house.

For the first time in years she felt childhood memories crowding her mind—the backyard swing, the shaded spot beneath the locust where she and her sisters had shared summer picnics, the porch step where she'd sat dreaming, planning her life.

She swallowed a sudden lump in her throat. She'd never felt—hadn't permitted herself to feel—nostalgia for those long-ago years. Those memories had been overshadowed by other less pleasant events. Like scar tissue replacing once-smooth skin, the newer memories had obliterated the old ones. Like scar tissue, they'd formed a thick callus, immune to sensation, numb. Could she allow that barrier to give way?

She killed the motor but still sat in the car, postponing the moment when she would have to go inside. Instead, she surveyed the redbrick Colonial house, looking for changes since her last visit two years ago. She noticed new landscaping, new furniture on the porch. For some reason that annoyed her. *Why?* she asked herself. *Why should you expect everything to stay the same? You've changed, haven't you?* She fervently hoped so. She didn't want to be the same Jill Levin who'd first left this house eight and a half years ago.

She got out of the car and slammed the door. She couldn't postpone her arrival forever, but her feet dragged as she approached the house. When she opened this door, she'd have to face her past.

She rang the doorbell, and the familiar sound of the chimes evoked more memories. Of high school dates arriving for her and her sisters, of their whispered excitement as they tried to guess whose boyfriend was there, of waiting for Mickey. God, she was getting maudlin. She'd have to cut this out or she'd never get through the next few days.

The door opened. "Jill! Welcome home, honey."

Her mother had aged in the past two years. Lines showed around her mouth and at the corners of her eyes, but her hair was the same chestnut brown, though Jill suspected the hairdresser had a hand in that. As always, her mother smelled of Chanel.

"Hello, Mother." Jill crossed the threshold and stood stiffly in her mother's embrace. She might come home, she might participate in family gatherings, but she no longer felt the warmth that had once been a part of her relationship with her mother. And what she didn't feel, she couldn't express.

Her mother drew back to look at her, and Jill saw the disappointment in her eyes. She was sorry to have put it there, but she wasn't a hypocrite; she wouldn't dissemble. She busied herself removing her coat and gloves.

"How are you?" her mother asked, surveying her from her hairdo down to her shoes. Frank McMinn couldn't have given her a more thorough inspection. Jill braced for a critical remark, though logically she knew the time for criticism was long since past. She was an independent woman now, leading her own life. Her mistakes were her own.

"You look good," her mother said, and Jill's tension eased.

Funny, she thought, how you reverted to childhood reactions when you came home, regardless of how old you were, how confident you felt in other situations. "Thanks. You do, too," she said and followed her mother into the living room.

"Is Jill here?" Her sister Sherry, three years younger, came barreling down the stairs.

Jill grinned. Long ago she and Lisa had nicknamed Sherry "The Tornado." The name still fit.

Sherry threw her arms around Jill and hugged her. "Happy Chanukah! Happy homecoming!"

Jill hugged back. With Sherry at least, she felt comfortable. "You look great."

"I am great. I'm in love."

"Again?" Jill met her sister's eyes. Sherry had a penchant for falling intensely in love, but her passions were usually short-lived.

"This time's the real thing," Sherry assured her. "His name's David Rosen. You'll see how wonderful he is. He's coming in this weekend."

Jill felt a brief pang. Sherry in love. Lisa married with two children. What would her own life have been like if...

Sherry grabbed Jill's hand and pulled her over to the couch. "Gee, look at you. Tailored suit, silk blouse. The career woman."

The pang of envy faded. She liked what she was, what she'd accomplished. Even though the executive look wasn't her usual style.

"Lisa will be down in a minute," Sherry went on. "She's upstairs getting the kids ready."

Jill glanced past Sherry and saw her mother's troubled frown. "Don't worry, Mom," she said. "I'm sure Lisa and I can be civil." She knew the old anger had crept into her voice and felt it stiffen her spine, as well, but was unable to prevent it.

"Jill—" her mother chided.

"Esther," came a voice from the hall, "is that my little girl?"

"Yes, Joel," her mother called. "She's here."

Her father came into the living room. Though she hadn't been his little girl in years, Jill rose and gave him a kiss, inhaling the scent she always associated with him—Old Spice after-shave. He tasted faintly of Hershey kisses, his favorite snack, and a vice Jill shared.

He, too, had aged, even more than her mother. His hair, which had been peppered with gray when she'd last seen him, was burnished pewter now. The skin on his neck sagged. Jill felt a twinge. She'd always taken her father for granted. Someday he wouldn't be here anymore.

He sat next to Sherry and regarded Jill over the rims of his glasses. "We're glad to have you home for Chanukah, Jill. It's been a long time since I've had all my girls under one roof."

Jill didn't want to talk about why she visited so seldom. To hide her discomfort she looked around the room instead. The silver menorah, the eight-branched Chanukah candelabrum, sat on the credenza, ready for the candle-lighting ceremony. Packages wrapped in blue and silver surrounded it, and on the wall above it hung a banner that said "Happy Chanukah."

"Everything looks nice," she murmured.

"You're away from New York at a busy time," Esther Levin remarked. "Won't you be missing a lot of...functions?"

Jill's laugh was brittle. "Mother, if that's a subtle way of asking whether I'm seeing someone, the answer is no."

"Honey, you know I wouldn't pry." Esther's lips thinned.

Jill sighed. She seemed to have a talent for hurting her mother's feelings. "I'm sorry, Mom." Searching for a safer subject, she asked, "Can I help you with dinner?"

"All right." Her mother looked relieved. "Both of you can," she said, beckoning to Sherry.

Jill and Sherry followed their mother into the kitchen. Despite late-model appliances, the large room had an old-fashioned feel. The butcher-block counters were cluttered with dishes and utensils. Pies sat cooling on the table. Jill sniffed apples and cinnamon, and her mouth watered.

Here, Jill felt her tension dissolve. The kitchen held only happy memories. She could picture herself at seven, standing on a chair, helping her mother mix a cake or vying with her sisters for a chance to lick the bowl.

Esther opened the oven door and lifted the roaster lid, and the aroma of browning turkey filled the room. She cut a thin slice from the breast and held it out to Jill.

She tasted and sighed. "Mmm. Mother, I've eaten in New York's finest restaurants, and you're still the world's best cook."

Esther smiled and Jill congratulated herself. At last she'd said something that made her mother feel good. "What can we do?" she inquired automatically, though she knew Esther, a born organizer, would tell them without being asked. Jill often thought her mother would have made an excellent corporate executive, or perhaps an army general.

Esther gestured toward the refrigerator. "Sherry, take the salad out of the mold and put it on a plate. Jill, would you help me peel the rest of the potatoes? We're having a crowd tonight. We'll need lots of *latkes.*"

"*Latkes.*" Jill sighed. "Heaven." The potato pancakes, always served during Chanukah, were her favorite holiday food.

"Jill, aren't you doing something with a restaurant here?" Sherry asked over her shoulder.

Jill rummaged in the drawer for a knife. "Yes. Steak Expectations."

"I've eaten there."

Interested in her sister's reaction, Jill turned to look at her. "What did you think of it?"

Sherry began garnishing the salad. "Everyone has fun there. The way the grills are set up in the middle, people can mingle and talk to each other. Girls who are looking say it's a good place to meet guys, away from the singles bar atmosphere."

Jill made a mental note to check into that angle. Perhaps tomorrow she'd ask Ben Abrams. *Oh, Lord, Ben*

Abrams. She'd forgotten all about him. "Mom, I invited someone to dinner tonight. I hope you don't mind."

"Of course not. Who is it? Someone from your agency?"

"No, he's an old friend I ran into and, hopefully, he'll soon be our client. He's the advertising manager for Steak Expectations." She sighed inwardly as two pairs of eyes fastened on her expectantly, then continued, "His name's Ben Abrams."

"Ben Abrams," Esther repeated, apparently running down her list of hometown eligibles. "He's not from Cincinnati, is he?"

"No." She had no idea where Ben was from. "I met him in college." That was partially true. *He'd* been in college.

"Well, we're happy to have him."

Her mother disappeared into the pantry, and Sherry sidled over to Jill. "So who's this Abrams fellow? Someone special?"

Jill shook her head. "I told you. He's a business acquaintance and an old friend."

Sherry raised a brow. "How good a friend?"

"Don't read anything into this," Jill warned her. "I just ran into him today. And he's harmless."

Esther returned with a handful of potatoes. "Jill, let's get started. Sherry, you can peel, too."

"Mom, I—"

Jill pivoted at the sound of the familiar voice. Her sister Lisa stood in the doorway.

They had seen each other only twice in eight years. Their eyes met.

No one moved or spoke, as tension built. Jill felt as if they were stuck in a snapshot from the family album. Esther and Sherry stood frozen, part of the tableau, watching; but Jill's attention focused on Lisa. She knew she should say something, but she couldn't get out a word.

Finally Lisa broke the silence. "Hello, Jill. How are you?" she asked in a too-bright voice.

Jill felt cold. "I'm fine."

From the hallway came a childish voice. "Mommy, will you put my bow in?"

Jill watched as a dark-eyed little girl, her hair a curly cloud around her elfin face, came into the room. She was beautiful. The knife in Jill's hand clattered to the floor.

At the sound, the child came to a stop. She put her thumb in her mouth and eyed Jill suspiciously. "Who's that?" she mumbled around her thumb.

"That's your aunt Jill. Remember, I told you she'd be here? You've never met her," Lisa added, glancing at Jill, her look reproving. Then she motioned the child forward. "Tell her hi."

The little girl peered at Jill through long, dark lashes. "Hi," she said. "I'm Whitney. I'm three."

Jill's tongue froze, but she knew she had to get through this moment. "Hello, Whitney," she murmured.

Whitney regarded Jill a minute longer, then tugged at her mother's skirt. "My bow's in the bedroom, Mommy."

"Let's go get it." Sounding relieved, Lisa took her daughter's hand.

As she turned, a boy as dark as Whitney, with a head full of curly hair and an expression of total disgust on his face, stomped into the room, dragging a white shirt. "Mommy, do I have to wear this? I wanted to wear my Super Mario Brothers T-shirt."

"We'll talk about it, Kevin," Lisa muttered. "Meanwhile, say hello to your aunt Jill."

He gave her a disinterested glance. "'Lo," he mumbled, then turned back to Lisa. "Now can we talk about it?"

"In the bedroom," Lisa said firmly and steered both children out the door.

Jill watched Lisa disappear into the hallway. *Don't envy her. Don't feel anything,* she ordered herself. She picked up the knife she'd dropped, rinsed it and concentrated on the potatoes as if peeling them were the most important job of her life. By the time she finished, the doorbell had begun to ring and she didn't have time to think or feel anymore.

Within half an hour the house was filled with dozens of relatives—her father's two older brothers and their wives; Uncle Harris, husband of her mother's sister Sarah who'd died a number of years ago; various cousins—some single, some with spouses and children—and a few close family friends. Aunt Elaine and Uncle Joe Kaplan arrived, but Roz and Mickey weren't with them. Jill had been dreading a possible encounter with Mickey, but apparently he and Roz hadn't come to Cincinnati for the beginning of the holiday. That was a relief.

Jill received hugs, kisses on the cheek, polite questions from relatives about her life in New York and thinly veiled inquiries about her marital prospects.

She searched the crowd, looking for her grandmother. She'd been looking forward to seeing the tiny, energetic woman, one of the few people in her family—perhaps the only person—whose love for her was unconditional. "Where's Bubbi?" she asked Sherry.

"She's spending a few days in Washington with Aunt Leah. She'll be back Wednesday."

Disappointed, Jill escaped from the crowded living room and stole down the hall to the guest bathroom.

Her throat felt parched, and she took a paper cup from the dispenser, filled it and went back into the hallway, where she leaned against the wall, sipping and watching the guests mill about in the living room.

What was she doing here? Even though they were kin, she was no longer part of these people's lives, nor they of hers. She felt as if she were looking at them through a wall of glass. Oh, God, how was she going to get through this week? She gulped down the last of the water and crushed the cup between her fingers, wishing she could slip out of the house unnoticed and go back to her hotel.

"Aunt Jill?"

She hadn't noticed Whitney come up behind her. Hair bow in place now, Whitney wore a burgundy velvet dress with a lacy white collar. White leotards showed off chubby legs, and black patent Mary Janes completed her outfit. In her arms was a Cabbage Patch doll. She held it out to Jill and said, "This is Barbara Ellen. She's three, too."

Jill knelt to look at the doll and found herself staring into her niece's round brown eyes. She reached for the doll and, of its own accord, her hand moved and touched Whitney's cheek. *Soft. So soft.* She felt a lump in her throat, but pushed it down and said, "Barbara Ellen's very pretty."

"Thank you," Whitney said. "She came with a 'doption 'tificate."

Adoption certificate. That was standard for a Cabbage Patch doll, but the words hurt. The tears she'd suppressed a moment ago welled in Jill's eyes.

Whitney stared at her solemnly. "Don't cry, Aunt Jill. You're pretty, too."

Despite the tears, a laugh bubbled up. Jill swiped at her cheeks and hugged Whitney close. "Thank you," she whispered, then rose, fighting for composure. "Why don't we go see what's happening in the living room?"

As they entered the room she heard the doorbell chime. That had to be Ben, she thought. She took Whitney's hand and went to open the door.

He stood outside, the porch light shooting golden highlights through his hair.

"Hello," Jill said.

"Hi." He handed her a bottle of wine. "Happy Chanukah to you and your parents."

"Thanks. You shouldn't have."

"My pleasure," he assured her, then glanced down at the child clasping her hand. "Who's this?"

"This is my niece, Whitney."

"Happy Chanukah, Whitney," Ben said.

"I'm three," Whitney announced. "How old are you?"

Ben grinned. "Thirty."

"Thirty." Whitney mulled this over as Ben stepped inside. "Thirty's a lot more than three. Maybe as old as Grandpa."

"Not quite, but close," he said.

Jill met his eyes and they smiled at one another, enjoying the child. She released Whitney's hand. "Go see if Grandpa's ready to light the candles, honey." She took Ben's overcoat and hung it in the entry closet and gave the wine to her mother, who scrutinized Ben quickly but thoroughly, then smiled her approval.

"Come meet everyone," Jill told him. Careful to stress that he was a business associate, she introduced him to her father and some of the guests. When he met Sherry, he said, "You and Jill look like mirror images. You aren't twins, are you?"

"Three years apart," Sherry replied. Her gaze traveled over Ben, unabashedly appraising him as if he were a piece of merchandise on a sale rack.

Oh, Lord, Jill thought. *Save me from my family.* Ben, however, appeared unruffled by Sherry's scrutiny. Probably Prince Charming was used to women ogling him, Jill thought. Probably he enjoyed it.

"Excuse me. I have to get something," Sherry said. She gave Ben a wide smile and left the room.

He chuckled and turned back to Jill. "Three years apart. Your sister must be twenty-three. Is she finished with college?"

"She's in her first year of grad school. How'd you know how old she is?"

"I can subtract. I know how old you are."

"You do?" she asked, nonplussed.

"Sure. You were seventeen when we met. Nine years ago."

Goodness, the man had an amazing memory. While she—damn, she still couldn't recall their first meeting.

Ben leaned closer and whispered, "Don't bother pretending. I know you still don't remember me."

She looked up at him and saw that he was laughing. She blushed and he added, "You'd never make a poker player. Admit it. You haven't a clue about when we met."

"You're right," she confessed and was treated to another dimpled smile. "I guess that doesn't bother you."

"Nope. *I* remember. You will, too, eventually."

She stared at him, unsure what he was implying.

"Ben!" The husband of one of Jill's cousins came over and clapped Ben on the shoulder. "What a change to see you with clothes on."

Ben returned the greeting with a friendly smile. "Eric and I work out at the same health club," he explained to Jill. "We usually meet in the showers."

Eric said, "Listen, I want to talk to you about—"

Ben gave Jill an apologetic smile over his shoulder as Eric led him away.

She leaned against the wall, watching Ben. He appeared at ease with her relatives, more comfortable in these surroundings than she was. Even in the midst of the familiar crowd she felt alone. Then she saw her father coming toward her and forced a smile.

He put his hand on her shoulder. "Daydreaming?"

"Just watching."

"Almost time to light the candles," he said, then reached into his pocket and came up empty-handed.

"I'll get the matches for you," Jill offered, glad of an opportunity to be alone for a moment. "Where are they?"

"Where they've always been."

She went into the kitchen and got a book of matches from the cupboard where, for as long as she could remember, her mother had kept her Sabbath candlesticks. There they were in their usual place along with the Sabbath wine cup. Perhaps nothing of substance had changed, after all.

"Jill." She turned to see Sherry standing in the doorway, twirling a pair of eyeglasses by one earpiece. She held them out to Jill. "I brought you these."

Confused, Jill frowned at her. "I don't wear glasses."

"You should. Good grief, are you blind?"

"What do you mean?"

"Your friend out there is drop-dead gorgeous, or haven't you noticed?"

"Ben?" Jill glanced at the door. "Well, yes, he's nice looking, but—"

"Honey, every female from Whitney to Aunt Hannah, who must be seventy if she's a day, started salivating when he walked in the room."

"Okay," Jill said. "I admit he's more than just nice looking, but so what? We're just friends. And I told you, he's—"

"Harmless," Sherry mimicked. "Ben Abrams is about as harmless as a load of dynamite, and he's looking at you like you're the fuse."

"Don't be silly. Come on, Dad wants to light the candles."

"Okay, change the subject, but if you're smart—" Sherry waved the glasses in front of Jill's nose "—you'll put these on and take a good look back."

Before Jill could think of a suitable comeback, Sherry spun around and disappeared, leaving Jill standing in the middle of the kitchen, caught between amusement and annoyance.

As she returned to the living room, however, she resolved to put Sherry's words out of her mind. Dynamite, indeed! She had no interest in such nonsense. Still, when Ben's eyes met hers and he crossed the room toward her, she had to admit she felt a small tingle of anticipation. What if the dynamite went off?

"We're ready to light the candles," her father announced, taking the matches from Jill.

With Ben beside her, Jill joined the circle around the menorah. Ben stood close but made no attempt to touch her. Jill relaxed. Sherry must have been mistaken about him.

From the candle holder her father lifted the middle candle, the *shammash,* or "helper," with which he would light the others. His voice resonant, he recited the blessing, first in Hebrew, then in English. "Blessed art Thou, O Lord our God, ruler of the universe, who has commanded us to kindle the Chanukah lights." With the *shammash,* he lit one candle, for the first night of the festival, then returned the helper to its place.

How many years had she stood here, listening to her father repeat the ancient blessing, Jill thought. Growing up in innocence and wonder.

Sherry slipped into the circle beside Jill and reached for her hand. Hands clasped, they joined in the *Sheheche-yanu* prayer. "Blessed art Thou, O Lord our God, ruler of the universe, who has kept us in life, and sustained us, and enabled us to reach this season."

As Jill's voice mingled with the others, she was surprised to find she truly meant the words she spoke. She hadn't expected to feel anything. She rarely allowed herself to feel, but there it was... a tiny spark of gratitude, as insubstantial as the flame of the first Chanukah candle.

As the prayer died away, the group raised their voices in the traditional Chanukah song, "*Maoz Tzur,*' Rock of Ages." Ben's deep voice blended with her own. She glanced up at him and he smiled. He had a nice smile, she thought. It lit up his whole face.

"Dinner," announced Esther Levin. "Children in the breakfast room. You have a special table." Within moments she had the children seated and the adults in an orderly line for the buffet.

"Hungry?" Jill asked, smiling at Ben. She turned toward the dining room and he followed. He put a hand lightly on her shoulder. Immediately Jill stiffened and pulled away, and he dropped his hand.

If she turned and looked at him, what would she see in his eyes? Irritation at her response? Surprise? She didn't want to know. She stared straight ahead.

When they joined the line at the buffet, Ben beckoned to Sherry. "Come join us."

She sauntered over to him and smiled archly. "Want to share your dinner with *both* of us?"

"Of course. There's enough of me for two."

Sherry laughed, her eyes teasing. "Are you sure of that?"

"Uh-huh. Are you flirting with me, Ms. Levin?"

Sherry tossed her head. "Just keeping in practice. I haven't seen my boyfriend for a week."

All three chuckled, but Jill knew her laugh was forced. The confidence she felt at work was absent here. Unlike Sherry, who clearly relished male-female banter, Jill felt out of her element sparring with men.

She glanced at Ben through her lashes as he helped himself to dinner. He'd called himself an old friend, but many men started a relationship talking about friendship and then wanted more. And were angry when they didn't get it.

Dispirited, she began filling her plate. Just as she'd expected, there was far too much food. Turkey, dressing, several vegetables, two salads, rolls, and of course, *latkes*. Golden brown, round and crisp, to be eaten with applesauce or sour cream.

"I haven't eaten like this since I left home," Ben said to Esther, who stood at the end of the buffet.

"Where are you from, Ben?"

"Cleveland."

"Oh, that's nice."

From her mother's voice, Jill sensed other questions coming. Quickly she steered Ben away.

He sat between her and Sherry. From across the table, one of her uncles gave Ben a benevolent smile. "Lucky fellow, sitting between the two prettiest girls in the room. I'm Phil Levin. Uncle Phil, if you like." He extended a hand across the table.

Ben shook it and introduced himself.

Uncle Phil smiled at Jill. "We haven't seen you in a long time, Jilly. You should come home more often."

Why did he have to bring that up now? "I've been busy."

"Ah, the career woman. In my generation, young women were home raising families."

Jill couldn't prevent herself from flinching at her uncle's remark, but before she could reply, Sherry said, "And in *our* generation they're arguing cases before the Supreme Court, running companies, writing the commercials you see on TV, huh, Jill?" When Jill nodded, Sherry said, "You know, Jill wrote that wonderful toothpaste commercial... for Goal, wasn't it? 'Make brighter teeth your Goal.'"

"Dazzle," Jill corrected her. "How quickly they forget."

"Dazzle." Her uncle shook his head. "Personally, I use—"

"Don't tell her," Sherry interrupted. "She always has a purseful of samples of any product she's working on. And she'll torture you until you take one."

"Don't worry, darling. I'm too close to dentures to bother with toothpaste samples." Uncle Phil turned to Ben, his eyes twinkling mischievously. "So, young man," he remarked, "are you involved in the advertising game, too—persuading gullible consumers to spend their money on products they don't need?" He winked broadly.

Ben shook his head. "I used to work for an agency, and I'm still in the ad game, but now I'm on the other side of the table. I'm with the Wellner Corporation. We're hiring an ad agency to promote a new restaurant chain. What do you do, Uncle Phil?"

"I'm an accountant."

"Ah, the accounting game. Persuading gullible taxpayers to pay someone else to fill out their tax returns?"

Uncle Phil threw back his head and laughed appreciatively. "Touché, young man. I like you."

Jill chuckled, enjoying Ben's ability to trade barbs with her uncle. Then she glanced up and her laughter died.

Lisa stood directly across from her, behind the one empty chair at the table. Her eyes locked with Jill's, and she raised her chin as if daring Jill to challenge her right to take a seat. Jill kept silent.

Fortunately Sherry smoothed over the uncomfortable moment by introducing Lisa and Ben. Then Sherry leaned across the table. "Uncle Phil," she said, "here's another one of the 'now' women. Only this one does it all—raises a family *and* holds down a job."

"Lisa, darling, you're working?" Uncle Phil said.

She nodded, then her eyes darted to Jill's. "Surprised?"

She wasn't about to touch that one. Jill shook her head, but she *was* surprised. As far as she knew, Lisa had never aspired to anything other than marrying and raising a family.

Her sister smiled, a gleam of triumph in her eyes. "I got my real estate license in October." She addressed Uncle Phil, but Jill knew the words were meant for her.

"So, Ms. Now Woman," Uncle Phil inquired, "how do you manage all this?"

"Kevin's in second grade this year, and Whitney's in preschool. I'm working part-time now, but I'll increase my hours when they're older."

"What kind of real estate are you handling, Lisa?" Ben asked. "Commercial or residential?"

"Commercial." Again, the look of triumph.

Again Jill was astonished. Selling commercial real estate seemed so much more... demanding than residential. She made no comment, though, fearing Lisa might take any remark she made as criticism.

"Where's your handsome husband, Ms. Real Estate Salesperson?" Uncle Phil asked.

Jill had wondered that, too, but hadn't wanted to ask.

"Todd's home in Omaha, slaving away at the law firm." Lisa smiled fondly. "He'll be in Friday evening."

The conversation continued. Jill was glad Uncle Phil was nearby. With his good-natured teasing, he defused the unpleasantness between her and her sister. And Ben fulfilled his role as buffer nicely, too. Eventually the conversation, spiced with their tongue-in-cheek humor, veered off in other directions, and Jill settled back and enjoyed her meal.

When she had eaten so many *latkes* she was sure she couldn't hold another bite, dessert appeared. The apple pies she'd smelled earlier, carrot cake, honey cake, chocolate cake. Glad she didn't tend to put on weight, Jill took a sliver of pie and a generous slice of chocolate cake.

While the adults lingered over dessert and coffee, Jill could hear the scraping of chairs in the breakfast room as the children finished their meal. Within a few minutes the clamor of young, excited voices came from the living room.

Soon the grown-ups began heading for the living room, too, stopping on the way to compliment Esther on the meal. Ben added his own words of praise, and so did Jill; she was stuffed.

Then she heard Uncle Phil's voice. "Gather round, children."

"Come on," Jill said to Ben. "Uncle Phil always tells the Chanukah story after dinner."

When they entered the living room Jill saw that Phil had pulled a chair next to the credenza. Most of the children were seated in a circle on the floor in front of him, their faces turned to him eagerly. The adults found seats, some carrying in dining-room chairs, some sitting on the floor with the youngsters. She and Ben found two spaces on the sofa. Ben leaned back and put his arm along the back of the couch, but this time he didn't touch her shoulder, and Jill was surprised to feel a flicker of disappointment.

"Quiet, boys and girls," Uncle Phil said. "Listen, and I'll tell you why we're here tonight, celebrating this happy occasion."

"He always begins the same way," Jill whispered to Ben. "I've heard that opening since I was a little girl." Again, she experienced that bittersweet feeling of nostalgia. She had many sweet memories of childhood Chanukahs—candles and presents, games and treats. But other memories, painful ones, had almost eradicated those happy early images. *No,* she told herself. For tonight, she'd recall only the good times. She turned toward Uncle Phil.

"Long, long ago," he began, his voice deep and dramatic, "King Antiochus of Syria ruled over the land of Palestine. Now Antiochus believed that for his empire to be strong, all the people in it should be alike. They must think alike, worship alike."

Jill glanced at Ben. His lips were curved in a half smile, his eyes soft as if he, too, were remembering long-ago Chanukahs. He met her eyes and they smiled at one another, sharing the moment. Then Jill turned back to her uncle and let the story carry her along.

"So, because Antiochus was educated as a Greek, he decided that Palestine would become Greek in thought and custom and religion. He forbade all worship except the religion of Greece, and what did he do to the Temple in Jerusalem? Who can tell us?"

"Put Greek gods there," a ponytailed little girl answered.

Jill listened as Phil continued, "Yes, Antiochus defiled the Temple. He put a statue of the Greek god Zeus there and ordered the people to worship Zeus from then on. Many Jews did what the king said, but others did not want to live like Greeks. So the king sent his officers around the land to enforce the new religion. When they reached the town of Modin, they found an old priest, a pious man named Mattathias, who was the father of five sons. Who knows what Mattathias told the king's officers?"

"He told them, 'Let my people go,'" a youngster replied.

"That was Moses, silly. That's a different holiday," another child said with a disgusted look. "Mattathias said, 'Buzz off, you creeps.'"

"Not his exact words, but close enough," agreed Uncle Phil. "Mattathias said, 'I and my sons and my brethren will walk in the covenant of our fathers. We will not hearken to the king's words, to go aside from our faith.' And he called for others who believed as he did to join with him, and he and his sons and their followers fled to the hills."

"And what happened, Uncle Phil?" Whitney had inched closer and closer as he had been speaking, and now she stood in front of him, her eyes round, her thumb in her mouth. Phil lifted her into his lap. "Well, my darling, I'll tell you. Those brave men fought the king's forces. And Judah Maccabee, the son of Mattathias, became their leader."

"We learned a song about Judah Maccabee," one of the boys interrupted.

"Would you like to sing it now?" Phil asked. "Come here, Jared, and sing for us."

"Me, too," a little girl offered eagerly.

"Girls can't sing the Maccabee song," Jared informed her, his voice ripe with disgust.

Ben leaned toward Jill and whispered, "A budding male chauvinist. I can't wait to see how Uncle Phil handles this one."

"You know, Jared," Phil said, tapping his finger against his forehead, "I've heard that some of the members of Judah's band were women. Brave women. So, Amy, you can be their representative, and both of you can lead us in the song."

With a huffy, "I told you so," Amy got up and joined Jared at the front of the circle. The two began, and the rest of the children joined in the song.

"I'd like to be a Maccabee,
So strong and brave and bold—"

As childish voices rose in the lively tune, Jill felt a stab of the pain she usually kept buried deep inside. She'd just promised herself she wouldn't allow unhappy memories to emerge, but tonight on Chanukah, with the candles flickering and the melodies of the holiday echoing around her, those memories swelled and surfaced, threatening to overwhelm her.

"And fight and win each fight I'm in—"

Somewhere in another house, in another city, was another little girl, perhaps singing the same song.

"But I am only eight years old."

A child just Amy's age. A child Jill had seen only once, a child she would never know. Her daughter. Hers and Mickey Zimmerman's. Born on the first night of another Chanukah and never forgotten.

A child few people knew of, not even Mickey, her father. A child whose existence had been concealed. Only Jill's parents and sisters, her grandmother and one aunt were aware of the secret of Jill's past.

As the group applauded Jared and Amy, Jill clenched her fists in her lap. More than anything, she wanted to run out of the room, shut herself in a bedroom and cry. But she couldn't call attention to herself. Especially not with Ben, the client she wanted to impress, in the room. Well, wasn't that why she'd invited him? To prevent just this sort of scene. She bit down hard on her lip and made herself concentrate on Uncle Phil as he complimented the children on their singing, then continued the Chanukah story.

"Though the Maccabees' forces were small, their cause was just, and Judah Maccabee and his followers defeated the army of King Antiochus. On this very day, over two thousand years ago, they returned to the Temple in Jerusalem, purified it and prepared to rekindle the eternal light which burned over the altar."

He paused dramatically. "But they had a problem. Who can tell me what it was?"

"No oil!"

"Not enough oil!"

"Right," Phil said. "They had oil for only one day, and it would take eight days to get more. A serious problem, don't you agree?"

"Yes, but God sent a miracle," cried an eager voice.

"And what was that miracle?" Phil asked.

"The oil burned for eight days."

"Absolutely right. And that is why, boys and girls, we celebrate Chanukah, the Festival of Lights, for eight nights, adding one candle each night to remember the miracle in the Temple and to commemorate our people's brave fight to worship as they chose."

Children and adults clapped as he concluded the story. "And now, boys and girls," Phil said, "I think we have some presents for you."

His words were met with ohs and ahs of delight. Jill and Ben watched as Uncle Phil began handing out Chanukah gifts, then they wandered into the family room and joined a group of people who were laughing and talking. Sherry was among them, but Jill was relieved that Lisa wasn't.

Conversation ranged from the ups and downs of the stock market to the Cincinnati Bengals' chances in the NFL playoffs.

"If the Bengals beat the Jets Sunday and the Dolphins beat the Oilers on Monday night, the Bengals sew up the division," someone said.

"Provided," Ben added, "the Steelers also lose to the Raiders. On the other hand, if the Bengals lose Sunday..."

Confused by the intricacies of professional football, Jill tuned out the rest. Then she smiled to herself. Except for a few uncomfortable moments, this evening had turned out well. She sent a silent thank-you to Ben.

After a while guests started drifting away, parents rounding up tired youngsters. Jill saw Lisa heading for the stairway, carrying Whitney in one arm and holding Kevin's hand.

As they passed the family room, Whitney lifted her head from Lisa's shoulder. She struggled out of her mother's arms and shuffled sleepily across the room to Ben and Jill. Her curly hair was tangled, and a smudge of chocolate decorated one cheek. She paused in front of them and yawned. "Good night, Aunt Jill. Good night, Ben. Are you *Uncle* Ben?"

Ben shook his head.

"Oh. Well, do you want to kiss me good-night?"

"I'd love to." He lifted her into his arms and chose the cleaner of her cheeks for a kiss.

When he put her down, she turned to Jill. "You, too, Aunt Jill."

How could she refuse? As she bent toward her niece she again wondered wistfully about her own child, the child she would never know. Did she have a caring family? Was she as affectionate as Whitney?

Jill breathed in the scent of baby shampoo and chocolate as her lips touched the tender skin of Whitney's cheek. The child gave her a moist kiss in return, then yawned again and plodded back to the door where Lisa waited. With a longing in her heart that would remain forever unsatisfied, Jill watched her go.

When she turned back, she saw Ben glance at his watch. "I'd better call it a night," he said. "I have an early day tomorrow."

"Me, too. I'll get my coat and we can walk out together."

"Coat?" he asked, looking puzzled. "Where are you going?"

"Back to the hotel."

"You're not staying here?"

Jill shook her head. "I have work to do, and I need a quiet place. Besides, Hope's there, and our art director will be in tomorrow. Staying where they are is more convenient." His look was still questioning, but that was the only part of her reason she was willing to share with him.

"Let's tell your parents good-night," he suggested.

When they had said their goodbyes he opened the door and they stepped out into a chilly night. Away from the porch light the evening was dark and still. Stars winked from a clear velvet sky. Across the street two firs, their branches garlanded with golden Christmas lights, stood like fairy-tale trees. Snow crunched under their feet as they crossed the yard to Jill's car.

She reached for the door. "I guess I'll see you tomorrow."

He stepped closer.

She took a step back, her gloved fingers clutching the door handle as if it were an escape hatch.

But he simply smiled and said in a friendly tone, "Thanks for the evening. I enjoyed being with your family. Holidays can be lonely when you're away from home."

She nodded. "I'm glad you could come." She pulled the handle and heard the click as the lock opened behind her.

"I owe you an evening."

"Oh, no, that's not necessary," she said quickly, easing the door open an inch.

"But it is." He smiled down at her. "We'll make it a business dinner—an evening at Steak Expectations. How about eight tomorrow night?"

A business dinner. The tension in her shoulders eased. "Okay."

He reached behind her and pulled the door open the rest of the way. "See you tomorrow. Drive carefully."

BEN WATCHED AS she pulled away, then got into his car and headed home, thinking about the evening, about Jill. She was an enigma. Knowledgeable and self-assured at work; uptight at home. She'd changed since her teenage years. Then, she'd been outgoing and bubbly. Years ago she'd been as generous with her affection as Whitney. He remembered seeing her hug or kiss Mickey Zimmerman unselfconsciously. Now was another matter.

He wondered what had happened in her life to cause that change. He hadn't missed the tension in her body each time he'd touched her, or the nerves in her rigid stance, her wide, almost frightened eyes when they'd stood in front of the car just now.

What to do about Jill? He was still pondering the question as he entered his apartment. He shrugged off his overcoat, went to the small bar in the corner of the living room and poured himself a Scotch. Then he wandered to the window and stared out.

The street before him was quiet. A lone car drove slowly by, its headlights creating golden pools on the asphalt. An empty street, a solitary car.

Loneliness. He'd lived too long with that emotion, over two years now. Nights of standing at the window, watching the street, watching for someone who would never come back.

Everything he'd done—and especially the few women he'd dated—had seemed like substitutes, inadequate and disappointing after Karen. He'd spent the first year getting over her and what she'd done to him. Then he'd been unwilling and unable to involve himself in any sort of relationship. But a few months ago he'd sensed a change in himself, a renewed zest for life, a feeling of anticipation. And now...

Again he thought of Jill. He wanted to know her better, to understand her, to touch her. But how? She'd be here such a short time, and he sensed there were walls to scale, barriers that would take time and patience to surmount.

With a tired sigh he left the window and sat in his favorite armchair. As he sipped his drink, he let his eyes rove over the bookshelf. Books had been his companions during the lonely times. They'd been the source of inspiration, humor, escape. His gaze stopped at *The Truth About Advertising,* a book he'd enjoyed in college, used as a guide when he'd worked for the ad agency, and still reread on occasion. He reached for the book and thumbed idly through the pages.

Then his lips curved in sudden amusement. What he needed was an advertising campaign. A plan to win Jill's trust. He'd think of Jill as the consumer, himself as the product. All he had to do was convince the consumer she needed the product. He should be able to do that. After all, marketing strategy was his specialty.

She wouldn't respond to a high-pressure campaign, he was certain. No, what he needed was a low-key, soft-sell approach. Ideas playing in his head, he put the book back on the shelf.

In his bedroom he stripped off his clothes and lay down. In the quiet, moonlit room his thoughts remained on Jill and the clear message she'd given him: "Don't touch." But, as the night wore on and the moon rose higher, he set his imagination free. In his fantasy he touched and tasted and experienced her. And, as he drifted into sleep, he promised himself that before Jill left Cincinnati he'd make that fantasy come true.

CHAPTER THREE

BEN SAT IN HIS OFFICE, eyeing a thick sheaf of papers on his desk. The proposal from the Tolar Agency, one of three vying for the Steak Expectations account. The ideas were on target. The agency had zeroed in on the right market, determined the appropriate media and focused on a simple, appealing strategy: highlight the steaks. Trouble was, he couldn't get excited about the execution of the concept. He frowned at the print and billboard ads—a steak sizzling on the grill with the line Well Done! beneath it.

A knock interrupted him. Before he could respond, the door opened and Frank McMinn entered. Controlling the urge to greet him with a sarcastic remark, Ben raised a questioning brow at his superior. It galled him that Frank, always in a hurry, habitually barged into his office without waiting to be invited.

"That the Tolar campaign?" Frank inquired, his voice a shade too eager for Ben's taste.

"Yeah, I've been going over their proposal again."

"And?" Arms crossed over his chest, Frank waited.

"The ads are simple, attention getting and certainly clear, but—"

"But what?" Frank interrupted. Clearly, the "but" annoyed him.

"But the concept has nowhere to go. Let's say we use Well Done for six months, maybe a year. Then what? Do we go with Rare?"

"Why not?"

Patience, Ben told himself. "I think we can do better."

Frank scowled. Good Lord, the man had barely glanced at the second agency's material and, of course, Carnaby and Ross hadn't had time to submit theirs. Was McMinn already pressing for a decision?

"Why don't we hold off discussing this until the final proposal comes in?" Ben suggested in a conciliatory tone.

"Of course, but push this Carnaby and Ross group along. I want their stuff by Friday."

Ben stared at McMinn in astonishment. "Frank, their deadline is Monday."

"Change it."

Ben felt the stirring of anger but tamped it down. "We can't do that," he protested. "They've barely begun. Besides, they're due the same amount of time the other agencies had."

"If they're good, they can prove it by showing us something sooner," McMinn said and began to pace the room.

"Dammit, Frank—"

"Friday," McMinn repeated. He reached into his jacket pocket with a hand that shook visibly.

What was this? McMinn was high-strung, unpredictable, but shaky—never. Ben watched as McMinn muttered a curse and dropped his hand to his side.

"Frank," Ben said, fishing for a reason for his boss's nerves, "still miss your cigarettes?" McMinn had given up smoking months ago, quit cold turkey the day after his doctor had given him a stern warning. He prided himself on his success in kicking the habit and never failed to sermonize on the dangers of cigarettes whenever he had the chance.

McMinn sighed. "Sometimes, when— Never mind." He turned abruptly. "I'll talk with you later."

Ben stared after McMinn with a puzzled frown as the man strode from the room. What in hell was bothering Frank? Something personal, perhaps?

On the other hand, for several months now Ben had been hearing rumors of a plan for reorganization at Wellner. Susan, his secretary, who seemed to have a direct line of communication into every department, said if that happened, McMinn was on his way out. Maybe McMinn sensed his job was on the line. Ben knew reorganization could mean a change in his own situation, as well. The ideas he and Alan Jeffreys had been kicking around suddenly assumed more significance. Good thing the two of them were meeting tomorrow. They had some serious talking to do.

In the meantime, he thought with a grimace of distaste, he'd better call Hope Wilson and give her the news that her deadline had changed. He was damn sure she wouldn't be happy to hear it. Trust McMinn to make the decision and leave him with the dirty work. With an oath, he picked up the telephone.

"No, NO, NO! THE LOGO is a disaster! It absolutely must go! Immediately!" Exclamatory sentences were as much Dan Givens's forte as art direction.

"Come on, Dan," Jill cajoled him. "You can't start out by asking Wellner to trash their logo."

"It goes or I go."

Jill rolled her eyes and urged Dan out of the car. "Come inside. You'll like the interior better, I promise." He'd settle down eventually, she knew. He just felt compelled to denigrate anything not designed by his own hand.

Inside the restaurant Jill greeted the manager and said, "Would you mind just turning us loose at first? We'll try to stay out of your way."

Then she followed Dan into the main dining room, listening as he continued his critique of the premises in a stage whisper she prayed went unheard by the staff.

"The dining room's a catastrophe," he muttered. "No spark. No color. What *could* these idiots have been thinking of?" He waved a hand, dismissing the room.

Jill bit her lip to hold back a laugh. "Dan, you once told me that black and white make a statement."

"In a different context."

"Well, I doubt they'll redecorate to suit your taste. Besides, the dining room probably won't appear in the ads. Personally, I like the decor."

Dan shook his head and wandered off. Watching him, Jill chuckled. His ego was colossal, but his work was outstanding. Together they'd formed one of the best creative teams at Carnaby and Ross. For that, she'd put up with Satan himself.

"We'll need a shot of the meat," Dan called over his shoulder, and Jill made a note for the photographer they'd hired.

For an hour after that they worked steadily—Jill discussing customer response with the manager and Dan making notes and sketches. Then they returned to the Hyatt, where they were to meet with Hope in her suite. On the way Dan, as usual in such situations, proclaimed the sheer impossibility of creating a decent ad. As was her custom, Jill tuned him out.

As soon as Jill knocked on the door of the suite, Hope opened it, a hand on one hip and a scowl on her face. "I thought you'd never get here," she snapped.

Jill raised a brow. "And good morning to you. Having a pleasant day?"

"Not really. I was going over the budget, which was bad enough. Then Abrams called, asking how we're coming on the ads. He wants them yesterday."

Dan responded with a picturesque suggestion as to what Abrams could do with his ads.

Jill decided to jolly Hope out of her mood. "Come on. Things can't be that bad."

"No? Well, listen to this. Our deadline has been changed. It's no longer Monday. It's Friday."

"Friday!" Jill tossed her purse onto the table. Ben had seemed so easygoing yesterday. Now he wasn't just giving them a rough time, he was being damned unfair! No, not unfair. Unprofessional. Prince Charming had turned into Godzilla. "What did you tell him?"

"I tried every way I could think of to persuade him to give us until Monday, but he wouldn't budge. We meet Friday afternoon at three."

Jill snapped open her briefcase, took out a legal pad and slammed it on the table. Tonight when they had dinner she'd tell Ben Abrams what she thought about that. Aloud she said disgustedly, "Typical client. Pressure, pressure."

Hope nodded. "I told him we're making headway."

"Okay, we'll make some," Jill said. "We've put out ads in a hurry before."

"I know we have, and we can this time, too," Hope said, "but a principle's involved here. We were supposed to have until Monday, and Wellner reneged."

"So what choice do we have?" Jill asked, already knowing the answer.

"None," Hope replied as expected. "Let's go to work, gang. I do have some good news, though," she added as they sat down. "I talked to New York, and word's out that Wellner is expanding into other areas. They have a takeover of a motel chain in the works. The agency they pick for Steak Expectations may get that, as well. And that means big bucks. So come up with something sensational, you guys. *Fast!*"

Over sandwiches and iced tea they tossed ideas around. Though in New York Hope wouldn't normally be included in one of their brainstorming sessions, here Jill welcomed her input. She knew a good deal more about the client than Jill or Dan, and, with a deadline in three days, they needed every scrap of information they could get.

"My sister says the restaurant's a good place to meet people," Jill commented. "How can we use that?"

"Sizzling singles," Dan offered, and was immediately booed down.

Hope wrote a line with a flourish and held up her notepad. "The meating place?" she asked and received another round of boos.

"Let's focus on the do-it-yourself angle," Jill suggested.

"Yeah, a steak made of Lego blocks," Dan agreed.

"Lincoln Logs."

"Tinkertoys."

"Oh, come on," Hope groaned.

"No, wait a minute. Maybe we're on to something," Jill said. She grabbed her pad. "Okay, think of as many crazy ways as you can to make your own steak, and I'll write them down. We need to use the same concept in print ads and television, so think action."

"Think graphics," Dan ordered. "We need something to overshadow that ghastly logo. What *am* I going to do with it?"

This was Dan's typical complaint, and Jill chanted her standard answer. "Make it smaller, Danny."

Within half an hour they'd come up with dozens of ideas. Then they began the task of selecting the best ones.

"Let's go with the little old lady knitting a steak," Dan suggested. "In the TV segment the knitted steak can turn into a real one."

They chose three more ideas—a paint-by-numbers steak, an origami steak and the original idea, a steak built from Lego blocks.

"Want me to start sketching?" Dan asked.

Jill hesitated. "I like the concept, but...something's missing."

"Don't tell me we're back to square one," Dan grumbled. "What's missing?"

"Are we really getting across the idea that the customer's the cook?" Jill asked.

"Sure we are. Everything we've picked is a do-it-yourself project."

"I know, but..." Jill turned to Hope.

"With three days, I say we'd better go with what we have unless you get an inspiration in the next ten minutes," Hope said.

"Okay." Jill put her objections aside and began a rough draft of the copy while Dan sketched. They worked without stopping until Jill called a halt late in the afternoon.

"Thank God," Dan said. "I'm getting out of here before Ms. Scrooge changes her mind." Quickly he packed up his sketches and left.

"What's on your schedule for tonight?" Hope asked as Jill gathered her notes.

"I'm going by my family's and then to eat at Steak Expectations."

"Want some company for dinner?"

"Um ... actually, Ben Abrams offered to take me."

"Oh? The charm won you over, hmm?"

"No." Jill busied herself stuffing papers into her briefcase and tried to sound nonchalant. "Ben turned out to be an old friend I knew when I was in high school. He, uh, came to the Chanukah party with me last night."

"Ah."

Jill snapped the briefcase shut. "Cut it out, Hope. If I can capitalize on an 'in' with the client, why not?"

Hope spread her hands. "I haven't said a word."

"But you *thought* loud and clear. Look, I should be back here around ten. I'll call you then and tell you my impressions of the food service."

"And of—"

"Don't say it," Jill warned, heading for the door.

"The customers." Hope's tone was innocent but when Jill looked back she saw that her friend's eyes were full of mischief.

Jill stalked down the hall. First Sherry, now Hope. Wouldn't anyone leave her alone? Just because Ben Abrams was "drop-dead gorgeous," as Sherry had said, and warm *and* witty, did everyone think she should fall at his feet? Annoyed at her sister and her friend, and even more irritated at herself because she half suspected they were right—she *should* fall at his feet—Jill jabbed the elevator button.

She dropped off her notes in her room and took a quick glance in the mirror. Today, attired in black pants and a bulky houndstooth sweater splashed with colorful daisies, she felt more comfortable. Daisy-shaped houndstooth earrings with red centers, a find from an offbeat Manhattan boutique, completed her outfit. She wondered if Ben liked the casual look, then cursed herself for wondering.

On the way home she stopped to pick up several small presents for Whitney and Kevin and deliberately put Ben out of her mind.

At her parents' house she endured more of Sherry's teasing about Ben, as well as her mother's thinly veiled probes about their relationship. Which, she assured her mother, didn't exist beyond business.

Finally she asked, "Where's Lisa?"

"She went to visit a…ah, friend. She'll be back in time for candle-lighting," Esther said.

Jill noticed the hesitancy in her mother's voice but didn't question it. She was glad Lisa wasn't here. Now she didn't have to be constantly on edge, censoring every word, every gesture.

They sat in the living room, sipping coffee and talking. Finally Sherry excused herself. "Have to go check in with David," she explained.

"Keep an eye on your watch," her mother suggested wryly.

Jill grinned at her mother. "I bet your long distance bill's going to be a killer this month."

As Sherry left the room, the sound of the front door opening and two high-pitched voices told them Lisa and the children had returned. They came into the living room, their cheeks rosy with the late-afternoon cold that followed them into the house.

As soon as his coat was off, Kevin disappeared into the family room, and in a moment the sounds of shrieks, pops and the tinny music of cartoons blared from the television.

Lisa sat down across the room. *As far away from me as possible,* Jill observed. Well, that was okay with her.

Whitney skipped over to her grandmother and received a kiss. When Esther excused herself to check on dinner, Whitney climbed onto the sofa beside Jill. "Hi, Aunt Jill. We went visiting, and I got brownies. Do you like brownies?"

"I love them."

"Maybe you can come with us next time. They prob'ly have some more. We went to see a baby," she announced, scooting back against the cushions. "It was a girl baby, wasn't it, Mommy?"

"Yes."

"But she didn't have much hair. She looked funny."

"Her hair will grow," Lisa assured her.

"She doesn't *do* anything," Whitney went on, looking disgusted. "Cousin Roz said she's a wonderful baby, but she mostly just sleeps. I don't think that's so great."

"Cousin...Roz?" Jill echoed. Lisa and her children had gone to see Roz and Mickey's new baby. Jill felt a sense of betrayal as strong as it was illogical. She turned to Lisa for confirmation.

"Yes," Lisa admitted. "Roz and Mickey came in this morning."

"Lisa!" Their mother's voice, shocked and disapproving, came from the doorway.

"What?" Lisa asked.

Esther came into the living room. "I thought we—"

"Thought we what? Weren't going to say anything in front of Jill? Whitney said it, I didn't. Besides—" her voice rose in obvious exasperation "—how long are you going to keep walking on eggshells around Jill? Don't say this, don't say that. For goodness' sakes, what's wrong with my visiting Roz? We were roommates at Michigan. We've always been close." She crossed her arms over her chest and raised her chin as if daring Jill to defy her.

Whitney's eyes widened as she watched her mother. "What's Mommy mad about?" she asked. Her lip trembled and she put her thumb in her mouth.

Esther went to the child and stroked her hair. "Your mommy's not mad, sweetheart. She's just...talking to Aunt Jill. Why don't you come and help me set the table? Grandpa will be home soon." With a warning look at Lisa, she urged Whitney from the room.

Jill waited until they were out of earshot. "Whitney was right. You are mad. Why?"

"Why not?" Lisa's voice transmitted an irritation Jill couldn't understand. "Why should you dictate what I do? I have a right to visit whoever I want."

"I'm not saying you shouldn't have gone, but *I* have a right to my feelings." Jill sighed with frustration. How could she explain those feelings to Lisa, who had never experienced anything as shattering as giving up a child? No, Jill thought with resentment, Lisa had two beautiful, loving children whom she could see and touch every day.

"Why do you feel so bad?" her sister asked. "Because Roz got Mickey?"

Jill shook her head. Mickey wasn't the issue here.

"Because she has a baby? You could have kept yours."

Of all the things Lisa could have said, this hurt the most. Lisa had just stated what Jill had always believed—that she should have kept her child. With a flood of pain and anger, Jill said, "I wish I had. I wanted to even then, but I let Mom and Dad convince me to give her up."

"But you didn't have to," Lisa persisted.

Jill tightened her hands into fists. Suddenly, irrationally, she wanted to slap her sister, something she'd done only once in her life, during a similar argument about this same subject. Infuriated now, she shot out of her chair and marched toward Lisa. "Do you have to belabor the point? I didn't have to give her away, but I did, and I can't go back now. Do you have any idea how I feel, knowing Roz and Mickey have a baby, an adopted baby, at that?" Lisa opened her mouth, but before she could speak, Jill went on. "And how can you sit there, giving advice about something you can't even begin to comprehend?"

Lisa propped her hands on her hips. "Are you saying I'm not smart enough to understand?" Her voice crackled with fury.

"No, dammit." Jill spoke through gritted teeth. "I'm saying you don't want to understand. You never wanted to." She stood opposite her sister, with hands on hips, mirroring Lisa's pose but looming over her. Rage surged through Jill, kindling a red haze before her eyes.

She and Lisa faced each other mutely, breathing hard. Blips and squeals of cartoons from the family room filled the silence.

The front door slammed. Footsteps sounded from the entry hall.

"What's this?" Joel Levin's voice was quiet but commanding as he looked from one to the other.

"A . . . discussion," Lisa said, her face reddening.

"It's nothing." Chagrined to be caught in a face-off with her sister, Jill swung around, returned to the couch and sat down, thankful her legs hadn't given out as she walked.

Her father glowered at them. "I could hear both of you before I opened the front door. This isn't the first 'discussion' you two have had. Whatever your differences, it's time you resolved them. Starting now."

"I have a business appointment," Jill protested.

At that, Lisa mumbled something under her breath.

"It's true," Jill said, her voice still shaky with anger. "I have to go." Besides, one evening's discussion would hardly be enough to work through her differences with Lisa.

"Tomorrow, then," their father said. "At least that will give you some time to get yourselves under control."

"I won't be back tomorrow," Jill said, swallowing tears. Her hands trembled, and she clasped them in her lap. If this was what she had to endure when she came home, she'd wait until Lisa left before returning. And in the future—business or not—she'd time her visits to Cincinnati more carefully.

"Of course you will." Her father sat down beside her and put his hand gently on her shoulder. His touch comforted her, calmed her, the way it had when she was a little girl and she'd gone to him with her problems. "This is your home. You two are family. Someday, when your mother and I are gone, you girls will be each other's only family. Now we'll light the candles and give the little ones their gifts, and tomorrow you'll talk."

He left the room. Jill sat silently, staring down at her hands. Lisa, too, said nothing.

From the family room Jill heard Kevin's dismayed voice as the sound of the television died. "Grandpa! You turned it off in the middle of the Ninja Turtles."

"You'll watch the turtles tomorrow. Now we're going to light the Chanukah candles. Go get your grandmother and Whitney and Aunt Sherry." He returned to the living room, glanced at Jill and Lisa in turn, then got out the candles and put them in the menorah.

In a few moments Esther came into the room, looking anxiously from one daughter to the other.

"Everything's all right," Joel assured her. "Tomorrow these two are going to make a start at working things out, right, girls?"

Her father spoke in the same tone he'd used to smooth over arguments when they were children. But they weren't kids anymore, and this wasn't a dispute over which of them got to watch a favorite television show or who had talked too long on the phone. This misunderstanding wouldn't be so easily resolved. Nevertheless, Jill nodded and saw Lisa do the same. She wondered if they'd really be able to work things out tomorrow, but, all right—she was willing to try.

She joined her family as they gathered around the menorah. Her father lifted the *shammash* and began the blessing. The two small candles sputtered and caught, their flames wavering upward. As her father returned the *shammash* to its place, he added, "And may tomorrow night see for Jill and Lisa, not the flame of anger, but the glow of family harmony and love."

"Amen," Esther said fervently.

"Amen," Jill murmured, and heard her sister echo the word. She glanced cautiously at Lisa. Their eyes met, and for the first time in eight and a half years Jill felt a faint glimmer of hope and saw it reflected in Lisa's eyes.

JILL WAS TEMPTED to cancel her dinner plans. Drained
and exhausted from her encounter with Lisa, she wanted
only to crawl into bed and sleep. But this was a business
appointment, she reminded herself. The reason she was
in Cincinnati. And no way was she going to let Lisa distract her from her purpose here.

So she ran her brush vigorously through her hair and
took special pains with her makeup, erasing the smudges
left by the tears she'd shed driving back to the hotel,
stroking blusher across her pale cheeks and adding cherry
red lip gloss. She looked passable, she decided, standing
back from the mirror and surveying herself critically.
Making a good impression on the client was important.
And concentrating on business would take her thoughts
off family problems.

When she heard Ben's knock, she felt a flutter of excitement. More than she'd normally experience before a
business dinner. "Cool it," she cautioned herself. The
last thing she needed right now was to get worked up over
a man. Hadn't Lisa just reminded her how much trouble
that could cause? Still, she had trouble heeding her own
advice as she opened the door.

He stood in the hallway, dressed in thigh-hugging jeans
and a tan cable-knit sweater that complemented the
brown of his eyes. "Hello," he said and held out a small
box wrapped in blue and silver.

Jill stared at it, flustered. "What's this?"

"Chanukah gelt." With a teasing grin he pressed the
box into her hand.

She tore off the wrapping and, sure enough, inside was
a small box of the chocolates that in recent times had
taken the place of real gelt, or money, traditionally given
to children during Chanukah.

Jill smiled, delighted. "Thank you. How did you know I'm a chocoholic? You didn't remember that about me, too, did you?"

"I saw the size of your piece of cake last night."

Laughing, she peeled the gold foil off one of the coin-shaped chocolates and popped it into her mouth, then, with a sigh of pleasure, reached for another.

He took a playful swipe at her hand. "Don't spoil your dinner."

"Okay, Dad."

She dropped the chocolates into her purse, glad she hadn't called off the evening. She was going to enjoy herself, not only because Ben represented a major account, but because he was congenial, thoughtful...a friend.

But as they walked together down the corridor she noticed her heart's increased cadence and felt a flush on her cheeks as Ben ran his eyes over her thoroughly and appreciatively.

"You look nice," he said. "More like yourself."

The comment intrigued her. "How do you know the tailored suit yesterday wasn't the real me?"

"Just a guess. When I worked at McKane Willis, all the creatives were...informal."

"Translation—sloppy?"

He grinned. "*You* said that."

They stepped into a crowded elevator, and Jill couldn't avoid standing shoulder to shoulder with him. In such close proximity she was very aware of him—the wavy hair that hugged his collar, the scent she'd already begun to associate with him, even the tempo of his breathing.

She was also aware—and afraid—that he could easily become more than a business associate, more than a friend. But perhaps she'd already discouraged that. He made no attempt to touch her in the elevator, nor did he put his hand on her waist to guide her through the lobby.

He opened the car door for her, and when they were on their way he asked, "So how was your day?"

Instantly her pleasant mood changed. Considering the pressure he'd put on them to produce their ad campaign instantaneously, how did he think her day had been? While she had his attention, she'd speak her piece. Diplomatically, of course. "Productive but stressful," she said. "Creating on demand isn't easy."

He shrugged. "You knew you'd have to create on demand when you came here. Advertising always involves pressure. You don't have the luxury of locking yourself in an art studio or sitting at a computer until the muse appears."

"True, but we generally have a firm target date."

She saw his cheeks redden, but he said nothing.

Warming to her topic, she continued. "My team is good, we're fast, but you can't snap your fingers and expect an idea to just pop out. You should know that if you've worked in advertising."

"And *you* should try to look at the situation from the client's perspective. We have restaurants under construction, bills to pay. We can't hold them up."

"Surely you knew that when you set the original deadline. If we'd known you wanted the proposal earlier, we'd have been here sooner, but we didn't have that information." She tried to keep her voice level in spite of her irritation, but she felt herself losing control. Yet she went on. "We don't need unlimited time. Just what we were promised. According to Hope, you told her you wanted the proposal immediately if not sooner."

"I don't believe those were my exact words."

"Close enough."

She saw his jaw tighten and a muscle twitch in his
cheek. She'd been on target, but she'd also made him
angry. Lord, how had she managed to get into an argument with the advertising manager? She was far too direct to be a diplomat, she realized. She'd better try
softening her tone. And she certainly didn't want to give
the impression that her agency couldn't come through.
"Don't worry. We'll have the proposal ready by Friday." Then she added, "And I apologize for getting so
worked up."

He glanced at her. "I understand how you feel. Personally, I'd be happy to wait until Monday, but—"
Abruptly he broke off and turned away.

But, what? Had he already decided on another agency
and didn't want to give Carnaby and Ross any more
time? Was someone putting pressure on him? She wished
she could ask him, but she couldn't afford to pry.

He was silent now, his eyes on the road. She needed to
do something to smooth things over. Like change the
subject.

"When did you work at McKane Willis?" The Chi-
cago-based agency was one of the country's largest and
most respected. Jill had interviewed there herself.

"I was there for five years after I finished business
school." He turned and smiled at her, and Jill suspected
he was relieved that she hadn't questioned his half-
finished comment.

"And you left to work for Wellner?" she asked, surprised.

He laughed. "You sound shocked."

"I guess I am. I can't imagine leaving the ad agency."

"Advertising does get in your blood," he agreed, "but
I was the account supervisor on the Wellner's Chicken
account, and when the corporation offered me a job, I

decided to get a taste of life on the other side of the table."

"Have you enjoyed it?"

"At times," he answered vaguely, then added, "It has its good points."

"What?" she asked, genuinely interested.

"Having dinner with creative directors."

"I mean, seriously."

"I am serious."

She knew he was teasing, but she couldn't help feeling flattered. "Other good points, then."

He stopped at a traffic signal. "Being on the client side has less pressure."

"And less challenge."

"You're right."

Their eyes met for a moment and Jill thought she saw some disquiet in his, but perhaps she was imagining. Just because she couldn't picture working anywhere but the pressure cooker of an advertising agency, she shouldn't read job dissatisfaction into Ben's casual comment.

The light changed, and she asked, "Do you miss Chicago?"

"No, I prefer Cincinnati. It's a beautiful city, and I like the slower pace."

She didn't miss Cincinnati or its pace, but she didn't want to differ with him again, so she nodded. "I miss the hills here," she said, intending to be agreeable, but realizing she meant it. Sometimes the flat sidewalks, the cement canyons of Manhattan wore at her and she longed for the slopes and greenery of her hometown.

Ben nodded. "I like the friendliness here, too. Don't you miss that in New York?"

"I live on the Upper West Side. The area has more of a neighborhood feel than the East Side." Was that why she'd chosen the location? Perhaps, subconsciously, that had been her reason. "I live in an old building that reminds me of home—on the inside, at least." Goodness, she was learning all sorts of things about herself. She'd never connected her choice of living quarters with a longing for home. In fact, she'd thought of the job in New York as a chance to get as far away from home and family as possible. Maybe she'd taken home with her all along.

Ben pulled up at Steak Expectations. "How about a truce for the rest of the evening? We won't argue about deadlines, you can soak up the atmosphere and we'll enjoy ourselves, okay?"

"Deal." His suggestion pleased her. She'd had enough confrontation for one day.

They entered the restaurant and found the large dining room already crowded. People were milling around the grills, table-hopping, laughing, eating. Dress was informal and the spirit of fun and holiday cheer filled the air.

"Want to have a drink first?" Ben asked.

"I'll try the bar another night. Right now I'm starving."

"Then let's get right to the important part."

She nodded. "Yeah, to the meat of the evening."

Ben laughed. "I bet you started out as a copywriter," he said as the hostess showed them to a table.

"I did, and I still write most of the copy for my team, although in New York we have a junior copywriter, too." She opened her menu. Dan had been decidedly unimpressed with the layout, mumbling under his breath about the third-rate design job. "My art director would love to get his hands on this," she said, tapping her finger on the page.

"We've just had the menu redesigned," Ben said. "The proofs came in this morning. You might want to take a look at them next time you're in the office."

"Thanks, I'd like to, and I'm sure Dan would love to see them, too."

The waitress approached them and explained the menu and cooking procedure. Though she was sure Ben had heard it a hundred times, Jill wanted to experience the whole routine. Afterward they headed for the refrigerator cases that lined the back wall. The steaks were enormous, but they decided on two different cuts so Jill could sample both.

At the grill Ben took charge. "Go on and mingle," he suggested. "I like to cook."

Jill watched him brush a sauce on the steaks and remembered the ad she'd teasingly suggested to Hope yesterday. "He cooked my steak. That's how I knew our love was real." *Watch out, Jill,* she told herself sternly. *Don't bite off more than you can chew.* God, how corny. She wondered what Ben would say to that.

Leaving him to handle the culinary chores, she strolled around, enjoying the hiss of sizzling meat, the smell of charcoal. The mood here was one of lighthearted camaraderie. She saw perfect strangers exchanging cooking tips beside the grill. A gray-haired black man was showing a young couple of Indian descent where to position their steaks over the coals.

To Jill's surprise, most of the cooks were men. She approached a ruddy-faced fellow who'd just sent his wife back to the table and asked, "Enjoying the cooking?"

"Sure. Just like barbecuing in the summer."

"Nah. This beats cooking out. No mosquitoes," the man next to him said as he turned the chicken he was grilling.

Jill wandered on. "Come here often?" she asked a couple at the next grill.

"About once a month. It's an inexpensive way to get a good steak," the woman said.

"This is my night to splurge on cholesterol," her husband added.

Another couple, who were alternating between cooking, cuddling and kissing, told her they'd met in front of the grill. "So we come here on our 'monthaversaries,'" they explained. "This is the third one."

We met at the grill. That might work into an ad, Jill thought as she meandered back to Ben.

"Steaks are almost done," he said. "Why don't you start on the salad bar?"

The greens were crisp and tempting. Jill made their salads, chose plump, foil-wrapped potatoes from the warmer and heaped butter, sour cream, cheese and chives on them. Back at their table she took out a notepad and jotted down her impressions. Maybe they could use the concept of barbecuing without all the fuss. "No mosquitoes," she scribbled and underlined it.

"Dinner is served."

She looked up as Ben set down the sizzling, juicy-looking steaks. "They look good." She sniffed. "Smell good, too."

"And how do they taste?"

She cut a slice, tasted, then tried another. "Delicious," she announced, then grinned at him. "My compliments to the chef."

He raised a brow. "Is that our ad?"

"No." *But it could be!* She felt a flash of excitement. "Maybe," she told him. "How about a TV commercial with a...a customer...standing at the grill? He's surrounded by busboys, a waitress and...let's see, the cook.

Everyone's applauding his steak...and the cook puts his chef's cap on the customer's head and says, 'My compliments to the chef.' What do you think?"

"I like it."

She'd found the spark that had been missing this afternoon! And the advertising manager had even said he liked her idea! Jill felt like jumping up and down and applauding herself. "Really?" she asked.

"Really." His eyes sparkled with the same kind of enthusiasm she felt.

She grabbed her pencil and began scribbling furiously.

After a few minutes Ben's fingers closed around her pencil. "Going to work all evening?" he asked, his tone teasing.

"This *is* a business dinner," Jill reminded him, looking up. "And I'm on a deadline."

"Uh-uh. Truce, remember?"

She grinned at him. "Sorry."

Ben gazed at her, lost for a moment in the depths of her eyes. They were beautiful, as changeable as the sea. Her lashes were long and thick. He imagined them brushing his cheeks.

She bent over her pad again and he smiled to himself. She was only partially right. They were having a business dinner, but for him the evening was also a pleasure.

Here again was the Jill Levin he remembered from years ago. This evening he'd watched as she circulated among the customers, enjoying her bubbly enthusiasm, the way she drew people out. She clearly relished planning an ad campaign, and this was the ideal turf for conducting his own campaign. He'd concentrate on friendliness and pleasant conversation...and leave the next move up to her.

A few minutes later she looked up and smiled fully, and his breath caught in his throat. He wondered if she had any idea of the effect she had on him. No, he decided as he watched her take another bite of meat, she was completely unaware.

While they ate, she plied him with questions about the restaurant, stopping every now and then to make more notes.

Dessert was apple pie. "Not as good as your mother's," Ben remarked.

"She's famous for her cooking."

"Did you inherit her talent?"

"Nope. I make great fudge, but I don't spend much time in the kitchen. New York's so full of food, you could eat in a different restaurant every night of the year and not hit them all. When I want to eat in, I usually stop and pick up something at Zabar's. They have everything from gourmet on down."

"How about your sister—the married one? Is she a cook?"

Jill frowned. "I guess Lisa cooks. She has her husband to feed, and Kevin and Whitney."

"When I first saw you with Whitney, I thought she was your child."

He watched with surprise as the color drained from her face. "Wh-why did you think that?"

"I thought perhaps you were married. Lots of women use their maiden names professionally."

She relaxed visibly. "Uh-uh. No ring." She wiggled the fingers of her left hand. "Didn't you notice?"

"No." He hadn't looked. He'd been busy concentrating on her face yesterday. Then when she'd opened the door with the child beside her, he'd felt an intense wave of disappointment, but when she'd explained that Whitney was her niece, a surge of relief. Now he wondered why his mistaken assumption should have upset her.

Before he could ask her any more questions, Jill checked her watch. "I suppose we'd better go," she said abruptly. "You probably have to be up early, and so do I."

He had a feeling her sudden insistence on leaving was a convenient way to steer the conversation away from herself. He signaled the waitress. He'd go along for now, but he was in no hurry to end the evening. He wanted to sit with her and listen to her talk, let the sweet, light scent of her perfume drift around him, lose himself in her eyes. He'd have to think of a way to prolong their time together.

He glanced at the bar as they passed it. No, in her present mood she'd probably turn down a suggestion that they stay and have a drink. *Low key,* he reminded himself. He'd give her time to relax first.

Fifteen minutes later, when they entered the hotel, he suggested, "Let's have a drink before you go up." She hesitated, and he added, "It's barely ten."

"Okay."

In the bar they sat across from one another in a shadowed booth and sipped brandy. Music from twin grand pianos filled the room. The tunes were mellow and romantic, but Ben couldn't have said what they were. He was too engrossed in the music of Jill's voice, the melody of her laugh. He was tumbling fast and deep, and he didn't care.

Jill stared at his face in the dimness. Unfair for a man to be gifted with such warm, expressive eyes. For a male to boast, not just one, but two dimples so deep a woman would kill to have them. Or to dip her tongue into them.

The brandy must be going to her head. How could she be thinking of a client this way? Well, why not? She was only fantasizing, after all. There was no harm in that...was there?

"Tell me about yourself," he murmured. "How do you spend your time away from work?"

"I like to sail. I have friends on Long Island who have a boat, and I go out there on weekends sometimes. I like museums and trying new restaurants, and I love the New York Public Library. What about you?"

He told her about winter ski trips, about books and music he liked, about his parents, who had moved from Cleveland to Florida to retire in the sunshine and whom he visited several times a year.

Time slipped by, the piano music ended, conversation around them quieted, and still they sat. Jill forgot about business and thought only of Ben.

"Another drink?" The waitress's voice intruded on their private world.

Jill looked up, startled, then glanced at her watch in surprise. "It's nearly one. I'd better go up." She sighed.

In the lobby Ben put his arm lightly around her shoulder, and this time she didn't pull away. Tonight his touch seemed right.

In the now-empty elevator they stood silently, his arm still around her. Jill's heart began to pound. Would he kiss her? Would he want to come in? She wanted... She didn't know what she wanted.

The elevator doors slid open, and they walked slowly down the hall. At her room she opened her purse and searched for her key, then unlocked the door and pushed it ajar.

When she turned back, Ben stood inches away. Their eyes met, locked. Her pulse thudded. Involuntarily her gaze dropped to his mouth. She held her breath.

He lifted his hand to her cheek, brushed his fingertips down it. "Sleep well," he murmured and stepped back.

Jill blinked as he took another step away, then caught herself. "Good night. I . . . I enjoyed the evening," she managed to say before she slipped inside her room.

She shut the door behind her and leaned against the wall. She'd been so sure he was going to kiss her. She'd misread him, she guessed. He obviously thought of her as a colleague, nothing more. Well, wasn't that what she wanted?

No. Tonight, for the first time, she'd wanted a different ending to an evening with a man. And as she undressed and got into bed she felt an unfamiliar and unsatisfied longing.

Ben got into his car and put the key in the ignition but didn't turn it. Instead, he shut his eyes, willing his heartbeat to slow. He'd used all the control he could muster to keep from kissing Jill, especially after her eyes had strayed to his mouth and her lips had half parted expectantly. Now his body was feeling the effects of that control. He took another breath and told himself his low-key, soft-sell campaign had better work soon because he damn well couldn't keep it up much longer.

CHAPTER FOUR

JILL OPENED HER EYES and sat up abruptly. What time was—*Oh, good grief*. Nearly eight. Had the desk forgotten her wake-up call again? She had the telephone receiver in her hand, ready to call and give the operator an angry lecture, when she remembered. They *had* called. She'd squinted at the clock, seen that it was only six-thirty and pulled the covers over her head and gone back to sleep.

Now she groaned and swung her legs over the side of the bed. Rubbing her eyes, she plodded into the bathroom. She *hated* oversleeping, having to jump out of bed and rush to get dressed. She preferred waking up slowly... very slowly.

She turned on the cold water in the sink, splashed a liberal amount on her face and peered at herself in the mirror. "You look like you've been carousing till all hours," she told herself with disgust.

Ben shouldn't have suggested that after-dinner drink. "Sure, Jill," she told herself. "He dragged you into the bar and tied you to the chair." Why hadn't she cut the evening short? Because...

Because she'd wanted to be with him. Because she'd hoped, even believed, the gleam in his eyes was for her, Jill Levin, the woman. Not Ms. Levin, creative director at Carnaby and Ross. "Well, you were wrong," she grumbled as she turned on the shower and stepped inside.

She yelped as icy water hit her full blast. Jolting back from the spray, she managed to lean around it and shove the control toward Hot.

She stood still for a moment and enjoyed the steamy water sluicing over her, but then, of their own accord, her thoughts returned to Ben. He'd been a pleasant dinner companion, a charming host for the evening and nothing more. Monday she'd been worried he might make a pass. Last night he hadn't even tried to kiss her goodnight. Not even a friendly peck on the cheek. Nor had he said one word about seeing her again. She must have imagined his interest.

"For the best," she admonished herself. She could think of a dozen reasons a relationship with Ben would be a mistake. Trouble was, she could think of a dozen more why it would be heaven.

"No use wasting time on make-believe," she said as she stepped from the shower and rubbed her body briskly with a towel. At least he'd been receptive to her ad idea. That was what was important, what she had to concentrate on, she told herself.

Yet she felt decidedly out of sorts as she hurried to get dressed. In a futile effort to cheer herself, she put on a black tunic embroidered with hearts and shooting stars in exuberant colors, and added a pair of black earrings with long gold tassels.

Her spirits didn't improve when she entered the hotel coffee shop and found Hope and Dan finishing their breakfast. Jill sat and took a healthy gulp of the black coffee the waitress poured for her.

Dan looked pointedly at his watch. Hope raised a brow and started to say something, but Jill forestalled it by rising abruptly and heading for the buffet.

She wasn't hungry, but she filled her plate with a little of everything, not caring what she ate. When she returned to the table, Hope cleared her throat and remarked brightly, "Tired this morning?"

"A little."

"Out late, were we?"

Jill took a mouthful of egg, noticing now how much food she'd heaped on her plate and wondering what she was going to do with it. She mumbled something noncommittal.

"I called you at ten," Hope continued. "And at ten-thirty. And at eleven. Then I gave up."

"Mmm."

"Must have been a tough steak to take so long to finish."

Before Jill could reply, Dan rose and shoved his chair back. "I can't handle girl talk this early in the day. I'm going to get another muffin." He headed for the buffet.

"Well?" Hope coaxed.

"Oh, all right," Jill said crossly. "If you must know, we stopped for a drink and began talking, and the time just got away from me."

"Nothing wrong with that," Hope said. She sipped her coffee and eyed Jill thoughtfully. "Going to see him again?"

"Certainly. I'll see him on Friday when we make our presentation."

"I meant after hours."

"No!" Jill snapped. "He didn't—we didn't talk about that."

Hope wisely didn't comment.

Dan returned to the table and Jill concentrated on her breakfast.

Finally Dan tapped on his water glass with his spoon. "What I want to know," he said, "is whether you came up with anything useful for the ad."

Jill looked up and brightened immediately. "Yes. I got Abrams's tacit approval for—Dan, you're not going to like this, but wait until I finish—for a whole new concept—"

"New concept!" Dan's spoon fell with a clatter. "The woman is mad! We have two and a half days, and she wants to throw out everything and start over."

"Now listen to me, Danny. Don't say a word until I'm done. Here's what we'll do." Quickly she outlined the "compliments to the chef" idea she'd had the night before, watching as the scowl disappeared from Dan's face and his eyes brightened. By the time she finished, he was beaming.

He turned to Hope. "What can I say? She's a genius! A toast!" He raised his orange juice glass and Jill and Hope followed suit. "To the creative director of the decade!"

Hope applauded. "Hear, hear." Then she asked, "Are you sure we can have this ready by Friday?"

"Piece of cake," Dan assured her. "Now, what we need to tell the photographer—"

As Jill quickly finished her meal, they made plans.

Upstairs in Hope's suite, Jill scribbled the first draft of a newspaper ad on her ever-present legal pad. Though the three of them spread out in separate areas, they traded ideas back and forth, their enthusiasm running high. Jill felt the exhilaration that came from knowing she was on target with a concept. Nothing could top that feeling.

Nothing could surpass the energy the three of them generated as they worked together.

But as the hour passed she noticed thoughts intruding. Thoughts of Ben. Questions. Like why *hadn't* he said anything about seeing her again? He'd prolonged the evening, and several times she'd noticed him gazing at her almost as if he were caught in a spell. Just before he'd left her at the door, when he'd touched her cheek, his eyes had darkened, two deep brown pools of desire. Then he'd just... left. There had to be some explanation. There had—

"I said, how's the copy coming?" Dan's voice was several decibels above normal.

"Uh, fine. Just fine." And it had been, until the past five minutes when she'd started daydreaming. What was wrong with her? She didn't have time for that now. She went back to work, crossing out, revising and crossing out again, knowing she'd continue until the copy was perfect. She'd keep trimming and polishing until every phrase counted, every word sparkled like clear, sharp glass. But now she needed a break.

She stood, stretched and walked over to the table where Dan's pencil was flying over his paper. She leaned over his shoulder and looked at the sketches spread before him. "Danny, these are great," she said, then chuckled. "That one, with the guy in the plaid shirt cooking steak—he looks just like this fellow I talked to last night."

Last night. As soon as she said the words, her mind shifted back to the evening before. To divert herself, she picked up several other sketches, but she couldn't focus on them. She put them down again and went back to her work.

A few more minutes and her mind was wandering again, searching for a clue to what had gone wrong with Ben. A man didn't spend three hours making conversation with a woman if he wasn't interested. Three *unnecessary* hours, she reminded herself. Their business dinner had been over at ten. He'd had no reason to suggest that long, leisurely drink unless he'd wanted to be with her. So why nothing further?

The phone rang and she jumped. Could Ben be on the line? She listened to Hope's conversation and realized the caller was the photographer they'd hired, wanting to talk something over with Dan.

Again Jill returned to her copy, and again she couldn't concentrate. Suddenly she stopped and tossed her pencil aside. Was she some namby-pamby Victorian lady who didn't dare make advances toward a man, some Cinderella waiting for Prince Charming to show up with the glass slipper? This was almost the twenty-first century, for heaven's sake. If a woman wanted to see a man and he didn't ask her out, *she* asked *him*.

Jill stood. "What time is the photographer meeting us?"

"Two-thirty," Hope replied.

"I'm going over to Wellner headquarters," Jill announced, picking up her purse. "I need—" *What? Oh, I've got it.* "To look at the new menus they've designed." Before either of her colleagues could question her, she marched out of the room.

Twenty minutes later she arrived at Wellner's offices, half out of breath from her rush through the building.

The receptionist smiled politely. "Ms. Levin, may I help you?"

"I'd like to speak with Mr. Abrams," Jill said.

The woman glanced at her watch. "He's usually left for lunch by now, but I'll check for you." She punched in a number on the switchboard. Jill held her breath. If Ben wasn't in, she'd just wasted a lot of time she didn't really have.

The receptionist glanced at Jill and mouthed, "He's here," then said, "Mr. Abrams, I'm glad I caught you. Ms. Levin from Carnaby and Ross is here and would like to speak with you. Yes, I'll send her right back." She gave Jill directions to Ben's office.

As she walked down the corridor Jill mentally rehearsed the breezy invitation she'd practiced all the way over. She hadn't had much experience—in fact, she'd had no experience—with asking men out because, until today, she hadn't wanted to. Now she wished she'd been more interested in socializing with the opposite sex. "Keep it casual," she reminded herself.

But when she knocked and Ben opened his office door, the words she'd prepared escaped her. He was standing so close and his smile was so appealing, his eyes so bright, that all she could manage was "Hello."

"Hi." He motioned her inside. "What can I do for you?"

Ask him now. Instead she postponed the question. "I wonder if I could look at the new menus."

"Certainly," he said. "I'll ask Susan to get them for you." Then he added, "You can make yourself comfortable in here. I'm taking my lunch hour to shop for Chanukah gifts for my family. Always put it off too long. I'm not good at picking out presents."

"I am."

"Really?" His voice was expectant.

"An expert," Jill assured him. "I love shopping. If...if you'd like some help, I could go with you. After

I look at the menus," she added, having almost forgotten the reason she'd given for coming here.

His smile was lazy, seductive. "A shopping consultant. Just what I've been looking for. How long will you need with the menus?"

"Ten minutes."

"You've got it." He called his secretary and told her what Jill wanted, then added, "We can grab a sandwich while we're shopping if that's okay with you."

She should get back to the hotel. Hope and Dan would wonder what had happened to her, but the idea of spending an hour with Ben was too enticing to pass up. She'd work doubly hard later, she promised herself, stay up late if she had to. "Yes," she said.

"Good." Ben's voice was husky. His eyes caught hers, and she felt the intensity of his gaze all through her. She couldn't tear her eyes away from his. Even when his secretary breezed through the door and put the menus on the desk, Jill had to give herself an internal shake before she could move.

She went over the menus quickly, surprised that she was able to concentrate so well with Ben waiting for her across the room. When she finished, they were on their way. As they walked sedately through the office, took the elevator down and then dashed through the garage, Jill experienced the same guilty exhilaration she'd felt when she'd once cut class on a dare her junior year in high school. She was on a tight schedule today; she should be working, yet here she was, out with a devastatingly attractive man.

"What did you have in mind for your father?" she asked as they drove downtown.

Ben shrugged. "Shirts, tie, handkerchiefs, I don't know."

"Handkerchiefs?" Jill laughed. "You *are* a dud at shopping."

"A loser," he agreed amiably. "A shopping drop-out."

"Maybe I can educate you," she said. "Tell me about your dad. What does he like to do?"

Ben thought for a moment. "Read, play golf. Since he's retired, he's taken up cooking. Bakes bread almost every week, my mother says. And he's gotten interested in bird-watching."

"Well, there you are," Jill said in her best school-marm's voice. "Four presents already—a first edition, a golfing cap, a set of baking pans, binoculars." She grinned at him, feeling pleased with herself.

"I am suitably impressed," Ben said, pulling into a parking space. "Let's go."

They entered McAlpin's, one of Cincinnati's large department stores, crowded with noontime holiday shoppers jostling one another for space. Every wall and display case was bright with Christmas decorations— wreaths, boughs, bells; every counter was piled with a tempting array of gifts. Harried clerks waited on equally harried customers while Christmas carols played in the background.

Jill looked around her, wondering for a moment, as she always did, whether her daughter might be in the store, whether they might pass one another without even knowing it. She knew the thought was illogical. This was a school day, after all, but she couldn't prevent her thoughts from taking their habitual track.

Then she caught herself and smiled at Ben. "Shall we start with a book or go for the binoculars? Or how about binoculars *and* a book on birds?"

When Ben nodded, she headed for the book department, then stopped. "Oh, look."

Before them was Santa's Wonderland—a castle with a chubby Mrs. Santa in the doorway, assorted elves, all eight reindeer plus Rudolph with his nose blinking on and off, and a sleigh piled high with toys. Santa sat on a throne near the back of the scene, with boxes of candy canes by his side. Children were lined up waiting to talk to him, and Jill felt a lump well up in her throat as she watched a small boy scramble onto Santa's knee.

"Wanna get in line?" Ben murmured in her ear.

She turned to him. "Uh-uh, I—" She blinked back a tear.

He frowned. "What is it?"

"I . . . I just get all choked up when I watch kids."

She shrugged, trying to make light of her feelings, but Ben looked at her gravely and gently brushed the tear away with his fingertip. "It's okay. So do I," he said softly.

The tenderness in his voice, in his touch was the sweetest she'd ever known. He took her hand and they walked slowly toward the book department. With her fingers enclosed in his warm, firm grasp, Jill felt secure, shielded from the pain she always carried with her. She wondered, just for an instant, how it would feel to be held close by him, to be pressed against him, body to body, heart to heart. The thought was too frightening, the consequences too drastic. As they reached the book department she forced the idea away.

They chose a book on migratory birds, then went on to the camera department. At least half a dozen pairs of binoculars were on display. "We'll look at all of them," Jill decided. Ben rolled his eyes in mock despair.

The clerk unlocked the case and began setting binoculars on the counter. "We'll just try them and call you when we decide," Jill said, smiling at the woman's relieved look as she turned toward another customer.

Jill selected one pair and motioned for Ben to choose another. They turned toward the crowds behind them and focused.

"These are great," Ben remarked. "Look. On the escalator. See that fat man with all the packages?"

"Where?"

"Halfway down. I can see the buttons on his jacket."

"I can't," Jill said.

"Here. Try mine."

He held the binoculars up to her eyes, and she put up her hand to steady them. Their fingers touched, and for a moment Jill forgot the fat man, the binoculars, everything but Ben. The warmth of his smile, the deep baritone of his voice, the light touch of his fingers. Then he asked, "Can you see him?" and the store came back into focus.

"Yes, perfectly," she whispered. "Even the stain on his sleeve."

Ben took the binoculars back. "Where?"

"Left sleeve near the wrist. Coffee, I think."

He laughed. "Yep. Very observant."

They continued trying binoculars, arguing good-naturedly about the merits of each pair. Finally they settled on the first ones they'd tried.

"Okay, now for your mother," Jill said.

"I always get her a—"

"Don't tell me. Let me guess. A handkerchief and a box of bath powder. The same kind every year."

"No," he said. "A billfold."

Jill shook her head. "Just as bad. This year you're getting her a silk scarf." When he gave her a blank look, she added, " 'Wrap her in color. Surround her with silk.' I did an ad like that once for a department store." Then, because it seemed natural to do so, she grabbed Ben's hand and pulled him toward the scarf counter. "What's her favorite color?"

"Blue."

"Here's one." She picked up a signature scarf with a swirling pattern of blues, golds and browns and, with a dash of pure mischief, slipped it around Ben's neck and tied it with a flourish. "What do you think?"

He peered in the mirror. "I don't think it's me."

"Oh, it definitely is," Jill insisted. "The brown matches your eyes." And it did. In spite of the ridiculous picture he made with a lady's scarf tied around his neck, the colors accentuated his thick lashes, made his eyes seem wider and darker. Dreamy eyes. Eyes you could get lost in. Jill made herself turn away, concentrate on the lighthearted mood. "Or how about this?" She held up a garish green scarf with orange flowers.

"Ugh! We'll take the first one."

While their packages were wrapped, they stopped for Reuben sandwiches in the store's crowded restaurant, then picked up their gifts and headed back to Wellner headquarters. Ben walked Jill to her car. "Thanks for your help. My parents will be overwhelmed."

She smiled at him. "Could I interest you in a pizza tonight?"

"Yes, but it'll have to be late. I have to meet a business associate after work."

"Okay with me. I promised my family I'd come by when I finish this afternoon." She wasn't looking forward to the talk with Lisa, but she'd given her word.

"I'll pick you up at your hotel, then. Around nine?"

"Fine. See you later." She drove slowly down the ramp, unable to resist watching Ben in the rearview mirror. He stood still for a moment, gazing after her car, a half smile on his lips, then turned away.

Jill's heart soared as she drove back to the Hyatt. She turned on the radio and hummed along as Natalie Cole sang "Unforgettable."

For the first time in years she was interested, truly interested in a man. She felt expectant, exhilarated. And scared. Where was she heading?

BEN GRINNED AS HE SAT at his desk and leaned back. His campaign to win Jill was going just as he'd planned. In fact, better than he'd anticipated. Tonight he'd step it up a notch, he decided, his smile widening. He'd—

His phone rang, and he straightened and picked it up. "Ben Abrams."

"Mr. McMinn would like to see you in his office."

"Be right there." He strode down the hall, knocked and opened McMinn's door. "What's up, Fr—" He paused, surprised to see his boss with a cigarette in his hand and a full ashtray on his desk. Something must be seriously amiss for Frank to suddenly resume smoking. And not just smoking. *Chain*-smoking. "Is something wrong?" Ben asked carefully, taking a chair across the desk from his boss.

"You tell me," Frank snapped.

Ben stared, puzzled. "I don't know what you mean."

Frank took a long pull on his cigarette. "I understand you've been socializing with the creative director from Carnaby and Ross."

So, Ben thought, the office grapevine had been at work and in record time, too. His own secretary? No, Susan

was too loyal to gossip about him. Maybe McMinn's
secretary, a straitlaced woman who made no secret of her
disapproval of what she called "office hanky-panky,"
which included anything more intimate than a three-
minute conversation in the hallway.

He'd make light of the situation with Jill, Ben decided, because it was entirely innocent. Moreover, it was
none of Frank's business. "Ms. Levin and I are old
friends."

"You were shopping together in a department store
during your lunch hour."

"You make it sound as if we were having an orgy," Ben
retorted. "Yes, we went to pick up a few things. And it
was her idea."

"I don't care whose idea it was. It's a conflict of interest." Frank jabbed his cigarette on the side of the ashtray.

If McMinn had suddenly grown two heads, Ben
couldn't have been more shocked. "Frank, you can't be
serious." But he could see the man was dead serious. The
mild annoyance he'd experienced at Frank's disapproval
escalated to an anger he couldn't afford to express.
Keeping his voice mild, he leaned forward. "Ms. Levin
stopped by to look at our new menus. We went out for a
quick lunch, and she helped me pick out some Chanukah gifts for my family. It was no more a conflict of interest than your lunch with her and Ms. Wilson on
Monday."

"That was a business lunch. Yours was clearly social."

Ben thrust his hand into his pocket and clenched his
fist. "All right, I won't deny that. What's the point of
this, Frank?"

"I'm surprised you have to ask. We're in a touchy situation, choosing between three agencies. I won't have us accused of favoritism."

"I can assure you there'll be no favoritism on my part."

Frank's face turned a mottled red. "What are you implying by that? Favoritism on mine?"

Ben found it hard to follow Frank. None of his conversation made sense. "I'm not *implying* a damn thing," he said, feeling anger bubble through his veins. "I'm telling you straight out that a sandwich and a shopping trip won't destroy my objectivity."

"See that they don't."

Ben said nothing. He would remain unbiased; he knew he could.

Frank tapped his fingers on the desk. "Now, how soon is that proposal coming in?"

"Fr—"

The telephone rang, startling Ben. Frank usually had his secretary hold his calls when they met.

Now, however, Frank grabbed the receiver, almost dropping it in his haste to answer the call. "Yes," he said, listened for a moment, then wrote something on a pad. "Two o'clock Tuesday," he said in a low voice. "No, Glenda, I don't want you to go alone." He paused to listen, then said, "No, don't call Ellen. I want to go with you. I have time." His voice was gentle, reassuring, a decided contrast to his tone a few minutes ago. "I'll see you tonight." He put the receiver down slowly and stared blankly into space.

Finally, as if suddenly remembering Ben's presence, Frank shook his head and turned to him. "My wife is having some...treatments. Chemotherapy." He made an effort to keep his voice level, unemotional, but Ben could see the pain in his eyes.

Ben was shocked. He knew Glenda McMinn had had surgery recently, but he hadn't heard that it was anything serious. "I'm sorry," he said. His acquaintance with Glenda was limited to company socials, but he'd found her warm and charming, and he was sincerely sorry to hear that she was ill. "Is she—" What was the appropriate thing to say, he wondered, then settled for, "Is she doing well?"

Frank shook his head and reached for another cigarette. His hand trembled. "Chemotherapy's a long shot, but it's the best they could offer." He took a long drag on his cigarette. "The only thing they could offer," he added.

"I'm sorry," Ben repeated.

"Thanks," Frank said. Then with a noticeable effort, he straightened. "Where were we?"

"You were asking when the presentation from Carnaby and Ross is scheduled. It's Friday at three."

"Why not tomorrow?" Frank put his cigarette in the ashtray and drummed his fingers on the desk.

He's back to normal, Ben thought, his anger returning. He felt truly sorry about Frank's personal problems, but his sympathy for the man didn't diminish his disgust at Frank's unfairness toward Carnaby and Ross. He listened to the rhythmic tapping of McMinn's fingers, one of his boss's habits that never failed to annoy him. Then he took a deep breath and ordered himself to stay controlled. And in control.

He rose. "Their presentation isn't tomorrow because you already sliced two days off their timetable, and because I will not call them and chop off another." Without another word, without giving McMinn a chance to respond, he turned and strode out of the office, shutting the door behind him with a decisive click.

He scowled at McMinn's secretary as he passed her desk. The woman was an incurable prude. He was certain she was the one who'd reported his shopping trip with Jill to Frank. And probably to everyone else in the agency.

To hell with them, he decided as he strode into his office and slammed the door behind him. He had not the slightest intention of curtailing his time with Jill. Wellner might pay his salary, but they didn't own him.

Half an hour later Susan came in with some letters for him to sign. "Still fuming?" she asked.

"You noticed."

"Yeah, and I can't blame you. Cora was out of line telling McMinn about your shopping trip."

Ben muttered an oath. He'd been certain McMinn's secretary was the culprit, but how had Susan found out? "You know about that?" he said. "Good God, is there a hot line into every office in the company?"

"Cora sounded off about you in the lounge."

"Good Lord. To how many people?"

"Just to me," Susan assured him.

"And?"

"You know I don't pay any attention to her, and no one else does, either. She's nothing but an old fussbudget."

"Yeah, and she meddles in everyone's business. Just what I need," Ben muttered darkly.

"*I* think it's great that you went out with Miss Levin," Susan said.

"Thanks, but keep it under your hat, will you? I'm not interested in becoming a hot gossip item during coffee breaks."

"Ben, you know I don't talk about your personal business." Susan was clearly hurt.

"I know. You're my eyes and ears in this company and I appreciate that." He did. Ever since she'd come to work for him, Susan had fed him valuable tidbits of information. What her sources were, he had no idea. He did know she was one person in the organization whom he could trust implicitly.

Still, as he and Alan Jeffreys began their conversation after work that evening, he was glad they'd chosen an out-of-the-way spot for their meeting. He didn't need to run into anyone from Wellner, particularly since he was uncertain about whether to leave the company and strike out on his own. And he was doubly cautious about deciding now. He didn't want to leave Wellner impulsively just because he was angry.

He stared at the ice cubes in his glass as he stirred his Scotch and thought about the spread sheets Alan had shown him.

"So, what do you think?" Alan said, waving his hand at the computer printouts he'd arranged on the table.

"Looks promising," Ben said.

"Promising, hell! The possibilities are mind-boggling."

Ben chuckled. "Spoken like a true advertising man."

Alan leaned forward. "Seriously, Ben. Cincinnati...heck, the Midwest, is ready for a hotshot ad agency, one that's willing to try new approaches, take risks."

"Maybe."

"No maybe about it. People are tired of old, stodgy ads. The business is out there. Someone's gonna come along and grab it. Why not us?"

"Starting a business is a big undertaking."

Alan gave him a hard look. "You saying it's too big for you?"

"No, just trying to look before I leap. We both have good jobs—"

"Boring jobs. Half the time I feel brain dead."

Ben laughed. "Okay. Safe jobs, then."

"How safe? Didn't you tell me Wellner may be reorganizing? Next month you could be out on your—"

"Yeah, I know."

"So? Are you so enamored of your situation you don't want to leave it?"

Ben took a breath. "No." The anger he'd felt this afternoon surfaced again. "No," he repeated more strongly. "I've had about all I can stomach of McMinn."

"Then what's the holdup?"

Ben swirled the liquid in his glass. "Guess it's my background. I was brought up to 'make haste slowly.'" He glanced up, caught his friend's grin and matched it. "Let's see those figures again."

They perused the information Alan had assembled, discussing finances, contacts, staff.

"I hear Jay Graham is looking to make a move," Alan remarked. "He's one of the most innovative guys in the business. I could put out a feeler, see if he'd be open to taking on the creative department at a new agency."

A picture of Jill flashed across Ben's mind. To see her every day. To work with her. "Hold off on Graham," he said. "I have someone else in mind. The creative director I'm working with right now. She's as good as Graham, maybe better. At least, that's my initial impression. I haven't seen her presentation yet, but I will on Friday."

"Is she in Cincinnati now? I'd like to meet her," Alan said. "How about lunch tomorrow?"

"Whoa, let's not jump the gun. We haven't decided for sure about opening the agency and you already want to interview the staff. On the other hand . . ." He paused to consider. "You did say something about getting together to watch the Bengals game Sunday, didn't you? Maybe I'll bring her with me."

"To watch the football game?" At Ben's nod, Alan grinned. "Sounds like your interest in this creative director goes beyond business."

"Maybe."

"How long have you worked with her?"

Ben cleared his throat. "Since Monday."

Alan stared at Ben in openmouthed surprise for a moment, then threw back his head and guffawed. "Since *Monday*. And this from the guy who makes haste slowly!"

"I guess she swept me off my feet."

"She even has the man talking in clichés. I can't wait to meet her. I'm glad Trish and I will still be in town Sunday. We'll definitely plan on watching the game."

"When are you leaving?" Ben asked.

"We take off next Wednesday and head out to Denver for Christmas with my in-laws. Then we're leaving the kids with them and taking a few days for ourselves. Ski trip and second honeymoon. We'll be back around the third.''

"I'll have an answer for you by the time you get back," Ben assured him. "Once I get through selecting an ad agency for the chain, I'll be able to think straight. McMinn is really putting on the pressure."

"Okay. Just don't put the decision off too long." Alan began putting papers back in his briefcase. "Want another drink?"

Ben glanced at his watch and felt a rush of anticipation. "Uh-uh. I have plans for dinner."

"Ah, the creative director."

"Yeah, and—" He grinned as a thought crossed his mind. "I have a stop to make first."

CHAPTER FIVE

THE SHOOT AT Steak Expectations had gone well, Jill thought as she drove toward her parents' home. The photographer had promised the proofs no later than noon tomorrow. She was certain the copy she'd written ranked with her best. The ads were going to be nothing short of sensational, plus they would be ready by the Friday deadline.

And, of course, there'd been the shopping expedition with Ben. She broke into a smile, picturing him draped in the silk scarf, remembering the sound of his laughter, the way he'd stood gazing after her car as she drove away. Something was happening between them. Something special. And they had the evening before them to explore it.

But first, she had to deal with Lisa. What would they say to one another? Could they make a start at reconciliation after so many years of estrangement? Eight and a half years now, since the summer of her pregnancy, when everything had fallen apart.

Or perhaps their alienation had begun long before. She and Lisa had veered off in opposite directions during their adolescence. They'd had different interests, different goals. Lisa's life revolved around boys, parties, makeup; Jill had focused on school—the journalism club, the National Honor Society, student council. Not that she hadn't had her share of boyfriends, but they hadn't been the center of her world. Until Mickey.

She parked in front of the house and got out. Maybe this evening she'd find the answers to questions she'd never thought to ask. Maybe she and Lisa were mature enough now to address the issues between them. One thing she promised herself; she'd keep her cool.

She rang the bell, and her mother opened the door. "Come in. Coffee's almost ready, and I've just taken out a batch of cookies."

A reprieve. She wouldn't have to talk to Lisa right away. "Chocolate chip?" Jill asked hopefully, shrugging out of her coat and following her mother to the breakfast room.

The scent of freshly baked cookies met her. Lisa and Sherry were seated at the table with Whitney between them. Jill glanced apprehensively at Lisa and got a wary look in return. Clearly, Lisa was as nervous about the promised confrontation as she was.

Jill sat down, Esther poured coffee and they talked about the holiday, the latest news, the weather.

Jill supposed her mother had engineered this family tête-à-tête to calm her and Lisa. Doubtless Esther wanted to remind them of happier times, of after-school snacks when they'd sat at the table giggling over school gossip and commiserating with one another about homework and tests.

If that was her mother's plan, it wasn't working. Beneath the casual talk lurked strain. Jill felt herself becoming more and more edgy; yet she dreaded the talk with Lisa and wanted to postpone it as long as possible. She tried to concentrate on the conversation to take her mind off her sister.

"Jill, are you going to be here for the benefit Sunday evening?" Sherry asked.

Had she missed something? "What benefit?"

"You know. The annual Chanukah Ball for the Shirley Cohen Agency," Esther said.

The agency that had handled her child's adoption. Of all times for them to have a benefit, just when she was home. Jill shook her head. "I hadn't heard about it."

"Of course you have," her mother said. "Remember, I called and told you to bring something dressy."

The call had come while she was packing, and she'd tossed her blue chiffon into the suitcase. But her mother hadn't told her about a special affair; she'd simply said, "You'll need a cocktail dress." Jill knew she'd hardly have forgotten a mention of the Cohen Agency. She suppressed her irritation at her mother's lack of candor and tried to make up her mind.

She wavered. How could she go? How could she not? She searched for an excuse. "I'll probably have an early meeting Monday."

"The ball's right in your hotel. You can leave whenever you want," Esther said.

"Why don't you ask Ben?" Sherry suggested.

Again Jill vacillated. She wasn't sure she could face an entire evening focused on the Cohen Agency; yet she owed them her support. With Ben along, the evening would be easier. "All right," she said. "I'll ask him."

"Good! David will be here and Todd, too—right, Lisa? We'll have a great time," Sherry said. "They're having a raffle and they're giving away fabulous prizes. I'll show you." She jumped up and left the room. In a minute she returned with a list of items to be raffled off. Everyone exclaimed over them, but Jill felt her tension mounting. Thoughts of both Lisa and the Cohen Agency had every muscle in her body tightening. She glanced covertly at her sister and noticed Lisa fidgeting with her wedding band. Lisa looked up, and their eyes met.

Nothing would be gained by delaying their talk any longer. "Lisa?" Jill said.

Her sister nodded. "Mom, would you excuse us?"

Jill took a last swallow of coffee and stood. Lisa folded her napkin with exaggerated care as if postponing their confrontation one last instant. Then she, too, rose. "Let's talk in my room," she suggested.

Jill followed Lisa up the stairs and into her bedroom. As she sat down, Jill felt a strong sense of déjà vu. She'd spent so many hours here, curled up on the bed talking; seated on the floor while Lisa gave her a manicure; posed at the mirror, trying on a pair of her sister's earrings.

Had they been close then? They'd lived in the same house, shared the same background. Like all siblings, they'd clashed sometimes, gotten along at other times. They'd been comfortable with one another, but close? Jill sighed. She couldn't remember.

She glanced around her as Lisa shut the door. "The room's hardly changed."

Lisa nodded. Her high school graduation picture still sat on the dresser. Her old bulletin board hung on the wall, crowded with snapshots of her and various high school and college friends. A stuffed tiger presented to her when she'd been sweetheart of a high school fraternity sat on the shelf along with other mementos of adolescence.

Nothing had changed, and yet everything had. Jill felt tense and uncomfortable. Where once she'd sprawled easily, now she sat, stiff and awkward, on the edge of the bed.

Lisa settled cross-legged on the other bed. Hands in her lap, she twisted her wedding ring, pushing it up and down over her knuckle as she'd done downstairs at the table.

What should she say, Jill wondered. She and Lisa were strangers now, and she didn't know how to begin.

At last Lisa broke the silence. "It's been a long time."

"Yes."

"You don't come home much."

"I'm too busy." That was a lie, and they both knew it.

"You should make the time to come. Mom and Dad feel bad that you stay away."

Jill felt irritation build and tried to ignore it, without success. She clenched her fists. "Don't lecture me, Lisa."

"I'm not." Lisa sounded defensive. "I'm just telling you how they feel because *they* won't."

"All right, I hear you." Jill didn't want to talk about her parents' disappointment that she visited so rarely. She had reasons for staying away, but she didn't want to get into them with Lisa. "But that's not what we're here for."

"No. I suppose you want an apology for yesterday." Lisa raised her chin.

"That would be nice."

"Okay, I'm sorry."

Jill sighed. Lisa wasn't sorry, she could see, and if their conversation continued in this vein, they would accomplish nothing. "We aren't here just about yesterday," she pointed out. "We're here to talk."

"So talk."

Lisa wasn't going to make this easy, but they had to start somewhere. Jill took a breath and plunged in. "Why do you hate me, Lisa?"

Shock registered on Lisa's face. She evidently hadn't expected such a direct approach from Jill. "I don't hate you," she demurred. "I just find it hard to sympathize with your. . . problems and the way you went about solving them.''

"Are you that heartless?" Jill's voice rose. "I was seventeen, unmarried, pregnant.''

"Well," Lisa said, "you should have been more careful. You knew where babies come from.''

"Are you telling me that you and Todd never made love before you were married?"

Lisa blushed and stared down at the hands still moving nervously in her lap. "No, but we were careful.''

Jill snorted. "You were lucky. Look, I made a mistake, but I don't have to justify myself to you.''

"You made a mistake and then you took the easy way out.''

Now it was Jill's turn to be shocked. "Is that what you think? That giving up my baby was the *easy* way? Well, let me tell you. The easy thing would have been to keep quiet about the pregnancy, terminate it and no one would have been the wiser.''

"You considered doing that?" Lisa's expression was disapproving.

"Not for a minute. I'm just saying it would have been easier than facing Mom and Dad, living with their disappointment in me, putting up with your contempt—''

"You brought that on yourself. Someone as smart as you should have known better.''

Her sister's tone was suddenly more than Jill could bear. Anger, pain, frustration—all boiled over at once. "All right, Miss Perfect," she said, forgetting her vow to control her temper, "so *you* would never have gotten yourself into such a predicament. Good for you. But why couldn't you have been more understanding of me? Why did you have to make things worse?"

"In what way?"

"You have a short memory, sister dear. You berated me when I was miserable and scared. You made me feel like a criminal. The least you could have done was keep out of it."

"Keep out of it," Lisa scoffed. "Your... condition affected my life, too."

Jill jumped up and began to pace. "You're talking about your blasted wedding. All you cared about was that your wedding come off without a hitch, that you walk down the aisle—"

"Without my sister showing the world that she was pregnant. Without you having to wear a maternity bridesmaid's dress."

"Oh, good grief, Lisa. I fit in the dress."

"Only because the dressmaker let it out at the last minute. You'd gained six inches in your waist in a week."

Jill swung around and faced Lisa, hands on her hips. "Two inches, and remember, she did fix it. You had your perfect wedding. No one suspected I was three months pregnant."

"Or that I had red marks under my makeup where you'd slapped me."

Jill flinched. "You called me a tramp."

Lisa said nothing.

No apology was forthcoming, Jill realized. Well, she could be bigger than her sister, apologize for that long-ago slap. She sat on the bed again. "I'm sorry I hit you that morning. I was wrong."

"It's one of the things I'll always remember about my wedding day."

Jill squeezed her eyes shut. She could still picture that morning. Lisa, clad in the dainty undergarments she would wear beneath her wedding gown, her dark hair flowing around her shoulders, her face flushed with anger. She remembered Lisa's bridal bouquet on the table behind her, the cloyingly sweet fragrance of gardenias. She'd hated that scent ever since.

She could see herself, the bridesmaid's dress half off, bunched around her thickening waist, still feel the tears of shame on her cheeks, hear Lisa's voice rising hysterically.

Every word Lisa had shrieked at her was indelibly imprinted in Jill's mind. "Look at you. There's no way that dress will fit. You're so smart, didn't you know this could happen? Didn't you think? Or didn't you care? Tramp, that's what you are, a—"

Unable to bear the sound of Lisa's voice, she'd reacted on impulse and swung at her sister. Her palm had connected with Lisa's cheek, the crack of the impact reverberating through the room like a shot.

They'd both collapsed in tears. And, although a skillful seamstress had salvaged the dress in time for Jill to walk down the aisle, neither she nor Lisa had ever forgiven or forgotten.

Jill opened her eyes and stared at her sister. "Oh, God, Lisa, don't you think I remember, too?" Her voice was thick with the same misery she'd felt on Lisa's wedding day. "I only wish I didn't remember so well."

For the first time she saw regret in her sister's eyes. "I'm sorry I called you a tramp."

Jill took a shaky breath. Lisa was not a person who apologized easily. The words she'd just spoken had cost her, Jill knew. "Thank you. I suppose you had no way of knowing what I went through that summer. You were happy and in love, caught up in planning your wedding and then in your own pregnancy. How could you relate to what I was experiencing, especially when you disapproved so strongly?"

"What I objected to," Lisa said quietly, "was what you did about the baby. How could you give away your own flesh and blood?"

"What choice did I have?"

"People always have choices."

She hated Lisa's holier-than-thou attitude. Come to think of it, she'd always hated it. Her sister had had a habit of admonishing the two younger girls in a superior tone that had never failed to stir Jill's ire. She glared at Lisa. "You're lecturing again. But since you're giving me the benefit of your wide experience, why don't you tell me what you would have done?"

"Kept the baby," Lisa answered promptly.

"Raised her alone?"

"If I had to. I can't imagine giving Whitney away. Or Kevin. Nothing...*no one*...could have taken them from me." Lisa looked like a mother lion, ready to fight to protect her cubs.

"You think I didn't care, don't you?"

"Did you?" Lisa asked.

"More than you can imagine. There hasn't been a day in my life that I haven't thought about my...my daughter, that I haven't wondered where she is and if she's happy. She...she haunts me."

"You're sorry you gave her up?" Lisa's voice softened.

"Every minute. If I could go back— But I can't. I was a kid at the time. Mom put tremendous pressure on me." When Lisa started to say something, Jill held up a hand. "I'm not blaming her. The final decision was mine. I'm just saying that she spent a lot of time telling me what she thought was best. And you know Mom."

Now Lisa's nod was understanding. "She can be pretty forceful."

"That's putting it mildly."

"I don't think she could have convinced me, though," Lisa said.

Her remark, her tone, shattered the momentary peace between them. "There you go again," Jill said, "drawing conclusions about a situation you know nothing about. You don't know what you would have done if you'd been in my shoes."

"I wouldn't—"

Jill stood, towering over her sister, and had the satisfaction of seeing Lisa flinch. "For the last time, Lisa, *you don't know*. When you were pregnant you were happily married to a man who wanted a baby as much as you did. I was alone, I was scared, I was too young to even think about what my options were. I listened to my parents. And why are we arguing about this eight years after the fact? I can't go back and change the past and you know that. Besides, in the long run, what happened affected my life, not yours. What do you have to be angry about now?"

Lisa dropped her eyes. "I . . . I don't know."

Jill was certain Lisa did know, that her sister had issues on her mind but wasn't ready to deal with them. What they were, Jill had no idea.

Both of them were silent. There seemed to be little more to say. Jill took a deep breath, shut her eyes and sat back on the bed, leaning against the headboard.

She'd vented long-held anger and she was relieved, but had she and Lisa achieved any kind of understanding or simply reached an impasse? They'd both spoken their minds, no doubt about that, but Jill suspected there were other barriers between them, higher and more difficult to scale. Just now, though, she was too drained to confront them.

She opened her eyes as Lisa said, "Dad's going to ask what we accomplished. What shall we say?"

Jill managed a faint smile. "Let's tell him we've established a truce. At least we've talked about all this for the first time in eight years. But there's more to say, isn't there?"

Lisa looked away. "Yes."

"Let's leave it for now." Jill stood. "I don't think I can deal with anything else tonight. If you feel like talking again, I'll be here until Tuesday morning. Come on. Let's go downstairs and see if Dad's ready to light the candles."

They trooped downstairs as Esther came out of the living room. She scanned their faces. "I was just about to call you. Everything all right?"

Jill held up her arms. "We're okay. See? No injuries." Behind her she heard Lisa's chuckle.

In the living room they found their father waiting, *shammash* candle in hand. He said the blessing, lit the three candles and put the *shammash* back in its place. Then he turned to Jill and Lisa. "Well, girls? Have you settled your differences?"

Jill smiled wryly. "Not completely, but—" she glanced at the candles glowing in the menorah "—I think we've shed some light on the issues."

"Good." He crossed the room, put an arm around each of them and squeezed. "The best Chanukah gift you two could give me is to be friends again."

"Sisters," Jill corrected and wondered if they could ever be friends.

"Now, then," Joel said, "time for presents."

Whitney and Kevin came forward eagerly and received several small packages each. Whitney got clothes for her Cabbage Patch doll, a pocket-size dollhouse with every amenity, and a new storybook, which Grandpa promised to read her at bedtime.

Kevin unwrapped the Ninja Turtle T-shirt Jill had bought the day before. "Okay!" he shouted, pulled off the shirt he was wearing and discarded it in favor of the new one.

After everyone had exclaimed over the gifts, Esther remarked, "By the way, Jill, Bubbi is back in town. She said she'd like to hear from you."

"Oh, wonderful," Jill said. "I was afraid I'd miss her. I'll call her this evening."

"Call after dinner," Esther told her. "Everything's ready."

"Thanks, Mom, but I'll pass tonight," Jill said.

"Why? You're not sick, are you?" Esther asked.

"No, I'm going out for a pizza at nine."

Sherry raised a brow. "Who with?"

"Ben Abrams," Jill said and waited for the inevitable razzing from her younger sister.

It wasn't long in coming. "Ah-ha! Three nights in a row. Fuse ready to ignite?"

To her consternation, Jill blushed. "Maybe," she admitted.

"Jill, why don't you have a snack?" Esther suggested. "You won't be eating until late."

Jill shook her head. "I need to get back to the hotel." She wanted some time to think about her talk with Lisa. But a few minutes later, as she drove back downtown, she found her thoughts were not on her talk with Lisa but on Ben and the evening to come.

WHEN BEN KNOCKED on her door, Jill was on the phone with Bubbi. "I have to go," she said. "My... friend's here." She referred to him as her friend, but privately she had begun to think of him as more than that. How much more, she wasn't sure yet.

"Have a good time," her grandmother said. "I'll see you at lunch tomorrow."

Jill opened the door. "Hi. Oh!" she said as she saw the package in his hand. "Another gift? You—"

"Shouldn't have?" he teased. "But this is Chanukah. Come on, open it." He followed her into the room and leaned against the dresser, watching as she tore the paper off.

She opened the box and found something soft, wrapped in tissue paper. She unwrapped the tissue. "A handkerchief," she said, unfolding the small, lace-edged square. "And this has to be—" she reached down into the box "—bath powder!"

She laughed, charmed by the gift, by the reference to her teasing him about his shopping habits. She wanted to hug him, and she took a step toward him. Then her natural reserve took over and she stopped. Instead she cocked her head to study the powder box. "Does this mean I remind you of your mother?"

"No way, lady." He grinned and shook his head emphatically. "No way in the world you remind me of my mother. Or my sister, either." He adopted an exaggerated leer, running his eyes over her body like a seasoned rake, and Jill laughed again.

But midway through his performance his teasing look faded, his eyes darkened and he stared at her with such an intense, heated gaze that Jill's heart began to thud.

At last he tore his eyes away. He picked up the coat she'd tossed on the chair and held it for her. As she slipped her arms into it, he leaned closer. She felt his warm breath on her neck, and she shivered.

"Cold?" he murmured in her ear.

She shook her head. She wanted to shut her eyes, rest her body against him and absorb him with all of her senses. His scent, his strength, his touch.

Fool, warned a voice inside her. *Haven't you learned anything in nine years?* She stepped away. "We should go."

In the car she gave him the address of the pizzeria and settled back. They chatted easily, taking up where they'd left off in the afternoon.

"Were the menus helpful?" Ben asked.

What menus? she almost answered, then remembered the ploy she'd used to see him. "Yes," she said. "I like the way you've changed them. They're more upscale. My art director was impressed, and, believe me, it takes a lot to impress him."

"Tell me about him."

"Dan? I suppose he's typical of most creative people. He's demanding, temperamental, egotistical."

Ben frowned. "Sounds hard to work with."

"At times. But he's incredibly talented and innovative. I think he's a genius. Not that I'd ever admit that to him."

"And you? Are you a genius, too, at what you do?"

Jill laughed. "I'll let you decide that when you see our presentation on Friday."

"I suppose you have a busy day tomorrow."

"Yeah, but if all goes well, we should be done by evening."

"Good. Some friends are having a crowd over for *latkes* around six. Think you'll be through in time to go with me?"

"I think so." Pleased that he'd asked, she vowed she'd make certain they were finished. Now, in turn, she would ask him for Sunday night. She'd been shy about doing that, but his invitation made it easier. "I wonder if you'd like to go to a fund-raiser with me Sunday night," she said.

"Thanks. I would," he said, looking as pleased by her invitation as she'd been by his.

"My whole family's going," Jill told him. "Sherry's boyfriend will be in for the weekend."

"Good. I'm looking forward to meeting the guy who caught that live-wire sister of yours. How about Uncle Phil? Will he be there?"

"Oh, I'm sure he will. He never misses benefits. He's a great supporter of Jewish causes."

"Who is the benefit for?" Ben asked.

"The..." Why was it so hard to say? She took a breath. "The Shirley Cohen Agency."

"The adoption agency?" he asked sharply.

"Y-yes."

He scowled. Why did he seem so irritated? What could he possibly have against the Shirley Cohen Agency? "W-would you rather not go?" she asked.

He hesitated a moment, then shrugged. "Of course I want to go."

Though he smiled at her, his manner seemed unconvincing. Still, she accepted what he said. "Okay. I'll find out the details and let you know tomorrow." She glanced out the window to see that they'd arrived in Clifton, the neighborhood surrounding the University of Cincinnati. "There's the restaurant, on the right. Romeo's."

"I'd say 'restaurant' is an exaggeration," Ben remarked a few minutes later when they stepped inside. The café was small and dark, with a few tables and half a dozen booths along one wall, nearly all of them occupied. Across the room stood a line of arcade games. Three young men clustered around one, watching a fourth manipulate the joystick on an aerospace game. At the other end of the line a lone man muttered aloud as he sent one of the Super Mario Brothers over an obstacle.

"Okay, so it's more of a hole-in-the-wall," Jill admitted. "But Romeo makes the best pizza in town. At least, he used to."

"You mean there really is a Romeo?" Ben asked.

"Sure is."

"Let's see if his pizza's still up to snuff," Ben suggested as they walked up to the counter at the back where a thin, mustachioed man stood ready to take their order. Behind him they could see two men in chef's regalia. One, using a long wooden paddle, shoved pizzas into an oven, the other tossed a circle of pizza dough into the air and caught it expertly.

Jill sniffed. Oregano, garlic, tomato, Italian sausage. She looked up at the menu printed on a wooden board suspended from the ceiling.

"What's your pleasure?" Ben asked.

Jill ran her eyes down the list. Everything sounded delicious, and she was starving. "Pepperoni," she decided. "Mushrooms. Black olives."

Ben wrinkled his nose. "No olives."

"Let's compromise. Half with olives, half without."

"Okay." They ordered a large pizza, salads and glasses of Chianti, then slid into one of the booths.

"This was my favorite hangout when I was in high school," Jill remarked. "I used to come here at least once a week for a pizza fix."

"And when you came home from college?"

"Uh...sure. Then, too." She hadn't come home from college. Cincinnati hadn't been "home" anymore but a place of painful memories.

"Where did you go to school?" he asked. "Obviously, not Ohio State."

"George Washington University." She'd gone to D.C.—to Maryland, actually—to stay with Aunt Leah during her pregnancy. *To keep me out of sight,* she thought, the hurt still intense, especially so tonight after her discussion with Lisa. The Cohen Agency's Washington branch had taken care of the adoption. Jill had stayed on in Washington after the baby came and enrolled in college the next semester, only weeks after giving birth.

"Did you like it?"

"Sure." Had she liked it? She couldn't remember. Her university years were a blur. She'd continued to live with her aunt, a Washington attorney who'd been widowed young and never remarried. Living off-campus, she'd never become involved in the college scene. Besides, her wounds had been too raw, her guilt too sharp to allow her to concentrate on anything but her studies. They'd been her salvation, kept her busy, helped her stay at least partially grounded in reality. Eventually she'd made a few girlfriends, but she'd discouraged all male overtures.

"Washington must have been an interesting place to live."

She nodded. She had vague memories of the White House, the Capitol, the Washington Monument. She hadn't appreciated the glamour, the excitement of the city. "But I like New York better."

The day after graduation she'd left Washington without a backward glance and moved to Manhattan, hoping to put the past behind her at last, to begin a new life. To a large extent she had succeeded. She was happy now. She enjoyed her work, had made good friends, even dated sporadically. She'd gained some success and, what was more important, a measure of contentment. Even though there were times when she felt like a war casualty, never quite healed, never quite forgetting the ordeal she'd experienced.

The man at the counter called their number and Ben picked up their order. Jill sampled the cold, crisp salad, the hot, spicy pizza. "As good as ever," she pronounced. "This place is Cincinnati's best kept secret."

"Not hard in a city that prefers chili over any other fast food," Ben remarked. "Want to talk Romeo into an ad?"

"Uh-uh. No ad campaign. Then his pizza wouldn't be a secret anymore."

They ate, talked, sipped wine. Ben returned to the counter and refilled their glasses of wine and brought them back to the table.

As they finished eating, noise from the other side of the room increased. Jill turned as a cheer went up from a group clustered around one of the video games. "What's going on?"

"Looks like someone's about to make a high score. Want to watch?"

"Sure."

They crossed the room and pushed their way into the crowd. A boy of about sixteen was guiding his plane through a maze. Flashes of electronic lightning, cannon blasts and bombs zoomed toward him while other planes dived at his, but, to the delight of the onlookers, he managed to evade them all. "He's gonna make it all the way," whispered the kid beside them in an awestruck voice, and Jill stood on tiptoe to get a better view.

Ben was in back of her, and as the crowd shifted he was pushed forward, so close against her she could feel the beat of his heart. He put his hands on her shoulders, and the zaps and whirs seemed to leap from the video machine straight into Jill's body. She tried to concentrate on the excitement of the game, but all she could focus on was the clamor inside her. Pulses of electricity seemed to arc through her, speeding her heartbeat, sapping her breath. Vaguely she noticed that the boy's score was increasing. So was her blood pressure.

When the kid finally won the game and a cheer went up, she let out the breath she'd been holding, assuming Ben would let her go. He didn't move.

The crowd around the machine began dispersing, the spectators congratulating the high-scoring youth, but Ben stood still. Jill glanced over her shoulder. "Shouldn't we sit down?"

"In a minute," he murmured, his lips almost grazing her cheek. "I like holding you."

They stood there, oblivious to the people around them. Finally Ben let out a breath and dropped his hands. He put an arm on her waist and guided her back to the booth. "Shall we go?" he asked and she nodded.

Outside, the temperature had dropped. Jill shivered, and Ben turned her toward him and pulled the lapels of her coat tight beneath her chin. He smiled down at her, slowly removed one of his gloves and lifted a hand to her hair, threading his fingers through the curls. "Like lace," he murmured.

"Your... your hand must be cold."

He shook his head. "Uh-uh, but your ear is." His finger, touching the lobe, now heated it. "We'd better get in the car."

They said very little as they drove back downtown. Ben reached for her hand. For an instant Jill thought of pulling away, but he clasped it firmly, and she left it in his.

The air seemed to vibrate between them. She knew without his saying a word that he wanted to make love to her. Desire communicated itself through his touch, through the glances he gave her as he drove.

She felt the same desire. She wanted him, but it was too soon. They hardly knew one another. She'd be gone in a few days, and although she longed for him, she was also afraid. Of intimacy with a man. Of Ben's reaction if he learned of her past. He'd acted so strangely for a moment when she'd mentioned the adoption agency. What would he think if he knew she'd used their services?

Ben parked at the hotel and came around to open the door for her. He took her arm and pulled her close against his side as she got out, kept his arm tightly around her as they went through the lobby and rode the elevator to her floor.

At her door, Jill got out her room key, but before she could insert it in the lock Ben took it from her. He opened the door and followed her in.

The light by the bed was on, but the rest of the room was in shadow. Jill reached for the switch, but he put his hand over hers and stopped her.

She stepped away from him. "Ben, I—"

"Relax. I'm just going to kiss you." He took a step closer, tipped her chin up and put his mouth on hers.

Just going to kiss you. Just? If this was "just" a kiss, she'd never been kissed before.

His arms held her so gently, his lips moved over hers so softly, but she felt as if he were devouring her. The tip of his tongue brushed her lips, coaxing them open, then retreated, only to advance again to dip into her mouth, then withdraw, enticing her to follow.

She heard his breath roaring in her ear, felt his heart speeding beneath her hands. She moaned and urged him closer, but he held back, never tightening his embrace, never deepening the kiss. He didn't need to. The light pressure against her mouth, the teasing dance of his tongue made her body go slack, made her dizzy with desire.

The kiss went on and on, and just when she thought she would shatter into pieces, he broke away. For a moment he stared into her eyes, then he lifted a finger and touched her hair. "Good night," he whispered. "Sleep well." He opened the door and was gone.

Jill sank down on the bed and lifted a trembling hand to her lips. Sleep well? However she slept, she knew her night would be filled with dreams—erotic dreams—of Ben.

CHAPTER SIX

"THIS IS WONDERFUL." Seated at the breakfast-room table in her grandmother's small house, Jill surveyed the lunch Bubbi had set out. Cold salmon, salad, and because Bubbi knew it was her favorite, a *kugel*—noodles combined with apples, nuts and raisins, sugar and cinnamon and baked to crisp perfection. Delicious. With the fork halfway to her mouth, Jill stopped to enjoy the tempting aroma. "Why do you suppose food always reminds me of home and family?"

The tiny, gray-haired woman who sat across from her smiled. "Who knows? I'm the same. Whenever I taste mint, I think of your grandfather, may he rest in peace. He loved a sprig of mint in his tea in the summer. You were so young when he died—do you remember him?"

"Yes, and the smell of his pipe tobacco and of the peppermint candies he used to give us."

Her grandmother's eyes stared into the past. "He was a good man. I hope you find someone as kind and compassionate."

Though a picture of Ben flashed through her mind, Jill shook her head. "I'm not looking."

"And why not?"

Bubbi sounded so indignant that Jill couldn't help laughing. "I have a career to think about."

"Pah! You think you can't have marriage *and* a career? Women of today—" she spoke the phrase as if it were in italics "—can have both."

"I'm surprised to hear you say that."

"You think because I'm an old lady I can't have modern ideas? I'm as up-to-date as you, maybe more."

Jill couldn't resist teasing. "I thought women's liberation came too late for you." She savored another bite of *kugel* as she waited for Bubbi's comeback.

Bubbi sniffed with disgust. "Women's liberation! Your generation thinks they invented it. Well, let me tell you, young lady, your zayde and I, God rest his soul, had...what do you call it? An equal partnership. We worked together in the store, we planned together, we raised our daughters together. Of course—" her voice trailed off "—I didn't burden him with the cooking and cleaning."

"No?"

"Of course not. My Aaron would have been lost in the kitchen."

"Bubbi, you're a contradiction."

Her grandmother ignored the comment and continued, "Now, your mother's generation, that's a different story. What did every one of them want? A man, of course. He should earn the living and she should raise the babies and do the housework. For some, it wasn't enough. My Esther, for example."

"Mother?" She was an organizer, true, but Jill had always thought her mother a typical homemaker, absorbed in her children, her house, Jewish women's organizations. Did Bubbi see a different picture?

"She would have liked a career."

Jill stared at her grandmother. Nothing could have surprised her more than Bubbi's remark. To her knowledge, her mother had always been goal oriented. If she wanted to do something, she did it. Hearing that she'd wanted a career, something she'd never had, astonished Jill. "Why didn't she go for it? Mother would have made a good executive. She's a dynamic lady."

Bubbi shrugged, cut another piece of *kugel* and put it on Jill's plate. "She's dynamic, yes, but did she follow her dreams? No. She didn't even question the dreams I had for her."

Another surprising statement. "What dreams did you have?"

"What dreams does any mother have? I wanted my daughters to have an easier life than I did. I thought being a homemaker would give Esther that. It didn't. I think being a housewife frustrated her. But she was like most daughters—she wanted to please her mother, so she lived out my dreams." Bubbi laughed wryly. "Instead of a career, Esther settled for being president of B'nai B'rith Women. She's the real contradiction."

"She always acted like being B'nai B'rith president was her greatest achievement in life."

Her grandmother nodded. "A substitute achievement, though. It's a shame Esther was born a few years too early."

"Do you really believe she stayed at home to please you?" Regardless of what Bubbi said, Jill found the idea hard to swallow.

"She would never admit it, but I think that was part of the reason." She glanced at the almost-empty casserole. "How about some more *kugel?*"

Jill shook her head. "I'm stuffed."

Bubbi began to clear the table. "Why are you so surprised about your mother?" She glanced curiously at Jill.

"Because," Jill answered, "I never thought of Mother having to please someone else. I guess when you're a kid you think grown-ups please only themselves."

"Pah! Girls spend their lives trying to please their mothers," Bubbi said. "You, for instance."

Jill rose and picked up her plate. Her expression was grim. "I'm afraid I didn't do a very good job of pleasing Mom."

Bubbi opened the dishwasher and bent to load it. "You made a mistake," she said without looking around, "and you suffered for it. Your mother suffered, too."

"Mother?" Jill gave a disgusted snort.

"She suffered." Bubbi's tone was emphatic.

"She never showed it. All I ever saw was her anger." Jill couldn't conceal her bitterness.

Bubbi straightened and looked at her. "Esther hides her pain well." She uncovered the cake plate that sat on the kitchen counter. "Are you too stuffed for dessert?"

Jill shook her head. "I'm never too stuffed for your German chocolate cake. But you'd better make it a small piece."

Bubbi cut the cake and they carried their dessert plates back to the table. Jill stabbed her fork into the cake. "Mother never gave me an ounce of support back then."

Bubbi sighed. "No, I guess not. She was...how do they say? She was fighting her own demons."

"What do you mean?"

"Ask her. Have you ever talked to her about that time?"

Jill shook her head.

Bubbi poured a cup of coffee and passed it to Jill, then poured another for herself. "You should. Talk to her, tell her how you felt. And listen."

The idea of talking to her mother made Jill uncomfortable. They'd never discussed their feelings about her
pregnancy. Decisions, plans, arrangements, yes. But
never feelings. She changed the subject. "I talked to Lisa
last night."

"Good. You two have held grudges much too long,"
Bubbi said, stirring cream into her coffee. "You need to
put your childhood feuds behind you."

"We're working at it."

"That I'm glad to hear. And next you'll talk to Esther."

"Maybe on another visit," Jill said.

"Why not now?"

"Talking to Lisa's one thing. But Mother is totally
different. I don't know if I can deal with what she'll have
to say."

"But you need to," Bubbi insisted. "You have to talk
about the past and then put it behind you." When Jill
started to protest that she had, Bubbi shook her head.
"You let the past run your life."

"I don't. I have exactly the kind of life I want."

"But you're not looking for a husband."

Jill grimaced. "What kind of modern woman are you,
Bubbi? Surely you realize that a 'woman of today'
doesn't need a man to make her life complete."

Bubbi shrugged. "Need, want. Two different things."

"I don't *want* a husband either."

"Haven't you ever met anyone who made you tingle?"

Jill began to laugh. "Made me tingle? You sound like
an old song. No, I—" She paused. She'd always been
able to talk to Bubbi about anything. Why not tell her
about the confusing, volatile feelings she'd had these past
few days? "Well..."

"Well?" Her grandmother's eyes twinkled.

Jill took a deep breath. "The other day I ran into someone I met a long time ago. I . . . I don't know how I feel about him."

"Is this someone a man of today? Is he like the women's magazines say?"

Jill chuckled. "Warm, caring, strong, yet vulnerable?"

"That's right. So, this man—he's strong and vulnerable?"

Jill grinned at Bubbi. Her grandmother was a whimsical mixture of yesterday and today. "Right."

"So what's not to like? Why are you having trouble deciding how you feel?"

Jill rested her chin on her hands and stared thoughtfully out the window at the snow-covered yard. "I'm afraid to get involved so fast."

"So? Get involved slowly. If love is *bashert,* if it's meant to be, you'll know."

"I . . . I guess I'm afraid to get involved at all."

Bubbi pushed her plate away. "What did I tell you? Again the past is controlling you. You're afraid because years ago you got mixed up with a man and things worked out badly."

Jill shook her head vehemently. Her grandmother didn't understand. "The situation with this man has nothing to do with the past. I hardly know him. Besides, he's in Cincinnati. I'm in New York. What's the point of getting into a relationship that has no future?"

"Is this my granddaughter talking? Pah! My Leah fell in love with a man who lived in Washington. So what did she do? She took a little vacation there, went to see the White House, the Capitol. She came back with an engagement ring." Bubbi nodded sagely. "You love this man, you'll find a job in Cincinnati. Or he'll find one in New York."

"Easier said than done," Jill answered.

"If that's the way you feel, then he's not worth the effort. Forget him."

Forget him? That, too, was easier said than done.

Bubbi waited a beat, then said, "But you don't like that idea, either."

She'd never been able to hide her feelings from Bubbi. "No, I don't. I . . . I don't know what I want."

"I think you do," Bubbi said gently, "but you're scared."

Jill stared into the blue eyes that looked back at her so knowingly, as if they could see her deepest thoughts, her hidden fears. "Yes," she whispered, "because—"

"Because," Bubbi prompted. When Jill said nothing, she continued. "Because you might make another mistake."

Jill nodded.

"You won't." Bubbi spoke with calm certainty.

Jill was touched by Bubbi's placid assurance. "You're the only one who's always had faith in me."

"The only one? You're exaggerating."

"Mother was disappointed in me. Lisa said I was a tramp."

"Pah! Forget what Lisa said." Bubbi stood and began stacking the plates and cups, the dishes clattering in the quiet room. "She spoke in anger. And you've made her words your . . . your—?"

"Slogan?" Jill asked, her voice shaky.

"If that's what you call it, yes. You see what I meant about letting the past control your life?" Bubbi sat down again and put her hand on Jill's shoulder, her touch gentle. "I don't want to see you close yourself off from love because of what happened long ago. You can't change the past, but you can go on."

Jill sighed. "Oh, Bubbi, I don't even know how this man feels."

"So you'll nudge him along and he'll tell you." The faded blue eyes gleamed and Jill could see vestiges of the coquette her grandmother must once have been.

"I would, but there's something else." Bubbi waited, and after a moment Jill continued. "Last night I asked him to the benefit for the Cohen Agency on Sunday. He seemed so pleased. Then, when I told him who the benefit was for, he...well, he sounded as if he disapproved."

"Could that be your imagination?"

"I don't think so. I can't help but wonder what he'd think if he knew."

"Maybe you're not ready to tell him yet, but when you are, if this young man cares for you, he'll understand."

"I wonder."

"Give him a chance. And if he doesn't understand, you didn't want him, anyway," Bubbi said firmly.

Jill smiled at that, but inside she wondered if her grandmother hadn't made everything sound a little too easy. Life had a way of throwing you a curve when you least expected it. Still, her grandmother always made her feel better, at least for a while.

"You know, Bubbi," she said, "I had a dream about you last night. I was walking down the street, wearing a red snowsuit I had when I was about five, and no matter how far I walked, I couldn't find our house. I sat down and started to cry and all of a sudden there you were, walking toward me, carrying this gigantic purse, as big as a suitcase. You gave me a handkerchief, then you took a pencil and paper out of the purse and said, 'You're not lost. Draw a map,' and you disappeared. Then I woke up.''

"So maybe I was telling you something about life." She patted Jill's shoulder.

Jill caught the wrinkled hand and squeezed. "Maybe you were. Thank you." She checked her watch. "I have to get back to work soon, but before I leave, why don't we have another piece of that chocolate cake?''

BEN SCANNED Beverly and Don Berger's family room. Half a dozen single men and women and an equal number of young marrieds with their children were scattered around. In one corner two dads had teamed up with their sons to play Nintendo. Their laughter echoed throughout the room. Three preschool girls were cuddled together in an armchair giggling, while several boys of the same age sat on the floor, moving plastic cartoon-character dolls through an elaborate adventure game they made up as they went along.

Two men were huddled in one corner, and if Ben guessed correctly, they were discussing the stock market. From the kitchen came the smell of *latkes* frying and the sound of laughter.

Ben had joined several men talking about football, but now he glanced across the room to where Jill sat in animated conversation with another small group.

She wore a knit pants outfit in vivid turquoise with a multicolored pattern of deep blue, raspberry and gold that reminded Ben of a Byzantine tapestry he'd once seen. Oversize gold hoops dangled from her ears. Although the other women in the room wore equally colorful clothing, Jill looked to him like a vibrant, exotic bird among a flock of sparrows. Her eyes sparkled, her smile flashed and he felt the desire he'd been working so hard to tame churn through him. She turned, caught him watching her and smiled slowly. The desire heated up another degree.

"Excuse me," he murmured to the man he was talking to—at this point, he couldn't even remember the fellow's name—and headed across the room, stopping beside Jill's chair.

Her thick mane of hair fell around her shoulders in lush waves. Her perfume wafted up to him, woodsy but sweet. She tipped her head back and looked at him, her earrings swaying, and patted the arm of her chair, setting an armful of bangle bracelets jangling. "We're talking about skiing," she told him.

They could have been talking about anything from aeronautics to Zen and he wouldn't have cared. He just wanted to be near her. Settling himself on the arm of her chair, he put a hand on her shoulder. She glanced sideways at his hand and he could have sworn he saw a smile. *You've come a long way, baby,* he thought. *A heck of a long way since Monday night.* He let his fingers toy with the ends of her hair.

She turned away and said something about the accommodations at Stowe. Ben admired the graceful way her hands moved when she talked. "Do you like Vermont?" she asked, glancing at him.

"Mmm," he said, concentrating on the texture of her curls.

Jill smiled up at him, a full smile this time. He wanted to nibble on that pouty lower lip, taste the honey of her mouth. He'd been thinking about doing that all day, even through a lengthy and annoying session with Frank McMinn late this afternoon.

The meeting with Frank had seemed interminable, and although Ben sympathized with his boss's personal problems, that didn't prevent him from becoming increasingly irritated as Frank whined about the delay in choosing an agency for the Steak Expectations account. Finally, totally fed up, Ben had slammed his hand on the desk. "Twenty-four hours, Frank, and you'll have my decision."

Frank checked his watch. "Six o'clock Friday. No later."

"Five forty-five if I can manage." *Earlier, if that'll shut you up.*

Frank got up and started for the door, then turned. "We'll announce the decision first thing Monday."

"Goes without saying," Ben agreed. *So why are we wasting time discussing it?*

With his hand on the doorknob, Frank hesitated while Ben clenched his jaw in silent fury. "Your decision has to be objective," he warned.

"Dammit, Frank, you've said that a dozen times in the past hour. It will be."

Frank nodded and left, and Ben longed for a stiff drink. Instead he let thoughts of Jill crowd Frank from his mind. So much about her intrigued him. Her sweetness, her enthusiasm for her job, the touch of shyness, the vulnerability he'd sensed.

Now, close enough to touch her at last, he smiled to himself. Thinking of her this afternoon had been pleasurable, but seeing her, sitting beside her, lit a spark inside him.

"Okay, everyone. Time to light the candles."

Everyone crowded around the menorah, this one an elaborate brass-and-silver piece. Beside it was a smaller version in blue-green Israeli Eilat stone. Don Berger raised the *shammash* and motioned his seven-year-old daughter to the smaller menorah. Together they chanted the blessing, each lighting four candles.

Ben stood watching, his arm around Jill. When the candles were lit, they looked at each other. "I see the glow of the candles in your eyes," he murmured.

Her smile was radiant. "That's how I feel," she said, "warm and bright."

He wanted to ask if he'd put those feelings there, or if she always felt that way during Chanukah. He wanted to kiss her right now, here with all the people around them. He wanted to take her home and make love to her.

"*Latkes,*" Beverly announced, cutting into his thoughts. Just as well. If he wasn't careful, his body would advertise exactly where his mind was headed, and while he intended to pursue his sales campaign with Jill in private, he certainly didn't want to broadcast his desires so blatantly.

"*Latkes,*" he repeated, though his supply of oxygen seemed to be diminishing rapidly. He joined the crowd, sat beside Jill at the dining-room table and enjoyed watching her savor the potato pancakes.

Afterward, Don Berger announced they would all play dreidel. The guests moved back into the family room and seated themselves in a circle in the middle of the floor while Don passed out handfuls of pennies.

"We all hafta have equal," one of the children reminded Don.

"Count 'em," he said, and the jingle of pennies mixed with the muttering of numbers.

"Twenty-'leven," one of the kids shouted.

"Twenty-*five*," a scornful young voice called out.

Jill sat cross-legged, her pennies piled on the floor in front of her. Ben lounged beside her, one elbow on the floor, his legs stretched out behind him.

"Hey, Abrams, sit up and pay attention," someone hollered.

Ben grinned and shook his head. From his vantage point he had a side view of Jill. The creamy skin of her cheek, the swell of softly rounded breasts beneath her sweater. He followed the slim line of her leg to a pair of ankle-high boots—Lord, she drove him mad.

"Okay." Don's deep voice silenced the crowd. "Everyone know how to play this game?"

"Yeah, but you're gonna tell us anyway," someone called.

"Right. Here we have a dreidel." He held up a four-sided top. "Here we have four Hebrew letters, *nun, gimmel, hay* and *shin,* one on each side." He turned the top from side to side.

Loud applause greeted him. "Hey, the guy can read Hebrew," a voice yelled.

"A genius!" someone else agreed.

Don ignored the good-natured jibes. "All right. Everyone put a penny in the pot." When all had complied, he said, "I'll spin the dreidel. If it lands on *nun*—"

"You get nothing," the group chorused.

"If it lands on *gimmel?*"

"You get the pot."

"Hay?"

"Half the pot."

"You're fast learners. *Shin?*"

"Put a penny in."

"Okay, people," Don said. "Play."

With no further urging, the boisterous crowd obeyed, and shouts of mirth, exclamations of delight or disgust filled the air, accompanied by the clinking of pennies and the plop of the dreidel as it tumbled on one side or another.

By the conclusion of the game, Jill had won fifteen cents. "A grand total of forty cents," she told Ben, letting the pennies sift through her fingers onto the floor. "How about you?"

"I'm in the hole." He rose and reached for her hand, intending to use this transition as an excuse to leave, but Beverly Berger called, "Chanukah gelt," and he knew he'd lost his opportunity. They'd stay until Jill had indulged her passion for chocolate. He tugged on a curl, pulling her close. "Don't eat too much," he warned. "I have plans for later."

"For later?" Jill felt a shiver of anticipation shoot up her spine. "What plans?"

"Surprise," he whispered, the dimple in his right cheek appearing. His eyes sparkled with mischief.

From his expression she supposed his surprise was something harmless, then remembered that Sherry had said Ben Abrams was as harmless as a load of dynamite. Before she could ask any more about his plans, Beverly came up to them with a handful of Chanukah gelt, and they were soon involved in conversation with her and several others.

"Jill, how long are you staying in Cincinnati?" one of the women asked.

"Until next Tuesday."

"Michael and I are having a few friends in Sunday evening. Why don't you join us?"

"Thanks, but we're going to a benefit that night."

"Who for?" someone else inquired.

"The Shirley Cohen Agency."

Silence. Uneasy silence. Suddenly everyone seemed to be concentrating on their hands, on the carpet. She glanced at Ben and saw him staring stony faced at the wall above the fireplace. She saw a couple of the people in the group eye him surreptitiously, then someone coughed nervously.

"Sounds nice," someone ventured.

Ben nodded. "It will be," he said, but his voice sounded flat.

What was going on? She felt as if she'd stepped into another dimension, where nothing made sense. What on earth had she said?

Beverly Berger changed the subject, and suddenly everyone seemed to be chattering with unusual animation.

Jill stole another glance at Ben. He was now talking to the man on his right as if nothing out of the ordinary had happened. Had she imagined the group's discomfort? No, she'd definitely said something that was, in this crowd at least, inappropriate. And that seemed to involve Ben. Perhaps there was a clue here to his puzzling reaction last night when she'd told him who the benefit was for.

What was it about the Cohen Agency that offended him? And why? She felt a sudden chill. She'd ask him to explain later. She wasn't sure she'd like what she would hear, but she needed to know.

Ben turned to her. "You're quiet, all of a sudden," he said softly. "Tired?"

She shook her head.

"Anxious about the presentation tomorrow?"

That wasn't the reason for her silence, but it was a logical excuse. "A little," she said.

"Let's go, then."

A few minutes later, as they walked to his car, he pulled her close. "You don't have anything to be nervous about tomorrow."

"I have a right. It's my first time."

He grinned at her. "I'd never have guessed. You're so confident about your work, I assumed you'd given dozens of presentations." He opened the car door for her.

When he got into the car, Jill gave him a rueful smile. "I shouldn't have admitted I'm a novice."

"Why? Everyone has a first time."

She sighed, relieved at his casual dismissal of her inexperience. "Right. Anyway, our campaign is fantastic. We're going to bowl you over, Mr. Advertising Manager."

"I sincerely hope so." He drove for a moment in silence, then remarked, "I suppose you'll be up for a promotion after this pitch."

"Hopefully."

"You'll have headhunters knocking on your door. Ever consider leaving Carnaby and Ross?"

"Not really."

"C and R's pretty conservative. Thought about a more forward-looking agency?"

Jill shrugged. "Most agencies are alike. Same circus, different clowns."

Ben chuckled at the familiar ad agency line, then said, "What about a small agency where you'd have more freedom?"

"I don't know."

"More . . . power?"

She smiled. "Now there's an interesting thought."

"You should keep it in mind. And speaking of advertising—" He reached into the glove compartment and brought out a sheet of paper. "Read this."

Jill squinted in the dark car. A flyer of some kind. She flipped on the overhead light to reveal shocking pink paper decorated with cupids and hearts and printed in flowing script.

" 'Indulge your fantasies,' " she read. " 'Gratify your appetites. Share an evening of bliss with a dynamic man'—" she raised a brow, and Ben responded with an innocent smile "—'whose lusts match your own.' *Lusts?*" This time she received a leer.

" 'To plunge into an episode of ecstasy, to turn the fourth night of Chanukah into an evening of rapture, you have only to say the word. Your driver awaits your command.' "

Amused, she folded the paper. How many men would think to advertise an evening's activity? How many men would know that nothing would delight her more than an ad? "Well, how can I turn that down?" she said with a laugh. "Drive on."

He whipped around a corner and Jill burst out laughing when he turned into Hyde Park Square and pulled into a parking space before a brightly lit store on the bottom floor of an apartment building. "Graeter's Ice Cream."

"So it is." Ben opened his door, came around to open hers. "Madame, your night of ecstasy awaits."

"You idiot," she said, still laughing. "I expected—"

"Yes?"

"A pleasure palace from the *Arabian Nights*. Sinbad's House of Sin. But this is better. I haven't been to Graeter's in—" She didn't want to say how long.

Inside, Jill and Ben sat at an old-fashioned ice cream table. A middle-aged waitress shuffled over to take their order, glancing at her watch as she stopped beside their table. "Almost closing time," she muttered.

Jill blithely ignored the woman's sullen reception. After all, as a New Yorker now, she'd become used to less-than-hospitable service in all kinds of places. Besides, she hadn't been to Graeter's in years and she intended to enjoy herself. "A turtle sundae," she decided.

"You?" The waitress turned to Ben.

"We'll share."

"You want two spoons, then?" She managed to convey the impression that, in her mind, only a barbarian would make such a request.

"Yes, please," he said solemnly and had the good sense to wait until the woman turned her back before laughing. "Congenial, isn't she?" he remarked, then reached into his jacket pocket, pulled out a small box and presented it to Jill.

"Not another gift! Oh, Ben, you're spoiling me."

"You deserve to be spoiled. Besides—" he grinned "—I couldn't resist this."

She opened the package. "Oh, good grief." She lifted out a pair of earrings. In place of typical teardrops hung shiny metal dreidels painted blue, with black Hebrew letters. Quickly she unscrewed the hoops she wore and fitted the dreidels into her ears, then shook her head to set the dreidels swinging. "They are absolutely perfect. Where did you find them?"

He shook his head and flicked one with a finger. "My secret. I'm glad you like them." He reached for her hand.

"Your order." The waitress placed the sundae before Jill, slapped the extra spoon down in front of Ben, and with another look at her watch, stalked off.

With the eye of a connoisseur, Jill surveyed the concoction before her—vanilla ice cream, walnuts, caramel and chocolate sauce—and sighed dreamily. She dipped her spoon in and let the smooth, thick ice cream roll over her tongue. "You're right. This is bliss."

"Let's see." Ben took a bite, then another.

So did Jill, but despite the ice cream, she felt warm all over. There was something...intimate about eating from the same dish, even in the brightly lit room with the waitress scowling at them from the corner. She wondered if Ben felt it, too. She sampled the chocolate sauce, then sighed. "Chocolate. Pure sensuality."

Watching her, Ben felt his gut tighten. Her expression was dreamy, her eyes half shut. Her tongue peeped out and licked a drop of cream from the corner of her mouth, and Ben swallowed convulsively. To him, *she* was sensuality incarnate; yet at the same time she had an innocence about her. She didn't seem aware of her effect on him.

"I, ah, guess I made a good choice," he croaked.

"Oh, you did." She smiled lazily and took another bite of ice cream.

Ben stifled a groan.

"I did an ad once for chocolates, the fancy kind you buy in stores like Bloomingdales. It was the best campaign of my life."

"Yeah?"

"Mmm. I had to try every kind of chocolate imaginable. My office was filled with Godiva and Barricini."

Ben reached across the table and linked his fingers with hers. "Paradise, huh?"

"Mmm-hmm. Much better than the campaign I just finished. That was toothpaste. I had samples falling off my shelves, toothpaste tubes for paperweights. At least I have healthy teeth."

Jill liked the feel of his hand in hers. She wished she could just sit here enjoying him, but she had questions that needed answering. Tonight. She put down her spoon.

"Ben," she said, her voice serious, "I want to ask you something." She took a breath, then plunged ahead. "When I mentioned the Cohen Agency last night, you seemed . . . uneasy. Then tonight, everyone was uncomfortable. Is there something I should know? Some reason you don't want to go Sunday night?"

He remained silent for so long she thought he wasn't going to answer, but finally he said, "You deserve an explanation." But instead of continuing, he stared down at their hands.

Anxiety clawed at Jill. What would Ben say about the Cohen Agency? Had he and Mickey been better friends than she thought? Perhaps he knew about her pregnancy and guessed that she had given her child up for adoption. No, that was ridiculous. That was her old self thinking, the Jill Bubbi had insisted let the past control her, the Jill whose nerves clenched whenever anything remotely connected with adoption was mentioned. Ben's misgivings were directed at the agency, she assured herself, not at her, and his friends were aware of his feelings. Nevertheless, as she waited for him to speak, she felt the trembling begin in her knees and crawl upward.

At last Ben raised his eyes. "A couple of years ago I was involved with a woman . . . deeply involved."

Oh, God, was he going to tell her he'd fathered a child who'd been given up for adoption?

"We'd planned . . . at least, *I'd* planned to get married, but things didn't work out. We parted in anger."

Jill saw the remnants of an old pain in his eyes. She put her free hand over his. No matter how badly she wanted to hear the rest of his explanation, she didn't want to put him through that distress. "Don't," she said softly. "Don't talk about it if it hurts too much."

He shook his head and smiled faintly. "I'm over the hurt. Karen left town after we split up, but a couple of months ago she moved back here."

Jealousy welled up, surprising Jill. Why should she feel possessive about a man she had no claim to, especially since their own involvement was fated to be so brief? Anyway, she had no reason to be jealous. Hadn't he just told her the affair was over?

Ben continued. "Karen's a social worker. She came back to Cincinnati to accept a job as director of social services for the Cohen Agency."

Relief surged through Jill. His former lover worked at the agency! So much for her fears. She quelled the urge to laugh hysterically. "Are you sure you feel comfortable going Sunday night?" she asked.

"Sure. Karen is past history."

Though she couldn't help but wonder if he was deluding himself, Jill accepted his assurance. Because she wanted it to be true. "Then Sunday's still on?" she said, picking up her spoon and taking another bite of ice cream.

"Mmm-hmm. How about tomorrow night?"

"I promised my family I'd go to the synagogue with them. Want to come for Sabbath dinner and go with us?"

"Why don't I meet you at services? I'll be working late."

He'd be evaluating their proposal, she thought, with twin pricks of excitement and anxiety. No, she wouldn't worry. Carnaby and Ross was going to snag this account.

Ben leaned toward her and, with a fingertip, caught a tiny dab of ice cream at the corner of her mouth, then, his eyes on hers, licked his finger. Jill felt her stomach plummet the way it did on a fast elevator ride.

"Want some more ice cream?"

She shook her head. Her voice was gone, lost somewhere amid the fluttering of her heart. Eyes locked with his, pulse thudding, she sat, unable to move. Finally she managed to whisper, "I should be getting back to the hotel. Tomorrow's a big day."

Their drive downtown was silent, each of them lost in their own thoughts. But their hands linked as they walked through the hotel lobby, their bodies touched as they stood in the elevator and, at the door to her room, Jill handed Ben her key without waiting for him to ask.

He was earning her trust, Ben thought, and promised himself he'd merit it. Though he wanted to sweep her up into his arms, carry her to the bed and make love to her until they were both sated, he wouldn't. Not yet.

Patience, he thought. He'd give her that. Because she needed it, and perhaps he did, too. He'd wanted her from the beginning, wanted to make love to her, wanted to make sure she'd remember him when she left. But what had begun as a lighthearted campaign to entice her into his arms had rapidly become something much more serious, and he wasn't sure of his own ground. They both needed to go slowly.

Inside her room he turned her toward him and unbuttoned her coat, slipped it from her shoulders and laid it aside, then took off his. When he reached for her again, her eyes were wide and dark. "Ben," she whispered, and he heard the uncertainty in her voice.

"Shh, just kiss me," he murmured, and she did. Her arms circled his neck, her lips parted and her eyelids fluttered closed.

Ben pulled her close, closer. *Slowly,* he told himself. *Go slowly.* So he kissed her softly, gently, and when he knew he couldn't hold back any longer he lifted his mouth from hers, laid his cheek against her hair and just held her.

Still. Be still. But he couldn't. Not with his heart hammering in his chest, his body tight and aching. Of their own accord his hands moved over her, stroking her back, slipping beneath her sweater to sample the smoothness of the skin along her rib cage, then moving upward until his finger brushed a taut nipple, and she gasped. His hand slid away.

"No!" Jill pleaded and covered his hand with hers, pressing it against her breast.

With a groan Ben gave up his fight for control. He pulled the sweater over her head, then with shaking fingers unfastened her bra and took her bare breast in his hand. At his touch she moaned, surely the most sensual sound he'd ever heard.

Ben forgot patience, forgot everything but the feel of her breast against his palm, the sound of her sighs, the taste of her mouth. Wildly, clumsily, he tore at the buttons of his shirt, until at last he could crush her against him. Flesh against flesh.

At the feel of his skin against hers, Jill sobbed out his name. Then he lifted her, holding her tight against his chest, and carried her to the bed.

Sherry's words exploded in her mind. *Dynamite. Fuse.* Then other words, older ones, Lisa's words. *Tramp. You're a tramp. You knew where babies come from. You knew—*

Ben laid her on the bed, followed her down, rained kisses over her.

Where babies come from. You knew.

"No!" Struggling against him, she sat up and covered her body with trembling hands. "No, please. I—"

Ben stared at her, dazed, as she pulled back against the headboard and jerked the spread over her breasts. He took a painful breath and tried to make sense of what had happened. Was this some sort of game? No, she was... terrified.

"What's wrong?" he rasped, reaching for the control he'd lost moments ago.

"I can't. I'm not—"

She was trembling. A tear slid down her cheek.

With an iron will he mastered the tremors vibrating through his own body. He shifted until he was beside her, then put his arms around her. "It's all right," he soothed. When she tried to pull away from his embrace, he whispered, "No, let me hold you."

He'd deal with his own ragged emotions later; for now, hers took precedence. He stroked her hair, rubbed her back, rocked her, calming her, protecting her. He felt her struggle against tears, then slowly begin to relax. When her trembling had stopped, he murmured, "All right now?"

She nodded, not looking at him.

"What happened?" he asked.

Her voice was so low he could hardly hear. "I'm not... protected."

Is that all? he wanted to say, but he sensed that wasn't what Jill needed to hear. In the frenzy of the moment he hadn't thought of protection, but that was easy to fix. "I'll take care of it," he assured her. "Next time, I'll protect you."

"Next time," she murmured, her voice uncertain.

He sat beside her, keeping his arm loosely around her shoulders until he was certain she was completely calm.

Then he turned her face to his and kissed her gently. "Go to sleep now," he told her. "I'll call you in the morning."

Jill watched him leave and shut the door behind him. She should get up and finish undressing, she knew, but she didn't have the strength to move. Not with her body aching with unfulfilled desire, her mind whirling in confusion. Her heart told her to take a chance on loving Ben; her head warned her of the folly of even considering it.

Do you want a replay of eight years ago? asked the voice of her old terrors. *Could you live with that again?*

Ben promised to protect me, she told that stern voice.

And if he doesn't? If there's one of those unforeseen accidents like before?

Mickey was a kid. Ben's an adult. So am I, she protested, wishing she could give in to her desires without qualms as so many other women did. But she couldn't, not when she knew so well the consequences that could result.

Long ago, after she'd given up her baby, she'd made a decision to forego intimacy. She'd never used birth control; she'd never needed it. And that was the ultimate form of protection, for the absence of birth control had forestalled any temptation to indulge in lovemaking, had kept her free of relationships. Until tonight.

She wondered what Ben had thought of her near panic. He'd accepted what she'd said about her lack of protection, but she was certain he hadn't realized the depth of her fear. How could he, without knowing what had happened so many years ago?

And how could she ever get up the courage to tell him?

CHAPTER SEVEN

THE SHRILL RINGING of the telephone caught Jill by surprise. She stumbled across the still-dark room and picked up the receiver. "H'lo."

"Still grouchy in the morning, I see."

"Lisa?" Her sister's voice brought her fully awake. "Why are you calling? Is something wrong?"

"No, I...ah...just thought we could talk some more, over breakfast, maybe. But if you're still sleeping..."

"I woke up early. I'd just gotten out of bed," Jill said. In fact, she'd hardly slept at all. She'd spent the night tossing and turning, torn between longing to call Ben and ask him to come back, and packing her bags and fleeing to New York. But that wasn't something she cared to discuss with her sister. "Why don't you come on down?" she suggested. "I'll try to be civil."

Lisa laughed. "I'll hold you to that. See you in thirty minutes."

This wasn't the best morning to continue her discussion with Lisa, Jill thought as she dressed hurriedly. With the events of last night still jangling her emotions and the presentation to Wellner only hours away, a third nerve-racking conversation with Lisa was the last thing she needed. "I'll be ready for a padded cell by the end of the day," she muttered.

Still, she wasn't sorry Lisa had called. Although they'd laid some of their old differences to rest the other evening, she knew they hadn't finished exploring the issues between them.

In the lobby she tried to read the morning paper while she waited for Lisa, but she couldn't concentrate. The headlines read like gibberish, and none of the articles made sense. Disgusted, she shoved the paper aside and watched the entrance.

When Lisa appeared a few minutes later, Jill hurried across the lobby to meet her. As usual, Lisa looked elegant, an amazing feat at this hour of the morning, Jill thought. Her sister's long black hair framed her face in a casual style that Jill suspected had taken the scissors of a skilled beautician and hours of practice on Lisa's part to perfect. Her tailored wool pants were worn with a vivid turquoise silk blouse that looked expensive and probably was. A leather signature bag, low-heeled pumps and understated gold jewelry completed her outfit.

Glancing at herself as she passed a mirrored wall, Jill imagined Lisa would see her as sloppy. She'd tied her hair back in a ponytail, pulled on a pair of jeans, the comfortable boots she favored and, with a nod to superstition, her lucky sweater. And, of course, she wore the dreidel earrings Ben had given her. Well, she and Lisa had always been a study in contrasts. Their clothes clashed; so did their personalities.

Jill pasted on a smile as she approached her sister. "Hi. Ready for some coffee?"

"Sure." Lisa's gaze skimmed over Jill's outfit. "You're not working this morning?"

Jill smiled to herself as she led the way to the coffee shop. "Yes, I am. My group's getting together at nine to go over our presentation. We're meeting with the Steak Expectations people this afternoon." She didn't bother mentioning that she was going to change before then.

Lisa ordered fruit and an English muffin for breakfast; Jill had an omelet, hash browns and toast.

"How do you eat so much and stay thin?" Lisa asked. "I'm constantly dieting and working out."

Jill shrugged. "Sometimes I have to diet if I go on a sweets binge, but we're different. Haven't you noticed?"

Lisa stared thoughtfully at her coffee cup. "And not just in metabolism."

"Or in our clothes."

Lisa's eyes traveled over Jill's attire, then she nodded. "Our life-styles have always been opposite, haven't they, even though we grew up in the same house. You were always such a tomboy as a kid."

"Yeah, and I still dress the part." Lisa laughed, and Jill went on. "I always preferred jeans over dresses, but you were Little Miss Scarlett, flouncing around in your designer party dresses." Lisa's eyes registered both astonishment and hurt, and Jill was immediately contrite. "I'm sorry. That was a catty thing to say."

Lisa concentrated on her muffin, buttering it with exaggerated care. She was better than Jill at controlling her emotions, but now her voice trembled. "Forget it."

But Jill couldn't. She was shocked at the resentment in her voice just now. She'd thought the feelings of hostility toward her sister's style were long gone, buried with her adolescence, but apparently that was a delusion. Jill realized that just moments ago, when Lisa had entered the lobby, she'd mentally derided every stitch of clothing her sister wore. And the feelings of resentment now expressed, were as strong as ever. "God, I hated you for that," she muttered.

Lisa gasped. "Hated me? For what?"

"For being so perfect."

Lisa's look of astonishment was almost comic. "You thought I was perfect?"

"Well, not exactly perfect, but you never seemed to get dirty."

Lisa burst out laughing, chuckling until her eyes filled with tears. "I was too wimpy to get dirty. You were the one with guts. I always wanted to be gutsy, too, but I couldn't. You, on the other hand, took chances."

Too many, Jill thought. And last night she'd almost taken another. No, she wouldn't think of that now.

Instead she smiled at Lisa. She hadn't realized her sister envied her spunk. Nor had she been aware that she didn't hate Lisa's ladylike perfection but was jealous of it. "I guess I always wanted to look and act just right like you did, but I could never quite bring it off. Remember when I broke my arm jumping out of the locust tree after Steven Goodman dared me?"

Lisa chuckled. "Yes."

"Steven was always getting into mischief and dragging me along with him."

"He's a hotshot prosecutor with the D.A.'s office now," Lisa told her.

"Going after troublemakers. That's ironic. I remember in high school he was always the one who thought up the practical jokes, like the time he and a bunch of guys spray-painted the assistant principal's car. Of course, by that time, *I'd* given up being a mischief maker and a tomboy."

"Yeah, in high school you were always studying." Lisa's voice sounded strange.

"I studied a lot," Jill agreed, "but I had fun, too."

"I suppose. I always remember you with your nose in a book."

"That's an exaggeration," Jill said, idly stirring her coffee. "I didn't study all the time, but I wanted to make good grades."

"Not just good." Lisa's mouth tightened into a disapproving line as she pushed her plate away. "Perfect. Straight A's." Her cheeks were flushed, and her voice had a shrill quality that Jill didn't understand.

Jill put down her spoon and stared at Lisa, puzzled. "Grades were important to me," she said.

"Oh, yes. You were the smart one, weren't you?"

"The . . . smart one?" The term sounded familiar.

"Wasn't that what Mother always said? The one who made A's in every subject, the one who was going to the best college, the one who was going to do something important. I'm sure she expects you to win the Nobel Prize someday."

Jill listened in astonishment. Anger revealed itself here, deep-seated and long suppressed. Hoping to lighten the mood, she said, "They don't give Nobels for writing advertising copy."

"I'm sure if Mother had her say, they would."

Tension hung in the air. The atmosphere between them wasn't easing. If anything, it was becoming more highly charged. "I guess Mother went overboard about my accomplishments."

"Oh, did she ever! She was always singing your praises. National Honor Society, student council . . ."

Suddenly Jill understood. Just as she'd resented Lisa's squeaky-clean perfection, Lisa must have been put off by her achievements. "You must've gotten tired of hearing about me," she offered.

Lisa reached for the carafe of coffee the waitress had left on their table and poured herself a fresh cup with a hand that shook noticeably. "You were Mother's fair-haired child. The one who was going to have it all."

"And you were the pretty one," Jill said, repeating what her mother had often said about Lisa. And also remembering that she hadn't liked it much.

"Pretty," Lisa scoffed. "Mother wasn't interested in pretty. She wanted smart. Being sweetheart of a high school fraternity didn't hold a candle to being yearbook editor."

"I'd have traded with you."

"Would you?" Lisa gazed at her thoughtfully, then shook her head. "I doubt it. In our family it was easier being you than me. When Mother realized all I really wanted out of college was to find the right husband, she was totally disappointed in me. You, on the other hand, were exactly what she wanted in a daughter." Her eyes shimmered with unshed tears.

Jill shook her head. "I did what she wanted for herself," she said softly. "Being a housewife frustrated her. She wanted her daughters to live out her dreams."

Lisa toyed with her teaspoon. "What makes you think that?"

"Something Bubbi said yesterday. Anyway, neither of us came up to her expectations." She grimaced. "I certainly managed to spoil them in a big way."

"I...I guess I felt it served you right." Lisa's voice was so low that for a moment Jill wasn't sure she'd understood her. Then Lisa raised her eyes and met Jill's, and Jill knew she'd heard correctly.

"I guess our...misunderstanding during my pregnancy went a lot farther back than either of us realized."

"Yeah," Lisa agreed. "I thought I was mad at you then for taking all the attention away from my wedding, but that wasn't the whole reason. Not only were you getting all the attention that summer, but you'd *always* been Mother's shining light." She stared into her cup. "I guess that sounds petty."

"No, just honest. I guess a lot of our anger at each other was misdirected. We were busy living out Mother's roles for us. No wonder we didn't have any idea how to relate to each other."

"And ended up resenting one another," Lisa observed. "I was even mad when you got braces and I didn't."

"Braces?"

"Yeah, they were another sign that Mother was grooming *you* for something special."

Jill shook her head. "I'd have been happy to give you my braces, but you didn't need them. You've always had perfect teeth."

"I know, but back then braces meant attention," Lisa chuckled.

Soon they were both laughing. At last Jill caught her breath. "Too bad we couldn't have talked about our feelings years ago."

"We were too young."

"And too angry," Jill added. "I was jealous of you for having what I wanted then—a man who loved you and wanted to marry you. There you were with what I needed and couldn't have."

"You'll have it someday." She touched Jill's hand.

Jill turned her palm up and grasped Lisa's—the first real contact between them in years, and it felt wonderful. Suddenly she wanted to confide in her sister, to share something of herself, to test the tentative bond they were forging. "Until now, I haven't let anyone get close. I haven't wanted to. I guess I've been too scared."

"And now?"

Jill smiled. "Maybe now things will change."

"I hope so," Lisa said. "I like him."

"Who?"

"Ben Abrams. Isn't that who we're talking about?"

"Maybe."

"Why maybe?" Lisa asked. "If he's as good as he seems, then go after him."

Jill folded her napkin. "We'll see." Reluctant to say more, she changed the subject. "Let's get back to you. Seems you're about to realize Mother's ambitions, Ms. Real Estate Broker."

Her sister grinned at her. "Maybe we'll both end up having it all."

"You're closer to that than I am," Jill said wistfully. "By a long shot."

Lisa squeezed Jill's hand. Her touch was comforting. The solace Jill had longed for once and hadn't received was finally being freely given. In her darker moments she'd imagined this happening—Lisa reaching out to her and herself spurning the offer of reconciliation, pushing her sister's hand away. She'd seen herself hurting Lisa, paying her back for the pain she'd inflicted. But now that the moment was at hand, she had no desire to retaliate. Peace was sweeter than revenge. The warmth of Lisa's touch spread through her, and she met her sister's eyes with a look of forgiveness and received one in return.

"I gave you a rough time, didn't I?" Lisa said. "I didn't realize until the other night how hard it's been for you to get over giving up your baby."

"I told you, I'll never get over it."

"Funny," Lisa mused. "I always thought once the baby was gone, you'd gotten on with your life without looking back."

"Could you have done that?" Jill asked.

"No, but as you just pointed out, we're different."

"I was . . . *am* still a mother. I loved my baby as much as you love Whitney or Kevin. She grew inside me for nine months, and I felt every movement, felt that miracle under my heart. We shared a body for all those months and . . . and then she was gone." With tears welling up, she added, "I never had a chance to know her. I never will."

"Maybe someday she'll want to find you."

" 'Someday,' even if that happens, won't make up for all the years I've missed. I feel like . . . like part of me was . . . was cut off."

"I'm sorry," Lisa whispered, "for everything."

They sat in shared silence until the waitress's voice intruded. "Can I get you anything else?"

Jill glanced at her, then smiled at Lisa. "No, thanks. I think we have everything we need."

WHEN JILL OPENED the door to her room, where she'd gone to pick up her briefcase, she heard the phone ringing.

Ben was on the line. "How are you this morning?" His voice was warm, concerned.

Jill felt a blush on her cheeks. "I'm fine."

"Sure?"

"Yes, of course."

"I'll see you tonight, then. And this afternoon. Ready for the big performance?"

"All ready," she said, her embarrassment over last night vanishing, replaced by anticipation. "Curtain goes up at three."

She could almost see him grin. "I'll be the guy in the aisle seat. Break a leg."

"Thanks."

She hung up, feeling exhilarated, confident about the afternoon. Five minutes later she was in Hope's suite, rehearsing.

Their run-through of the presentation went like clockwork, and by two-thirty she, Hope and Dan were on their way to Wellner headquarters. Even the weather, cool and clear, seemed to bode well for them. As they drove through downtown Cincinnati, the sun sparkled against the store windows, turning Christmas ornaments into colorful jewels.

Jill smoothed her navy skirt. Her matching navy jacket had a forest-green windowpane check, her tailored blouse was white silk. She wore a gold choker and long gold filigree earrings, and she was sure that even Frank Mc-Minn—even her mother—could find no fault with her appearance today.

When they arrived at Wellner headquarters, the receptionist ushered them into a large conference room. Plush executive chairs in maroon surrounded a rectangular teak table. A large easel dominated one side of the room. Methodically, Dan began arranging displays and storyboards.

At exactly three o'clock Frank McMinn entered the room. He shook hands with Hope and the rest of them with businesslike precision, then sat down, checking the crease in his trousers. He glanced at the clock on the wall, then at the door, tapping his fingers on the table. A few minutes later Ben strolled in, followed by the vice president of marketing and several other Wellner executives.

Ben caught Jill's eye and his lips curved in a slow smile. He nodded almost imperceptibly, and she felt a warm glow. In a few hours they'd be together again. What would happen this time? Would caution win out, or would she follow her heart?

"Ms. Wilson," McMinn said, "are you ready to start?"

Hope nodded and walked to the front of the room. As Hope began, Jill forced herself to block out Ben, to forget everything but the presentation.

Ben watched Jill straighten in her chair, then lean forward to concentrate on her colleague. If there were nerves beneath Jill's professional facade, they didn't show. She was the epitome of the up-and-coming young Madison Avenue executive. But to him, she was more. Under that muted, conservative suit was the body of a temptress, a body he'd only glimpsed but which had filled his dreams through a long, restless night.

Reluctantly he tore his attention from Jill and focused on Hope as she explained the concept behind Carnaby and Ross's proposed campaign.

"What is unique about Steak Expectations isn't the steaks but the customer as cook, so we capitalize on that, make it appealing, exciting. We tell customers, 'Come to the restaurant where you're in charge.' We nullify the image of the customers slaving over a hot grill by convincing them they're not just the *cook* but the *chef*."

Right on, Ben thought. The Carnaby and Ross team had a good concept, and Hope presented it well.

Hope continued. "And we emphasize that *anyone* can be a successful chef, by using models of both sexes and of different ages. We choose models who look like someone the customer knows, his next-door neighbor or someone she'd see in the checkout line at the supermarket. You'll see our concept at work now as Mr. Givens shows you the artwork, and then Ms. Levin will go over the copy.''

Hope sat down and Ben watched the art director place the first print ad on the easel. As Jill had said, the man was flamboyant—slate gray suit, tie with swirls of purple, powder blue and silver, and a diamond stud in one ear. But he was good, damn good, Ben could see, as he eyed the photo Dan displayed. In it a rangy, fortyish man wearing a chef's hat was surrounded by restaurant staff—busboys, waitress, hostess, kitchen worker—all obviously cheering him on.

Then Jill rose, and Ben felt his heart contract, his muscles tighten. She was on display, under scrutiny, and he wanted her to succeed, not just for her but for himself, too. As if they were linked together. One. He hadn't bought her a gift for this fifth night of Chanukah; suddenly he knew what he would give her.

She walked to the easel, her step brisk. Her voice, as she began to read her copy, was confident. ''At Steak Expectations, you're in charge. Select your own steak from our menu of prime beef. Or choose chicken or our catch of the day. Broil your choice to your own specifications, season it to your taste. Add a plump potato with all the fixings, a crisp salad with your choice from our edible rainbow of vegetables. And sit down to a delectable meal of your own creation. Our compliments to the chef!''

Damn, Ben thought, she was good. He wanted her for the position of creative director when he and Alan opened their agency. In the past two days ''if'' had become ''when'' in Ben's mind, as he grew increasingly frustrated with McMinn, less tolerant of his boss's moods.

Jill and Givens showed the storyboards they'd created for TV commercials, similar to the print ad, with the restaurant staff applauding the "chef" and the customer looking thoroughly pleased with himself as he surveyed his culinary creation.

Then the creative team was finished. When Jill walked back to her seat, Ben caught her eye. He wanted to give her a thumbs-up sign, to wink at her, to tell her what a great job she'd done. Of course he couldn't. But a smile was acceptable. Roger Harris, marketing VP, and even McMinn were smiling at the Carnaby and Ross team, so Ben did, too. But he looked directly into Jill's eyes; his smile was for her alone.

Now Hope summarized, made suggestions for building on the concept over time, and the presentation was over.

Ben joined the other Wellner executives clustering around the presenters. He shook hands with Hope, then with Givens, made the standard complimentary remarks offered prior to a final decision. Then he turned to Jill. Again he longed to pull her into his arms and hug her, to tell her how elated he was with her presentation. Instead he grasped her hand for a politely impersonal handshake and let his eyes say it all.

Her adrenaline still pumping, Jill smiled at Ben, being careful to make it the same smile she'd given the others. Though he murmured something businesslike when he shook her hand, his eyes, deep and brown, sent a personal message.

For a moment the conversation around them receded, the people on either side of them seemed to fade away and she and Ben were the only two people in the room.

I want you. She heard the words as clearly as if he'd spoken them aloud. Maybe it was the exhilaration of the moment, maybe the heart-to-heart conversation with Lisa this morning, but she knew she was ready to cross the line she'd drawn for herself so many years ago. Tonight she'd take that final step and make love with Ben.

Ben felt the warmth of her hand in his, read her silent message. *Yes. Tonight.* He knew her thoughts with a confident certainty, read them in the beat of her pulse beneath his hand, in the curve of her lips, the soft cadence of her breath.

He stood silently, watching as she dropped his hand, turned away and joined her colleagues filing out of the conference room.

"Got a busy weekend planned?" Roger Harris asked.

"Mmm," Ben answered, thinking of the evening ahead. Bemused, he walked toward his office. There should be background music tonight. A violin concerto. He should stop by the florist, put a vase of roses on the dresser, candles on the nightstands. He imagined the candlelight flickering over Jill's body. Beautiful.

At his desk he opened the folders from Tolar and HG and B along with the one Hope had handed him a few moments ago. He'd cautioned himself that he had to be impartial. Under no circumstances did he want McMinn to accuse him of a conflict of interest; therefore he spent a good hour going over each campaign thoroughly. When he finished, he leaned back and stretched. He had no doubt in his mind. Carnaby and Ross had far and away the best concept, the slickest execution.

Turning on his computer, he typed out a memo to McMinn, stating his decision that the account should go to Carnaby and Ross. Then he took the memo to McMinn's office himself. Frank had already gone, but his secretary took the envelope into his office and Ben saw her put it on Frank's desk. Ben glanced at his watch. Five forty-seven. *Okay, Frank. I met your deadline.*

Ben returned to his office. He had a good two hours of work to clear off his desk before he left, but for the moment his thoughts drifted back to Jill and the night to come.

Should he get red roses or pink? Or a mix? He shook his head. He wouldn't stop for flowers, wouldn't set out candles. Whatever Jill's fears were, they wouldn't be appeased in that way. Her anxiety would only be magnified by a staged seduction. Tonight there'd be no candlelight, no flowers. Just the two of them together, alone in a quiet room.

"I THINK WE'VE GOT IT!" Hope's voice radiated excitement and confidence as she, Jill and Dan congregated at the Hyatt's bar.

"To Carnaby and Ross." Jill raised her wineglass.

"To us!" Dan corrected, lifting his own.

"We were great, weren't we?" Jill crowed. "Did you see the looks they gave each other?" She turned to Hope. "I'm not being overly optimistic, am I?"

"Absolutely not. I've done a lot of presentations, and I've never seen one go so well." She shot Jill a sly smile. "Maybe you'll get some inside info this weekend. You are seeing Abrams, aren't you?"

"Yes. I won't pump him, though."

"But if he should drop a hint—"

"I'll be listening," she promised. "What do you two have planned for the weekend?"

"I'm off to Cleveland," Hope said. "I have a couple of friends there."

"I'm outa here, too," Dan said, taking a sip of his drink. "I'm visiting family in Akron. I'll be back Sunday night."

"What time are you leaving, Hope?" Jill asked. "Do you have time for a shopping spree? I feel like rewarding myself for the presentation."

"Let's go."

They took the Skywalk, an elevated, glass-enclosed walkway that ran between Cincinnati's downtown hotels, shops and restaurants. As they strolled along, Jill looked around her with pleasure. "Different from the slushy sidewalks of New York, huh?" she remarked.

"Yeah, but I like 'em there—the noise, the crowds, even the smells." She glanced at Jill with interest. "This is the first time I've heard you say anything positive about Cincinnati."

"Well, there's a saying that Cincinnatians are like weeds. You can pull them out of here, but they come right back."

Hope raised a brow. "So home is where the heart is? Or has the charming Mr. Abrams changed your outlook?"

"Um, both maybe. My sister and I talked this morning, and we're beginning to work out our differences. We should have done that years ago."

"You probably weren't ready to listen to each other then."

"I suppose," Jill said.

"So, now you're comfortable with your family again?" Hope inquired.

"Not completely. I have other things to work out ... other people to deal with."

"Families are so complex," Hope agreed, then added, "You didn't answer my second question."

"What?"

"You know what. The one about Ben."

"He's charming, all right."

"And I guess that's all you're going to say. Okay, I won't hound you. By the way, what are we going to buy ourselves?"

They grinned at each other in perfect understanding. "Earrings," they chorused.

"Let's go outside," Jill suggested, and they abandoned the Skywalk for a side street at ground level. Jill, who was ahead, had almost passed a tiny boutique between two larger stores when Hope halted and exclaimed, "This is it! Take a look in that window."

Jill backed up. Earrings of every size, color and shape crammed the window and the store behind it. "Okay!"

Inside, she stared around her, awestruck. "Where on earth do we start?"

"Anywhere."

They spent nearly an hour, Jill trying on the most outlandish earrings she could find, Hope opting for more conservative pairs. "I don't see how you can wear that stuff without pulling your ears down to your elbows," she commented as Jill contemplated a pair of rectangular malachite drops, then a large copper button with an array of spiral wires hanging from it. "How about these? Can you believe 'em?" She held up a multicolored carousel with three tiers of animals—a zebra, a camel and a lion.

"Let me see." Jill grabbed for them.

"Uh-uh, lady. Even the most creative of creatives—even Dan—would roll over and die if you walked into the office in these. Forget it."

"Okay, but how about these?" Jill held up a pair of lapis and crystal with double teardrops.

"They'll be perfect for your blue dress. Take them," Hope advised. "And I'll get these." She picked out an understated pair of onyx-and-silver ovals.

They left the store, pleased with their purchases. "And," Jill pointed out as they headed back to the hotel, "whether we get the account or not, we'll have the best-looking ears in the Big Apple."

A SNOWY WHITE CLOTH covered the Levins' dining-room table. A *challah,* the braided egg bread served on Sabbaths and holy days, was placed at one end of the table. At the other was the kiddush cup, filled with crimson wine. A pair of Sabbath candles in gleaming silver holders flickered on the sideboard.

Jill glanced around the table. Her father sat at the head, his eyes shining with pleasure as they roamed over his family, all together for the first time in years. Jill had heard his voice catch with emotion as he'd said the kiddush, the blessing over the wine.

Her mother, more controlled, busied herself with serving. Jill stared at her thoughtfully, wondering if Esther had ever been conscious of the animosity she'd created between her daughters. Wondering if she was aware of the emotional blows she'd inflicted during those awful months of Jill's pregnancy. Perhaps the time had come to find out. She and Lisa had made a start at talking through their differences, but confronting her mother would be much more difficult. And much more painful.

But tonight wasn't the time to think about that. This was an evening to disregard the tensions that lurked beneath the surface and to concentrate on the positive.

Jill smiled, glancing at Bubbi. Attired in a navy silk dress, her grandmother sat across from Whitney and

Kevin, glowing with pleasure as she watched her great-grandchildren.

Beside Bubbi was Sherry. Her "wonderful" David had arrived this afternoon. As Sherry had described, he was good-looking in a boy-next-door way, with clear blue eyes and an engaging grin. He and Sherry stayed close to one another, touching at every opportunity.

Lisa's husband, Todd, had rushed in just before dinner. He'd lifted Whitney high in the air, swooped her down for a hug, ruffled Kevin's hair and pulled Lisa into his arms for a quick kiss and a look that promised more. Seeing them together, Jill felt the familiar pain of longing, but the bitterness that had been so much a part of her relationship with Lisa was absent. Instead, she felt cleansed, whole.

She'd forgiven her sister. Would she be able to do the same with her mother? And more importantly, would she someday be able to forgive herself? Perhaps. When the family had gathered earlier for the lighting of the Chanukah candles—five of them now—Jill thought their glow had held the promise of a brighter future.

When dinner was over, Joel pushed back his chair. "Get your coats, everyone. Friday night services start at eight sharp."

Jill went up to Sherry's room to comb her hair. She surveyed herself critically in the full-length mirror on Sherry's closet door. She hadn't packed an outfit suitable for the synagogue so she'd borrowed a dress of Sherry's. Not her style at all, she thought. For one thing, the dress was black. For another, it had a white collar and cuffs that gave it a demure look. "Something's not right," she complained as Sherry came up behind her.

Sherry cocked her head. "Your earrings are too flashy. I'll get you a pair of mine."

She rummaged through her drawer and returned with a pair of simple round gold earrings that were a perfect match for the buttons at the cuffs and collar.

Jill took off the pair she'd worn—quadruple loops in alternating black and gold—and put on Sherry's. "These aren't me."

"The gypsy look isn't in for synagogue. Come on, before Dad pitches a fit."

Jill took one last glance at herself and wondered if Ben would recognize her in this disguise, then followed Sherry downstairs.

As they trooped down the sidewalk, Lisa turned to Jill. "Todd's driving Mom's car. Come with us."

The offer meant more than was apparent on the surface. Jill knew it was a confirmation of their renewed relationship. "Okay," Jill replied, feeling she belonged with Lisa at last.

She got into the back seat with Whitney and Kevin. Whitney cuddled against her as they drove along. "Did you live in Grandma's house when you were a little girl?" she asked.

"Yes, I did, just like your mommy. I played softball in that park." She pointed out the window. "And there's Skyline Chili where we used to go after the softball games."

"Will you take me there, Aunt Jill?"

"Sure," Jill answered.

"Tomorrow? For lunch?"

"It's a date." Jill turned to Kevin. "Want to come along?"

Kevin shook his head. "I'm going to Jared's," he said. "We're gonna play Nintendo."

Whitney tugged at Jill's arm. "Can I have french fries?"

"Yes, and ice cream for dessert if you want." Again she felt that familiar pang. Did her daughter like french fries? What flavor of ice cream was her favorite? She pushed the thought away. She'd never know the answers to her questions.

They turned into the already crowded parking lot of B'nai Zion Synagogue. A moment later her father's car pulled up beside them. Jill edged over to Sherry as soon as she got out of the car. "Stay close to me," she whispered. "I won't recognize half the people who come up to me, and I'll be embarrassed."

Sherry laughed. Jill's poor memory for faces was legendary. "I'll introduce them to David... loudly," she promised.

Inside, the organ was playing as seats filled up. They found places near the front, taking up an entire row. Jill hadn't been here in years, but the synagogue hadn't changed. Designed in a stark, modern style, it still afforded a sense of timelessness, a connection between this generation and those of centuries past. The Eternal Light was suspended above the altar as it was in countless synagogues. Maroon velvet curtains decorated with religious symbols hung before the ark where the Torahs, the Books of Moses, were kept. Around the sanctuary, windows of stained glass depicted scenes from the Bible—the burning bush, Moses carrying the tablets with the Ten Commandments, the binding of Isaac.

After the congregants joined in *"Lechah Dodi,"* the song welcoming the Sabbath, Rabbi Benson, who had been the senior rabbi here ever since Jill could remember, stepped forward and began the service. "Praised be Thou, O Lord our God, ruler of the universe, who with Thy word bringest on the evening twilight and with Thy wisdom openest the gates of the heavens."

Jill opened her Sabbath prayer book. She loved the familiarity of Friday night—the unchanging order of the service, the old prayers with their well-loved tunes.

When the service was over, they filed out. Old friends came up to greet them as they headed for the hall where refreshments were being served. True to her word, Sherry announced each in ringing tones. Jill chatted with former schoolmates, many now married, with relatives, and with friends of her parents. As she talked she scanned the room for the one person she wanted to see. Ben.

Then she heard his voice behind her, felt his hand on her shoulder. Heart thudding, she turned.

He took both her hands in his. "You were magnificent this afternoon."

"Thank you. I thought the presentation went well."

"You're being modest. It was spectacular. I wanted to tell you then, but..." He kept her hands in his. "You look beautiful tonight."

So did he. The brown of his jacket enhanced the deep mahogany of his eyes. Eyes that were staring into hers as if they couldn't break away.

"Can we slip out," he asked, "or is there someone you want to see?"

"I—"

"Ben, hi." Sherry appeared beside them. "How nice to run into you." She gave Jill a sly grin, then added, sotto voce, "This is Ben Abrams."

Jill choked with laughter. "I recognized him."

"Good for you. She doesn't remember faces," Sherry said to Ben.

"I found that out on Monday," he said.

"I'd say she was suffering from premature senility," Sherry continued, "but she's always been that way. Come on." She took his arm. "I want you to meet David. Remember, I told you about him."

Keeping Jill close beside him, Ben walked along with Sherry. She made the introductions, then said, "We're going out for a drink in a few minutes. You two will join us, won't you?"

Jill didn't want to. She wanted to be alone with Ben. She met his eyes and saw reluctance, then resignation.

"Sure," he said. Then he murmured in Jill's ear, "But not for long."

That was okay with her. "Let me introduce you to my grandmother before we go," she said, searching the crowd for Bubbi. Jill finally located her, deep in conversation with a distinguished-looking white-haired gentleman, and hurried over to her with Ben in tow. "Bubbi, this is Ben Abrams."

Her grandmother put out her hand. "So, you are the meat man, right?"

Ben looked nonplussed for a moment, then he grinned. "Yes. You'll have to come to Steak Expectations and try our steaks."

Bubbi shook her head. "At my age I go to a restaurant where someone else does the cooking." She gave her companion a sidelong glance, and he nodded.

Flirt, Jill thought. *And how old is she? At least seventy-five.*

Bubbi continued. "Cooking at a restaurant is for young people."

"Then you'll have to come with us and let us cook for you."

"That I would consider," Bubbi told him, then gestured toward the table behind her, which was laden with sweets. "Have you tried some of the strudel? Not that it's as good as mine."

Ben shook his head. "We're going out to get a snack."

"Enjoy yourselves, then," Bubbi said.

Jill leaned over and kissed her, and Bubbi whispered, "A nice young man. This one you should take seriously. Don't let him slip through your fingers."

"Shh, he might hear you," Jill whispered back.

"So?" Bubbi looked up at her, eyes twinkling. Jill shook her head and gave her another hug, then turned back to Ben.

They said good-night to her parents and stepped outside to find that the temperature had dropped. Heavy clouds hid the stars and promised snow.

"We'll go down to the Riverfront. That okay with everybody?" Todd said. There were murmurs of agreement, then Todd added, "Let's take one car. Ben, we can drop you two off here afterward."

Jill, Ben, Sherry and David piled into the back. Jill perched on the edge of the crowded seat. She put her hand on the back of the driver's seat and leaned forward, but Ben pulled her back against him. Immediately the cold she'd felt outside disappeared, replaced by a delicious feeling of warmth. His fingers traced her palm, his breath stirred the hair behind her ear, and when he laughed at something David said, she felt the deep rumble of his chest against her back. She felt a sense of belonging she hadn't known in years. Closeness with her sisters, of course, but Ben was the core of it. And she knew a thrill of anticipation, imagining how the evening would end.

They drove to the Riverfront and found a small, intimate club with dim lighting, old-fashioned wooden booths and a combo that played jazz. Tonight, in deference to the season, the band interspersed an occasional Christmas carol.

Jill ordered hot buttered rum. She sat between Ben and Lisa and tried to concentrate on the lively conversation flowing around her, but everyone could have been speaking Swahili for all she could follow. Every time Ben's arm touched hers it set off tiny brush fires of excitement. Every time his eyes met hers and she saw the desire in their depths, she felt the flames within her grow higher, hotter.

Ben slipped his arm around her shoulder, let his fingers slide through her hair and gently outline the shape of her ear. Jill sighed. He heard and turned to her, his smile intimate, his thigh pressed against hers. She felt languid, dreamy, yet impatient for this part of the evening to end.

Conversation continued, another round of drinks was ordered and Jill's tension mounted. No one seemed in a hurry to end the evening. Even Ben made no suggestion that they leave. Was she imagining the current flowing between them?

Minutes passed, or maybe hours. Finally Todd glanced at Lisa, gave her a lazy smile and said, "It's been a long day. Why don't we head back?" He signaled the waiter, who seemed to take an inordinate amount of time bringing the check, then they left.

As they drove back toward the synagogue Jill's heart began to hammer. As the moment she'd thought of all day approached, she felt a mixture of anxiety and exhilaration, and she didn't know which was stronger.

Todd turned into B'nai Zion's parking lot, stopped the car and everyone said good-night. When she'd gotten out of the car and Ben had shut the door behind her, Jill wasn't sure if she'd said goodbye to her family or not. Her nerves were so tightly strung she wasn't certain of anything, least of all what she was going to do now that she and Ben were alone.

She was vaguely aware of the chilly darkness, the emptiness of the parking lot, the sound of Todd's car driving away. Then she heard Ben's voice, warm with amusement, close to her ear. "Come on. You'll turn into an icicle if you don't get in the car."

Automatically she moved toward the car and got in.

Ben sat behind the wheel, put the keys in the ignition, but made no move to turn on the motor. Instead he turned to face her, took one of her hands in his and with his other hand gently touched her cheek. "Come home with me," he said, his voice deep, seductive.

The moment was here. The moment she'd ached for, feared. Suddenly there were no doubts, no misgivings. This was what she wanted. This was right. "Yes," she breathed.

Ben traced a finger over her lips and urged her closer for a long, sweet kiss. Then he turned the switch, and the car moved forward.

CHAPTER EIGHT

BEN'S TOWN HOUSE WAS an old, refurbished one nestled on the side of Mount Adams. He opened the door and stepped back so she could enter, but Jill paused on the threshold. This was a moment she wanted to remember. The opening of another door.

Her memories of lovemaking with Mickey were vague, obscured by the anguish that had come after. She had hazy images of groping, of frenzy. They had been young, elated with their sexuality, their aliveness. They'd delighted in sensations, but they hadn't probed beneath the surface. With Ben she sensed everything would be different.

He turned to her, concern showing on his face. "Are you okay? Having second thoughts?"

"No." He'd interpreted her hesitation as fear. She wasn't sure she could explain the reason she'd stopped or that she even wanted to try. Instead she said, "I was just looking at the room."

"Like it?"

"Yes." High ceiling, hardwood floors with a couple of dhurrie rugs scattered about, dark leather couch and armchairs you could curl up in, tall bookshelves filled with books, a watercolor of a forested lake. She liked the room very much. It felt like...home.

She stood for another moment, uncertain what to do next.

Ben stepped behind her and helped her off with her coat, then leaned forward and kissed the back of her neck. His breath was warm. "Sit down," he said. "I'll get us something to drink."

She sat on the couch, breathing in the scent of leather, and watched Ben walk over to a small bar in the corner of the room. In a moment he returned with two snifters of brandy.

He handed her one and sat beside her, swirled the golden liquid in his glass, then reached into his pocket and took out a small box. He held it out to her. "Your present for the fifth night of Chanukah."

She truly hadn't expected another gift. Pleased, excited, she unwrapped it. "Oh, Ben," she breathed as she lifted out a small silver heart on a chain.

"It's a symbol of my heart," he told her gravely. "I've given you that, too."

They weren't just pretty words, she could see that. He meant them. She wished she had some words to give him in return, but she wasn't ready yet. So she concentrated on the gift. Fastening the chain around her neck, she said, "This is beautiful. I should have something for you, too."

"Oh, you do," he murmured, moving closer, fingering the silver heart where it rested above her own. "I've imagined you here," he said, and his lips curved. "When you were giving your presentation this afternoon, I pictured you in this room, in my arms."

Jill felt her breath catch in her throat, felt a wave of warmth suffuse her body. Her voice gone, she watched as Ben gently took the brandy snifter from her and set it on the table, put his hands on her shoulders and drew her close. "Kiss me," he murmured.

She did. Slowly, almost shyly, she put her arms around him and covered his lips with hers. Their kiss was soft, gentle as the touch of spring. No pressure, only the first tender meeting of new lovers. No rush. They had time, time for passion to build. And she knew it would.

Gently he urged her lips apart, and their tongues met, retreated, then advanced again in a teasing courting dance. Gradually their kisses deepened, their mouths fused, as if they could absorb one another's innermost hidden secrets.

At last Ben drew his mouth away and looked into Jill's eyes. He stroked her cheek as he had in the car. "Let me love you."

Again she nodded. "Yes."

He touched his mouth to hers. "Don't be afraid."

"I'm not." She'd spoken the truth. Gone were her fears of last night, of all the nights before. Fears of pregnancy, of intimacy. She trusted him. She wanted him.

Ben took her hand, drew her to her feet and led her to his bedroom. Light from the living room illuminated it with a pale glow. He paused by the bed and took her into his arms. No longer soft, now his kiss spoke of desire still leashed but simmering, ready to burst forth.

He began to undress her, unfastening the buttons at her collar and cuffs, drawing her dress down and letting it fall around her feet. He bent and kissed her shoulders, tracing the line of them with his tongue, murmuring over their smoothness.

She wanted to see him. She reached for his tie, but her fingers were clumsy. Had he expected proficiency? She glanced at him, wondering if she'd see disappointment in his eyes. But she saw only desire. He lifted her hands and kissed her palms, then undid the tie himself.

Willing her fingers to cooperate this time, Jill began unbuttoning his shirt. Carefully she opened one button, then another, and spread the garment back to reveal his chest. Tentatively, then with growing assurance, she ran her fingers over him. Dark, curling hair. Soft, like a kitten's, against smooth, firm skin, against strong bone and taut muscle. He was beautiful. She wanted to tell him, but words wouldn't come. So she used her hands and lips and tongue to show him what she couldn't say.

He unfastened her bra. Her breasts felt swollen, heavy, the nipples tight with desire. He touched the silver heart that lay between her breasts, first with his finger, then with his lips. He took her breast in his hand, caressing it slowly, thoroughly, as if he wanted to memorize its weight, its shape, its texture.

Then he bent and took her nipple in his mouth. Jill gasped. She'd never felt like this, never imagined feeling like this. As if she were on fire. As if she were melting from the heat.

Why had she been afraid of this... this passion, this wonder? What could be more beautiful than knowing that within minutes you would be united with the man you wanted, the man you... loved? The realization of love flowed through her heart, through her body.

Ben lifted her into his arms and laid her on the bed. He pulled down her panty hose, his lips following his hands, kissing her exposed skin, setting it ablaze. He kissed her ankles, her feet. She moaned, writhed, reached for him. He came to her, shedding his trousers, his shirt, almost ripping them off in his haste. "Kiss me again," he urged.

And she did. Enthralled, fascinated, she explored him. The texture of his skin—his cheeks scratchy with a shadow of beard, his shoulders smooth, his thighs rough and hair covered. The taste of him—the tang of salt from the sweat on his shoulders, the flavor of brandy on his tongue. The scent of him—vestiges of after-shave, musky odor of desire, of man. Everywhere she touched, everywhere she looked, there was something new to experience.

This was what love was, she realized. Not a frenzied mating, but a deep, consummate discovery of one another. They had begun already, learning about one another emotionally; now this step, the physical exploration, unfolded naturally.

She'd always imagined men and women talking as they made love, always wondered, when the time came, what she'd say. But now she knew that words were unnecessary. She and Ben could communicate everything with fingertip touches, soft moans, intense glances.

He pulled her closer. She felt the rhythm of his heart, racing madly. She heard his breathing quicken, shorten. He drew away and rose from the bed.

He stood silhouetted in the faint light. Male, virile. Ready.

She felt one last flash of panic, but he opened the drawer of his nightstand. "I'm going to protect you," he said, and her fear subsided.

Jill watched as he took out a packet, opened it, sheathed himself.

He turned back to her, knelt above her. In that last second her breath stopped, the blood raced through her veins and her body opened to him.

He entered her. She cried out with pain, with pleasure. And then she forgot everything but the heat of him, the rhythm of their movements and the glorious feeling of oneness.

The fires of desire built, swelled, exploded. She shattered, felt Ben's last powerful thrust before he, too, climaxed. And finally she experienced the delicious, slow settling back to earth.

They lay still, wrapped in each other's arms. Ben brushed the damp hair from her face. "Are you okay?"

"Yes." She was suddenly shy again. She didn't know what to say, what Ben expected. So she said nothing.

Ben continued to stroke her hair. Then he sat up and moved away from her, and Jill felt the sting of rejection. Was he disappointed in her?

But he bent over the bed and kissed her. "I'll be right back," he whispered. "Don't go 'way."

She watched him walk out of the room, unabashedly naked, boldly masculine, outrageously sexy—and hers, she thought possessively. For the moment, anyway.

She pulled the sheet up over her breasts and waited. In a minute he returned, carrying their brandy snifters. He stopped at the side of the bed and stared down at her, then set the glasses on the nightstand. "You're still wearing your earrings," he said.

Automatically her hand went to her earlobe. Yes, the earring was there, but removing her jewelry had been the last thing on her mind. "I guess I forgot about them."

Ben grinned. "And I didn't notice them, they're so plain." He sat on the edge of the bed. "Let me." Grasping her lobe gently between two fingers, he unfastened the gold button...slowly. Jill's breath quickened; so did his. He set the earring aside and covered the space where it had been with warm, moist kisses. His tongue dipped inside her ear, sending shivers through her.

Her hands tightened on the sheets. "I...I'll do the other one," she croaked.

"No problem." He reached across her, his arm brushing her shoulder, and gave the same thorough attention to the other ear. By the time he finished she felt as weak as if he'd made love to her all over again.

Ben gave her a slow, sexy smile. Then he straightened and reached for the brandy snifters. He handed one to her, plumped up the pillows and got into bed beside her.

Jill welcomed the brandy. Glad to have something to concentrate on, she raised the glass to her lips. The sheet slipped, exposing her. Quickly she tried to cover herself, but Ben caught her hand. "Leave the sheet down. I want to look at your breasts." He brushed a nipple with his thumb. "They're beautiful. You're beautiful."

Jill shook her head. *Lisa* was beautiful.

Ben's glance was tender, amused. "You don't believe me, do you? But you are. If I were writing an ad for you, I'd say, 'She's exotic, bewitching.'" He trailed his fingers across her cheek, and she sighed.

"I'd say, 'Her eyes are changeable, mysterious. Her breasts are the color of honey, their taste even sweeter.'" He placed light, airy kisses on each breast in turn, and she trembled.

"But," he went on, "I wouldn't write that ad. I don't want to share you...with anyone." He tipped her face up for a long, brandy-laced kiss, and she moaned.

With his lips on hers, his eyes gazing at her admiringly, Jill felt beautiful. She felt loved.

They sipped their brandy amid whispered words, kisses and caresses. When they were finished, Jill said, "I should go."

"No. Spend the night. I want to wake up with you in my bed."

She hesitated as guilt reared its head. *Ridiculous. You're a big girl, Jill. You can do what you want.* "I'll stay," she said.

"Good." He pulled her into his arms, and they made love again. And again.

BEN WOKE EARLY the next morning. He lay in bed, savoring the feeling of waking with Jill beside him. Her head resting on his shoulder, she slept deeply, her lips slightly parted, still swollen from his kisses during their last furious coupling just a few hours ago.

Though he'd learned every secret of her body, she was still an enigma to him. She wasn't a virgin, but she had an innocence about her. She'd cried out that first time, as if his entry were painful. Perhaps it had been; her passageway was tight. Her experience in lovemaking must be limited. But she'd learned quickly under his tutelage, he thought with satisfaction. The final time they'd come together, she'd been as unrestrained, as avid as he.

He kissed her cheek, but she didn't stir. Even when he gently disengaged himself from her, she slept undisturbed. He took one last lingering look at her before he pulled a pair of jeans and a sweater out of his closet and left the bedroom.

He got into the shower, relishing the rush of steamy water over his body. He felt exhilarated, more alive than he'd been in months. Today he was certain he could conquer the world. That was what love did to you...what real love did. He'd fancied himself in love with Karen, but his feelings for her seemed tame in comparison to the emotions he was experiencing now. Joy, passion, wonder. God, even being away from Jill's side for scant moments had him longing for her. Crazy. He was crazy in love with her.

With a wry smile he thought of his strategy to lure Jill to his bed. He'd started with basic desire, but by the end of his campaign, he'd been the one captivated, caught in a web of his own making.

And it wasn't over yet. Because now he had another goal in mind, a much more serious one. He wanted Jill, not just in his bed, but in his life forever. Home, hearth, family.

"Okay, Abrams," he murmured as he stepped from the shower, "time to get the next stage of your campaign in gear." Thank goodness Carnaby and Ross had come up with an exceptional ad campaign for Steak Expectations. That guaranteed Jill's returning to Cincinnati frequently and assured him they would be in regular contact. This way he could use their business meetings as a backdrop to convince her she couldn't live without him. And when he and Alan opened their own agency, he'd persuade Jill to join them.

He toweled himself dry, shaved and pulled on his clothes, then padded barefoot into the kitchen. Whistling softly, he filled the coffee maker.

When the coffee was ready, he fixed a tray with two cups and headed back to the bedroom. He stood for a moment, enjoying the sight of Jill, her hair spread across the pillow, her hand curled beneath her cheek, the soft swell of her breast visible above the sheet.

He set the tray down beside the bed and bent over her. "Wake up, sleepyhead," he murmured in her ear.

Her eyes flew open and she gasped, then gave an embarrassed laugh. "I . . . I forgot where I was."

He chuckled. "Remember now?"

She nodded and blushed.

She was so adorable, her eyes wide, her cheeks pink. He sat beside her and covered her face with kisses. "Glad to be here?"

"Mmm-hmm."

"Want some coffee?"

"I'd love some." She sat up, pulling the sheet with her.

Ben's smile was tender, amused. "Still shy?"

"I . . . yes. I don't have much experience in . . . this."

"This?" he repeated in a teasing tone and saw the color rise in her cheeks.

Her chin came up. "Don't pretend you don't know what I am talking about. Spending the night. Sleeping around." Her voice trembled.

Ben was surprised at the surge of anger that ran through him at her words. He caught her chin in his hand. "Hey, this isn't sleeping around, and it doesn't require a résumé listing previous experience. This is something special between the two of us. I call it making love."

"Oh."

He saw the relief in her eyes and the lessening of tension and felt his irritation fade. His grip on her chin softened, and he urged her close so their lips could meet.

"I like calling it making love," she whispered against his mouth.

"Me, too," he agreed. "Want some more practice?"

Her laugh was free, joyous. "Later. Didn't you bring in some coffee?"

He turned to pick up the cup. "Spoilsport."

"Sorry. I'm not good for much of anything until I've had my caffeine."

"Wanna test that out?"

She laughed again and held out her hand. "Coffee, Mr. Abrams."

He sat on the edge of the bed, drinking his coffee as she sipped hers. He enjoyed the sound of her laughter, the delicate early-morning fragrance of her body.

When they finished their coffee, he suggested, "Come watch while I make breakfast."

"Coffee in bed. Breakfast. You're spoiling me rotten," she answered. "At least let me help."

"You're on. I'll be in the kitchen." Although he would have enjoyed watching her dress, he'd indulge her need for privacy. He went to the closet and took out a shirt. "This'll be more comfortable for breakfast." He handed it to her and left the room.

Jill watched him go. Was this really happening to her? This delicious feeling of being pampered, loved by a man. What better gift could she have asked for in this season of giving? She fingered the tiny silver heart resting between her breasts, remembering Ben's words when he'd given it to her. *It's a symbol of my heart. I've given you that, too.* Had he really meant those words, or were they part of the typical male line—tell a woman what she wants to hear until he gets what he wants her to give?

No, she wouldn't let herself believe that of Ben. He wasn't a kid as Mickey had been during their adolescent affair. Besides, Ben was too sincere. She could see it in his eyes. His beautiful, chocolate-colored eyes.

Smiling to herself, she stretched luxuriously and got out of bed. A glance out the window told her the promise of snow last night had been fulfilled. The ground was covered with a pristine blanket of white. Seeing it, Jill felt a euphoria she thought she'd left behind with her childhood. She wanted to skip outside, throw snowballs at passersby and fall backward into drifts, leaving the imprint of a snow angel.

After a quick shower she reached for Ben's shirt, but instead of putting it on she held it to her cheek, breathing in the scent that clung to it. The scent of her lover.

She'd never had occasion to use that word before. Or
to think about what it implied. Closeness. Sharing.

What could she allow herself to share with Ben? The
story of her past? God, no. Not yet, anyway. She deserved some time to enjoy their relationship, to let it grow
unencumbered by her past mistakes. Later, she'd tell him.
Her mind made up on that score, she ran a brush through
her hair and strolled into the kitchen.

Ben stood with his back to her looking out the window, but as soon as she stepped into the room he turned
as if he sensed her presence.

He ran his eyes over her thoroughly and appreciatively. His lips curved into a smile that warmed Jill down
to her toes. "I like you in my shirt. Last night you looked
like a cameo, sweet and innocent. Today—" he grinned
and let his gaze settled where the shirt just skimmed her
thighs "—today you look like a temptress."

"Are you tempted?" The archness in her voice surprised her. She was learning the role of lover quickly.

"Don't push me." He came to her and hauled her
against him for a long, thorough kiss. When he finally
drew away, they were both half out of breath.

"Shall we start cooking?" Jill panted.

Ben laughed and shook his head. "Honey, we already
have. I know I'm way past the boiling point."

Jill gave him a punch on the shoulder. "Be serious,
Ben. I'm starving."

Between laughter and kisses they managed to prepare
their meal. Jill took charge of the scrambled eggs, adding grated cheese and canned mushrooms, and Ben set
the table, warmed frozen muffins and poured fresh cups
of coffee.

They sat across the table from one another in his small,
old-fashioned kitchen. He tasted a forkful of eggs and

raised his coffee cup in a toast. "My compliments to the chef."

Jill was pleased that he'd used the key phrase from her campaign. That could only bode well for Carnaby and Ross. She fluttered her lashes. "Thank you, sir."

"And you told me you couldn't cook," he chided. "You must be your mother's daughter, after all."

Involuntarily, Jill stiffened. *Was* she her mother's daughter? Did she want to be? Was she even certain who the woman she called mother really was? She'd confronted Lisa this week. As Bubbi had said, the time had come to talk with her mother, as well. Today. This afternoon.

She hoped Ben didn't notice her discomfort at his words, but his gaze searched her face as if he wanted to see into her mind. She shifted in her chair and deliberately changed the subject. "Looks like we'll get some more snow."

Ben followed her gaze to the sky outside the window. Thick, pewter-colored clouds bulged with moisture ready to be released at any moment.

"This weather makes me want to go outside and play," Jill continued.

"Makes me want to stay inside and play." He smiled lazily, and Jill watched with fascination as his dimples emerged. "We could spend the day in bed."

"That's an attractive idea, but I have plans for lunch."

Immediately his smile faded. He was hurt, Jill realized, and hastened to add, "With Whitney. I promised to take her to Skyline Chili. Want to join us?"

"A lunch date with a young lady who's destined to be a world-class heartbreaker? How can I refuse, especially when her aunt is part of the deal?"

They lingered over coffee, did the dishes together, and afterward Ben drove her back to the hotel to change. "I'll wait for you downstairs," he said. "Pack an overnight bag, okay?"

Jill didn't need any further urging. Their time together was growing short, and she wanted to make every minute count. She put on a favorite pair of royal blue sweats and fastened her dreidel earrings. Then she tossed some necessities into a carry-on bag, and hurried back to Ben.

As soon as they arrived at her parents', Whitney came tearing into the living room. "I'm ready, Aunt Jill." Noticing Ben, she slid to a halt and with natural female flirtatiousness sidled up to him. "Are you coming with us?"

"I sure am," he answered. "Is that okay?"

"Uh-huh, if you like chili." She slipped her hand into his.

"What did I tell you?" Ben murmured to Jill. "She's a femme fatale already."

"Takes after her mom," Jill said without rancor. She was beginning to understand and even appreciate the differences between her and Lisa.

"Put on your mittens before you go out, Whitney," Lisa said.

While Ben helped Whitney comply, Jill glanced at her sister, who leaned against the door frame, and saw Lisa's fond smile as she watched her daughter. What was it like to be a mother, a real mother, not just a woman who'd gone through the birth process? As much as she'd loved her own daughter, as much as she yearned for her, Jill would never experience the day-to-day knowledge of her child, or of motherhood.

What goals did Lisa have for Whitney? What wounds might she, because of those goals, inadvertently inflict? Jill wondered if you had to be a mother yourself before you could understand your own parent.

Whitney put one mitten-encased hand in Jill's and the other in Ben's, and the three of them started on their way. At the porch step Ben asked Whitney, "Want us to fly you down?"

"Okay."

To the child's intense delight, he and Jill swung her up and over the step and set her down on the sidewalk. She stared at the yard. "It snowed a lot, didn't it?" She looked up at Ben, a baffled expression on her face. "Where does the snow go when it melts?"

"Ask Aunt Jill," he suggested.

"It turns into water," Jill explained dutifully. "Some of it soaks in the ground, and the rest goes back up in the air."

Whitney pondered this for a moment. "Like upside-down rain?"

"No. You can't see it. It's called water vapor."

"If you can't see it, then why's it got a name?"

"Because... because it just does. Let's get in the car, honey—before she asks for another scientific explanation," she muttered.

On the way to Skyline Chili, Whitney chattered non-stop about a variety of subjects: the new clothes she'd acquired for her Cabbage Patch doll, a set of false teeth she'd discovered at Poppy's—"He's my other grandpa, the one at home in Omaha," she explained—the upcoming wedding of Miss Marcia, her preschool teacher.

At the restaurant she crawled into the booth beside Jill, scrambled up on her knees and inquired, "What did you have for lunch when you were three, Aunt Jill?"

"Five-way chili. Chili with everything," Jill replied.

"Did you have that, too, Ben?"

"No, honey. I didn't live here when I was three."

"Oh, did you live in Omaha?" Whitney inquired with interest.

Probably, Jill thought, Omaha and Cincinnati were the only two cities Whitney knew about.

When Ben shook his head, Whitney's brow furrowed. "I looked out of the window on the plane," she said, "and I didn't see any other places to live. Just grass. Did you live in the grass, Ben?"

He met Jill's laughing eyes and explained, "No, I lived in another city, called Cleveland."

Whitney considered this but didn't appear convinced such a place existed.

"Have you decided what you want, sweetie?" Jill asked her.

Whitney finally chose the chili dog. Jill's meal was punctuated by several rescues of the chili bowl, which threatened to fall into Whitney's lap with alarming regularity, and three trips to the bathroom. "I just love restaurant potties," Whitney confided.

When the meal was over, Jill shook her head at Whitney's chili-covered cheeks. "Let's go clean up," she said, precipitating yet another visit to the ladies' room.

"You're great with kids," Ben remarked when she and Whitney returned to the table.

The casual comment struck her like a blow. She knew he meant nothing by it, nothing but an offhand compliment, but it hurt. Her hands began to shake. Sliding into the booth, she overturned a glass of water. As the glass shattered on the floor, splashing water around her feet, Jill felt her eyes fill with tears. She was overreacting. She knew it, but she couldn't seem to control herself.

"Hey, it's okay," Ben said. "It's just a glass." He motioned to the busboy, then turned back to Jill. "Are you all right? Did you cut yourself?"

"No, I was startled that's all."

Stupid, she chastised herself. *Silly to let these things upset you.* She'd heard remarks like that before, but in New York, not in Cincinnati, the scene of all her earlier pain. Her heart was pounding and she was certain her face was pale, but she managed to shrug as the busboy cleaned up the broken glass.

Ben still studied her thoughtfully, but he said nothing except, "Ready to go?"

Back in the car, he said, "I want to stop at Kroger's. I thought we'd eat in tonight."

At the grocery store he bought supplies, while Jill and Whitney trailed after him. He tossed a box of pancake mix into the cart. "For breakfast," he murmured and gave Jill an intimate smile.

On the way out Whitney halted before a vending machine that featured plastic containers filled with rings and bracelets. "Can I have a ring?" she asked.

"Why not?" Ben produced a coin.

Whitney insisted on inserting the coin herself. When her selection fell into her hands, she examined it with delight. "What's it called?"

"It must be a ruby," Ben said solemnly. He opened the plastic container and took out the ring. "Put out your hand, honey."

Whitney held out her hand, turning it back and forth, and nodded her approval. "It's nice. Miss Marcia got a ring. She says when you get one from a boy, you're 'gaged. Are we 'gaged, Ben?"

"I think thirty's a little old for you. Maybe we're just good friends."

She considered that a moment, then nodded. "Okay. Are you and Aunt Jill good friends, too?"

"Very good friends." He gave Jill a heated glance.

Whitney was quiet on the way back, absorbed in admiring her ring.

When they turned down her parents' street, Ben said to Jill, "I have some work to do at home. I'll let you visit with your family and come back for you around six. How's that?"

"Fine."

Jill was disappointed to see a blue Honda parked in the driveway. She'd hoped for a chance to talk to her mother, but with company there, she wouldn't have the time or the privacy.

With a light kiss on the cheek, Ben left her at the door. Jill followed Whitney inside. From the living room she could hear voices . . . and the sound of a baby fussing.

A feeling of dread assailed her. She paused in the entry hall, but she couldn't postpone going in. Clutching her hands together tightly, she took a step forward.

Seated on the sofa, baby in her arms, was one of the two people in the world Jill least wanted to see.

"Jill," she said, "hi. I was hoping you'd be here. It's been a long time."

Jill took a long, steadying breath. "Hello, Roz," she said. "How are you?"

CHAPTER NINE

"I'M WONDERFUL," Roz said, and she clearly was. Her short cap of red-brown curls framed a face that glowed with happiness. Her green eyes sparkled. "And here's the reason." She nodded toward the baby in her arms. "This is Sarah. Come take a look."

Because she could hardly avoid doing so, Jill walked across the room on feet that felt like iron. She met Sherry's eye and saw sympathy, and that gave her the strength to do what she had to do.

She approached the couch and looked down at the blanket-swathed bundle. Blue-black eyes. A head covered with fine black curls, one of which was sassily tied with a pink ribbon. Tiny fists flailing at the air. A Cupid's-bow mouth, which was presently emitting sounds of discontent.

"She's been a little fussy, but she's better now. She likes to be held," Roz explained with a mother's certainty. She rocked Sarah gently, and the baby quieted.

"She's . . . beautiful," Jill whispered.

"Want to hold her?"

No! God, no! "I don't want to upset her." The excuse was a lame one, but maybe it would give Roz second thoughts.

"She won't mind a bit. Sit down."

Jill knew she couldn't stand another minute, no matter what. Her legs, which had been so heavy seconds ago, had begun to wobble. Carefully she seated herself on the sofa and held out her arms for Roz and Mickey's child.

How tiny she was. How soft. How absolutely perfect. Her eyes fastened on the baby's face, Jill was aware of Roz's voice beside her.

"She's nine weeks old today. We got her when she was two days. Uncle Harris was so pleased that we named her after Aunt Sarah. She's a wonderful baby. We're so lucky. She's already sleeping through the night, no colic—"

"That's nice." *Enough, please. I can't listen to any more.*

But Roz continued. "She weighs twelve pounds already, such a little fatty. Yes," she added, leaning over to chuck Sarah under the chin, "you're a little piggy, aren't you?"

Sarah's tiny mouth spread into an endearing baby smile, and Jill felt her heart splinter into pieces.

"You wouldn't believe what a great daddy Mickey has turned out to be." Roz beamed. "He bathes her and burps her, even changes her. I think he was born to be a father."

But not to my child. The pain was so potent Jill thought she would surely shatter. But she didn't. She sat holding the baby, biting her lip to keep back the tears.

She looked up and, through a blur, saw Lisa's compassionate expression.

"Roz, are you still active in the sisterhood at your synagogue?" Lisa asked in what Jill realized was an attempt to steer Roz away from the subject at hand.

"Oh, I'm taking a break from committee work to enjoy Sarah. We've hardly even left her yet. I'm sure we will, but so far I haven't wanted to, and honestly, Mickey won't hear of it. He—"

The baby shifted in Jill's arms and whimpered.

"Okay, sugar, come back to Mommy." Roz took the child from Jill.

Just as she'd taken her from the woman who'd given birth to her. Jill knew her thought was unfair to Roz. Roz had simply been the beneficiary of someone else's misfortune.

"There. Don't cry," Roz crooned to the baby. "Mommy loves you."

But you aren't her only mommy. Somewhere, some girl or woman gave Sarah life, but no one will ever acknowledge her other mother. No one will know what a huge, aching void that woman will always carry with her.

"Well," Sherry said brightly, "anyone read any good books lately?"

Lisa jumped into the conversation. "There's a new Julian St. Clair mystery out, *Night of the Dragon.* I've been looking for it, but it's sold out everywhere. Have you read it?"

Between the two of them, Sherry and Lisa managed to distract Roz from baby talk. Jill sat silently, unmoving, her thoughts on hold, as conversation flowed about her.

She heard footsteps and saw her mother come into the room. "Jill," Esther said, "I didn't hear the door. Whitney just found me and told me you were back. Everything all right?"

You know it's not. But she appreciated her mother's concern. "Fine."

"Roz, why don't you let me put Sarah down in the bedroom?" Esther suggested. "She looks like she's falling asleep."

"Thanks, Aunt Esther. I'll do it," Roz said and got up.

Jill sent a silent thank-you to her mother and breathed a relieved sigh. If she didn't have to look at Sarah, maybe she could—

The sound of the back door slamming, masculine voices and heavy footsteps interrupted her thoughts. Her mother and sisters exchanged nervous looks, and Jill knew what was about to happen.

She reached deep inside for strength, for stoicism, as three men walked into the room. Her brother-in-law, Todd, Sherry's David . . . and Mickey Zimmerman.

He and Roz met halfway across the room.

"Hi, honey," she said. She shifted the baby and stood on tiptoe to kiss his cheek.

"Hi," he echoed and bent to plant a light kiss on Sarah's curls. Then he glanced over the baby's head, and his eyes met Jill's.

She saw surprised recognition, a look of unease, then a forced smile. "Hello, Jill," he said and walked toward her across the room.

Jill had pictured this meeting many times, but never in her imagination had it occurred with Mickey's child in attendance.

Though more than eight years had passed, she could picture their last encounter as though it had happened yesterday. They'd broken up six weeks earlier, but when she'd learned she was pregnant she'd told her parents they were trying for a reconciliation, and she'd gone to Columbus to talk to him.

She could still see the two of them sitting in the front seat of Mickey's car, hear their last conversation, even feel the faint spring breeze that had wafted through the open window.

She remembered Mickey sitting behind the wheel, dressed in jeans and scuffed sneakers and an Ohio State

T-shirt, his hair tousled where his fingers had raked it, his expression stunned and angry, his voice curt as he gave her a suggestion so foreign to her values she could never even consider it—to terminate the pregnancy.

She wondered whether the warring emotions she felt today showed in her expression as he came closer. She wasn't even sure she could name them all. A deep, molten anger that he had wanted someone else's child and rejected his own. Sorrow that neither of them would ever know that product of their infatuation—she could no longer call what they'd shared "love." But surprisingly absent was any sort of feeling for Mickey himself. As if the slate had been wiped clean, any trace of that long-ago ardor had been erased. *Ben,* she thought. Her love for Ben had replaced any lingering feelings she'd held for Mickey.

He put out his hand. "How are you?"

"I'm fine. And you?" She congratulated herself that her voice was steady; so was her hand.

"Doing well." He glanced over his shoulder at Roz. Clearly, he didn't want to mention the baby. "You're looking good," he added. "What are you doing with yourself?"

"I'm working for a New York ad agency." Certainly in her fantasies of their meeting she'd never imagined this inane conversation. She'd envisioned something meaningful, some resolution of the past.

"That's nice." He glanced at Roz again. "Honey, if Sarah's asleep, maybe we should take her home."

"All right." Roz put Sarah in her carrier and said her goodbyes to the rest of the group, then joined Mickey. "Jill, I'm so glad to have seen you. It's been too long. Will you be at the benefit tomorrow night?"

Jill nodded.

Mickey took the baby carrier from Roz. "What benefit?" he muttered.

"You know. For the Cohen Agency. We can't miss that."

Mickey nodded. For a frozen moment his eyes locked with Jill's. She wondered how he'd feel if he knew that the agency had handled the adoption of his own child. But, of course, he didn't even know he had a child. His eyes slid away from Jill's and he said, "We'll see you there."

WHEN JILL HEARD the outside door shut behind Mickey and Roz, she stood. "Excuse me."

"Where are you going?" Sherry asked.

"Upstairs for a while."

"I'll go with you," Sherry offered.

"Me, too," Lisa said. "We'll be back in a little while," she said to Todd and David.

Flanked by her sisters, Jill crossed the room. Although she was drained from the encounter with Roz and Mickey, she gained strength from Lisa and Sherry's support. The succor she'd always needed was finally at hand.

Since Lisa's children were using Jill's old bedroom, they went to Sherry's and curled up on the bed.

"That was tough for you," Sherry said.

"Yes, but having you...*both* of you there made it easier."

"How did you feel, seeing Mickey again?" Sherry asked.

"Mickey? I didn't feel much of anything. Seeing the baby hurt."

"You handled it well," Lisa said.

"On the outside, maybe. Inside I was pretty shaky."
She sighed. "It's ironic, isn't it, that Roz and Mickey had
to adopt?"

Before either of her sisters could respond, the door
opened and their mother came in, a worried frown on her
face. "Jill, are you all right? I wish I could have pre-
vented that. I had no idea that Roz would drop by, especially with the baby." She tugged at an earring, an
uncharacteristically nervous gesture.

Jill felt the need to reassure her mother. "I know you
didn't."

"Do you think Roz knows about...about Jill's baby?"
Sherry asked.

"I doubt it," Esther said.

"Lisa, you know Roz better than anyone," Sherry
continued. "What do you think?"

"I'm absolutely certain Roz doesn't know anything
except that Jill and Mickey dated for a few months. She's
such a sensitive person—when we roomed together our
sophomore year, she would fall apart over the silliest,
most trivial incidents. If she knew that Mickey had fathered a child, I'm sure she'd be devastated, particularly
since she's infertile."

"And," Esther added, "if Roz knew that Jill—well,
she'd never bring her baby here. Fortunately, we never
told anyone but Bubbi and Aunt Leah about Jill's pregnancy." Her lips tightened into a thin line.

A disapproving thin line, Jill thought. She rubbed her
temple, where a headache had begun to throb. Lisa might
have forgiven her past indiscretions, but her mother obviously hadn't. Probably never would, she thought
tiredly.

"Jill, you look exhausted," Lisa said.

Exhausted was too tame a word to describe the way she felt. She was totally depleted, as if every ounce of energy had been sapped from her. "I think I'll lie down for a while."

"I'll get you a robe," Sherry offered, going to her closet.

Jill kicked off her shoes and pulled off her sweats. She slipped into the fleecy blue robe Sherry handed her and drew it around her. Soft. She needed softness.

Her mother turned off the light and Sherry closed the blinds. Jill lay down. With a tenderness Jill hadn't known her sister possessed, Lisa drew the cover over her, then left the room.

Jill shut her eyes, but she couldn't shut out the image of Sarah's smile, the kind of adorable smile she'd seen on the infant in a baby food ad that had once been touted around her office. She couldn't shut out the sound of Sarah's whimper or the gurgle that had accompanied her smile. And she couldn't ease the longing in her heart for another baby girl, a baby who by some painful coincidence, some curious trick of fate, she'd always called Sarah.

AN HOUR LATER, having slept deeply, Jill awoke. She was disoriented at first, then everything came back to her at once, and for a moment she felt physically ill.

But she shook the sick feeling off. She'd seen Mickey again, seen his new baby. The meeting was over and done with. She hadn't fallen apart or become hysterical. Now she could put it behind her.

Of one thing she was certain, though—this was not the time to talk with her mother. She didn't want to add any more emotional stress to the day.

She lay still for a moment, staring at the ceiling, then peered at the clock on Sherry's bedside table. Three-thirty. Plenty of time to pick up a Chanukah present for Ben. He'd given her something every night, and she hadn't gotten him a single thing, but she knew the perfect gift for tonight. She started to get up, then became aware of a soft tapping at the door. "Come in," she called.

The door opened and Whitney tiptoed in. She approached the bed slowly, then peered anxiously at Jill. "Grandma said you weren't feeling well. Did the chili give you a tummy ache?"

What a sweetheart. "No, honey, I just had a headache. I'm fine now."

"Then can I sit on the bed?"

"Sure. Hop up."

Whitney scrambled up on the bed, then held up the book she'd brought with her. "Would you like to read me a story?"

"I'd love to."

Whitney handed Jill a dog-eared Dr. Seuss book and cuddled up beside her. Jill read the well-loved tale of *The Cat in the Hat,* with Whitney chiming in at intervals and both of them laughing over the antics of the cat and the zany illustrations. By the time she'd half finished the story, Jill knew she'd lost her heart to Whitney.

When Jill closed the book she ruffled Whitney's raven curls and said, "I have to run pick up a present. Would you like to come along?"

"Okay. I'll ask Mommy."

Jill slipped her clothes on, ran a comb through her hair and went downstairs to find Whitney already in her snowsuit.

"Mommy said yes."

"So I see. Let me get Grandma's car keys and we'll be on our way."

Forty-five minutes later, her spirits revived from shopping for Ben, she and Whitney drove home through an early gray twilight. Snow was already falling by the time they reached the house. Inside, they found Lisa and Todd, Sherry and David playing Trivial Pursuit. "Come join us," David suggested.

"You may be sorry. I'm a trivia buff," Jill warned.

She met her match in David, who knew all sorts of obscure facts, like the burial place of Pocahontas and the number of hearts in an octopus.

When they were midway through the game, their father came in and settled down, with a tired sigh, to read the evening paper. After a while he got up and counted out candles for the menorah. The doorbell rang as he straightened the last candle in its holder.

Jill jumped up. "That'll be Ben."

"Again?" Sherry teased.

Jill made a face at her and ran to get the door.

He smelled of fresh air, of leather...of man. He opened his arms and she went into them for a quick kiss, then pulled him into the house. "We're just finishing a game of Trivial Pursuit. Do you mind waiting?"

"If you want to finish, you must be winning," Ben guessed.

"You're right. We're heading for a photo finish—David or me." She led him into the living room where he greeted the boisterous group around the game table and pulled up a chair to watch. He laid a hand over the back of Jill's chair, and she leaned into it as if she were a kitten seeking out the touch of a well-loved person.

Jill missed her question, and so did Lisa, then David took his turn. "Okay, this is it," he chortled. "Where is the Wimbledon tennis tournament played?" He paused dramatically, then intoned, "Wimbledon, England. And the winner is . . . David Rosen."

Jill booed. "Unfair question."

"Uh-uh. The better man won. Want to join us for another round, Ben?"

"No, thanks. We'd better go."

Joel Levin came over to the table. "How about waiting until I light the candles?"

"I'd like that," Ben said.

Lisa rounded up the rest of the family, and, as they had every night, they gathered around the menorah.

Tonight six candles shone in their holders. Six tiny flames were reflected in the pane of the darkened window across from the credenza. Above them the *shammash* glittered.

Jill studied the candles. *Six nights.* How her life had changed in this short time. She felt as if each candle, each night, had added more light, more warmth. Ben, Lisa, the advertising campaign. Her life seemed suddenly alight with a golden glow.

Of course, there were still dark places. She had yet to come to terms with her guilt and anguish over giving away her baby. And the talk with her mother was still to come. But two days were left, she thought optimistically.

"Amen," her father said and the others echoed it.

Soon Jill and Ben took their leave, turning down Esther's invitation to stay for dinner.

"Would you rather have stayed?" Ben asked as they negotiated the slippery walkway, rapidly disappearing beneath a fresh coating of snow.

Jill shook her head. "I'd rather be alone with you."

He hugged her tighter against him. "I'm glad."

When they reached his town house the snow was falling faster, swirling around them and leaving tiny flakes that melted on their jackets.

"Mmm, a nice night to stay in," Jill said as Ben opened the door. Again she noticed that she felt at home here, as if this place were already a part of her. She hated to think that in three days she'd be going back to New York.

"I'd offer to build a fire, but I don't have a fireplace," Ben said. "So we'll have to keep each other warm." He pulled her close. "Body heat should do it." Then he grinned. "But first we eat."

"I brought you something," Jill said, thrusting the box she'd wrapped in paper decorated with dreidels and menorahs into his hands.

Ben got a box of equal size from the coffee table and presented it to her. "Happy sixth night of Chanukah."

They sat down and both tore eagerly at the wrappings. Jill finished first, opened her box and burst out laughing. Ben opened his and joined in as they held up their identical gifts. "A Bengals sweatshirt," they chorused. Ben gave her a bear hug and pulled her into his lap.

Jill laughed until she collapsed against his chest. "You're such a Bengals fan, I thought the sweatshirt would be perfect."

"And I was hoping you'd catch my Bengalmania. You haven't forgotten we're going to my friend Alan's tomorrow to watch the game?"

She shook her head as she reached for the hem of the sweatshirt she wore. "Shall we put our new sweatshirts on?"

"Uh-uh, lady. If you pull that top off now, we'll have to postpone our dinner."

"I wouldn't want to do that. I'm starved. Let's get to work." She got off Ben's lap and tugged his arm.

"There's nothing to do. Dinner's ready, and the table's set. All you have to do, Ms. Levin, is enjoy."

He led her to the breakfast nook, stopping on the way to turn on the compact disc player. The strains of *La Traviata* filled the room.

The table was set with a red-checked cloth. A thick candle in a wax-encrusted bottle served as the centerpiece. Ben filled their glasses with red wine and brought out two chilled salad bowls. From the oven he produced a loaf of warm garlic bread. Then, with a flourish, he placed a casserole of spaghetti and meat sauce before her. "Madame, for your dining pleasure, spaghetti à la Abrams."

Jill's mouth watered as she inhaled the rich aromas of tomato sauce and spices. "Smells wonderful." Ben spooned a hearty helping onto her plate, and she tasted. "Mmm, it is wonderful. My—"

He joined in. "Compliments to the chef."

They began the meal with laughter and delight in one another. They finished it replete with good food, heady with wine, beguiled by Verdi's music. Together they cleared the table and put the kitchen to rights, then of one accord they headed for Ben's bedroom.

There they moved leisurely, almost in slow motion, taking the time to explore and exclaim over one another's bodies. They kissed lightly, tenderly, deeply, or urgently as passion moved them.

Jill loved undressing Ben, loved the ability she had to excite him with a brush of her fingers, a flick of her tongue. She let her hands run slowly down his body, watching his nipples harden as hers had, seeing his muscles quiver when she trailed a light caress across his stomach. His thigh muscles clenched as she slipped her hands inside the waistband of his briefs. Slowly, lazily, she drew them down, exposing him inch by inch, touching him only with her eyes. His chest rose and fell with shallow, panting breaths; his hands tightened into fists.

She stood back and raked his body with a scorching gaze, from his eyes, past his chest and downward where his arousal arrested her attention.

She felt brazen. She felt powerful. "I want you," she murmured.

"God, yes," he groaned and reached behind him for the packet on the nightstand.

But Jill took it from his hand. "Let me." She opened it and turned to him.

His breath caught in a gasp as she took him in her hand. He caught her shoulders. "Jill—"

"Shh." She fitted the shield into place and pulled him close. "Come here."

They fell across the bed. She kept her eyes locked with his as, with a moan, he entered her. As he plunged inside, she gave a soft cry of triumph. He was hers.

LATER . . . MUCH LATER, they checked the TV guide and found an old Cary Grant movie on the late show. Now they were in bed, propped against the pillows, with a big bowl of popcorn between them.

"This is the only way to go to the movies," Ben said, reaching for a handful of popcorn.

Jill smiled. They hadn't watched much of the movie. In fact, she'd be hard put to say what the plot was. Her attention had been on Ben and his on her. They'd joked and laughed, fed each other popcorn and only occasionally turned their attention to the TV screen.

As the on-screen lovers came together for a last clinch, Ben sighed with satisfaction and put the empty popcorn bowl on the floor. "Good movie."

Jill raised a brow. "How would you know?"

He grinned. "I've seen it before."

"That explains it." She stretched and wiggled her toes.

"You wear polish on your toes."

"Mmm-hmm." She held up a foot and wiggled again.

"Sexy." He moved to the end of the bed and lifted her foot in his hand. "Nice." He nibbled at a toe and chuckled when Jill squirmed. "Does it tickle?"

"No, it . . . it—"

"Yes?" He put his mouth over her toe and sucked gently.

"It . . . oh, Ben."

"Tell me," he prompted, raining light, breathy kisses over the sensitive sole of her foot.

"You're driving me crazy."

He dropped her foot and pulled her into his arms. "Show me."

She did. Twice.

Afterward, as they lay half-dozing in each other's arms, Ben yawned. "I should turn off the television."

"Yeah. I think what we're seeing now isn't even the late late show."

"Nope," he agreed, sitting up. "It's a test pattern."

Enjoying the sight of his unclothed body, Jill watched him cross the room. "You have dimples," she remarked.

He flipped off the TV and turned back to smile at her. Male satisfaction was written on his face. "Yeah. My mother tells me they're my best feature. She says they turn women on." His walk, as he came back to bed, could only be described as a swagger.

Jill cocked her head. "I doubt most women see these dimples."

"Why?"

"Because," she said and grabbed for his buttocks as he tumbled onto the bed, "they're right here."

"You're getting too cocky, Ms. Levin." He pinned her with a wrestling hold. "Give?"

She struggled for a moment, then capitulated. "Give."

"Good." He pulled her against him and, cuddled spoon fashion, they fell asleep.

THEY WOKE EARLY the next morning. After a leisurely breakfast, Jill suggested, "Let's go for a walk."

Since the Bengals were playing at noon, they put on their matching sweatshirts. Outfitted with boots, caps and mittens, they strolled down the quiet street.

The sun had come out this morning. The clouds had disappeared, and in their place was a sky so clear and blue that it looked like a painting of the ideal winter day. The ground lay under a blanket of pure white snow that reflected the sunshine with a blinding light. Or perhaps, Jill thought, the happiness she felt made the world seem perfect.

She scooped up a handful of snow, patted it into a ball and pitched it at the nearest tree. Then she twirled in a circle. "Oh, it's beautiful, isn't it? There's nothing like a good Ohio snowfall. Snow in New York is dirty and slushy."

"Tell me more about your life in New York."

She considered his request for a moment. "I told you most of it the other night. My life's pretty ordinary. I get up, go to work at a job I love, and come home."

"What about weekends? You told me you like sailing, museums, reading. What else?"

"I do a little volunteer work."

"What kind?" he asked.

"Tutoring."

She didn't elaborate on the fact that she gave her time to a tutoring program for unmarried pregnant teenagers, and thankfully, Ben merely said, "That's great."

"What about—" He hesitated, then went on. "I can't believe you aren't involved with anyone."

She glanced at him in surprise and anger. "Do you really think I'd go to bed with you if I was involved with another man?"

"No, of course not. I . . . I'm sorry." She saw vulnerability in his expression and heard a forced lightness as he said, "Why hasn't someone grabbed you?"

At his reaction, her anger fled, and she shrugged. "I haven't found anyone who interested me."

Looking relieved, he smiled and tossed a snowball of his own. "Lucky for me."

Ben's question made Jill wonder about his love life. "When I met you, I couldn't believe an attractive, sexy man like you wasn't involved with anyone, either."

"I haven't been for some time." He stared into the distance for a moment, then turned to her, his expression solemn. "I suppose it's time I told you the whole story about Karen."

CHAPTER TEN

JILL REACHED FOR BEN'S hand. She felt a prick of fear. Did she really want to hear this? "You don't have to tell me."

"I need to. I want you to understand who I am, where I'm coming from."

By mutual agreement they turned back toward Ben's house, walking hand in hand.

"I met Karen just after I moved to Cincinnati," Ben began. "We were introduced at a party and we hit it off right away. Within a month we moved in together. We were perfect for each other it seemed. Both of us were career oriented, we had the same interests and the chemistry was sure as hell there. For the first six months everything was great between us. We—or at least I—began talking about marriage. Karen was in the middle of a job change and she said she couldn't make plans until she was settled in her new position. Then everything began to unravel."

He stared down at the sidewalk as if he might find the reason there. Jill waited silently.

Finally he continued. "Karen had taken a job with a teenage drug abuse program that also had facilities in Cleveland and Chicago, and that necessitated some traveling."

When he fell silent, Jill asked, "Was that the problem? Did you mind her being gone?"

"No, I missed her, of course, but my job involves some out-of-town trips, too, so I understood . . . at first, anyway." His face turned stony as he went on. "After a while, her trips became more frequent, and they lasted longer. Sometimes she was gone on weekends, too. We argued about it, but she managed to convince me that this was important to her career . . . and far be it from me to stand in the way of my future wife's career." He laughed harshly.

"What happened?" Jill asked.

Ben stooped and picked up a handful of snow, then, without bothering to form it into a ball, flung it down again. "One Saturday she got a call from her supervisor at work. When I told her Karen was still in Chicago on her business trip, the woman didn't know what I was talking about. The next evening I was waiting for Karen at the door. Before she took two steps, I asked her what the hell was going on. She told me."

Jill held her breath.

He stuffed his hands into his pockets and stared straight ahead. A muscle jumped in his cheek. "Seems she'd met this fellow on one of her first trips to Chicago, and one thing led to another. To put it bluntly, she had something going with him. When I asked her if it was fair to me *or* to him, she said she wasn't deliberately hurting either one of us, but, hey, if it bothered me . . .

"I told her it damn well bothered me, and she said in that case she'd better move out. All that talk of marriage? Well, it was just talk."

Jill's eyes filled with tears. How could the woman have been so callous? She tightened her fingers around Ben's. "Oh, Ben. I'm sorry."

"She packed up that night. A few weeks later she moved to Chicago. I guess things didn't work out for her there because I heard from friends that she's back in Cincinnati, working for the adoption agency."

"Have you seen her?"

"Nope. Haven't seen her, haven't wanted to."

"But you'll see her tonight," Jill said softly.

Ben paused in midstride, turned to her and put his hands on her shoulders. "Jill, I'm over Karen. I'll admit I was pretty torn up when she left, but I survived. Now I don't feel anything for her. Or against her. She's... history." He cupped Jill's chin in his hand. "You do believe me, don't you?"

"Yes." She did believe him. She only hoped when he saw Karen tonight he would still believe it himself.

Ben pulled her closer. Oblivious to passing motorists, to a man crossing a nearby lawn to retrieve his Sunday paper, he kissed her. His lips were cold but the kiss was hot, desperate. "Believe me, Jill," he said.

She touched his cheek with her mittened hand. "I do."

They turned into Ben's yard and walked slowly toward the door. Once inside, he said thoughtfully, "One thing I learned from my affair with Karen was the value of trust. If a relationship isn't built on that, it has nowhere to go."

Jill nodded. Ben, too, had scars. Though he'd given her an opening to tell him about her own past, she said nothing. Her thoughts focused on his pain, his suffering.

They were both quiet as they drove to Alan's house to watch the football game, but once they arrived, Ben's mood brightened and hers did, too.

Trish Jeffreys was a warm, effervescent woman who immediately made Jill feel at home. Alan's wry sense of humor was appealing, and their children, four-year-old Amanda and three-year-old Brad, were adorable.

"Time for lunch," Trish announced soon after Jill and Ben arrived.

The men greeted her statement with loud boos. "Come on, Patricia!" Alan protested. "The game starts in fifteen minutes. If we start eating now, we'll miss the kick-off."

"My love, I've taken that into consideration," Trish countered. She pointed to four TV tables stacked against the wall. "Voilà!"

"Did I or did I not marry a genius?"

"Nope, you married a fellow football fan," Trish declared.

"I'll help you get lunch ready," Jill offered, and the two women went into the kitchen. Laughing and chattering like old friends, they arranged platters of cold cuts, raw vegetables and potato salad.

Jill liked Trish and envied her. She had two bright-eyed kids, a husband she obviously adored and a lovely home. Trish mentioned that she worked full-time as a high-school counselor.

"How do you manage everything so well?" Jill asked.

"I have a good day-care center, household help twice a week and a wonderful husband who pitches in whenever I need him."

"Your life sounds perfect." It was hard to keep a wistful note from her voice.

"Come on." Trish laughed. "Alan and I have our disagreements, the kids get crabby, the housekeeper came down with flu in November and was out for two weeks, but other than that, you're right. My life is perfect."

When they brought the food into the living room they found Ben and Alan studying a stack of papers. The two men looked up almost guiltily when Trish called, "Okay, everyone, no work today. Let's dig in."

While they ate, Alan remarked to Jill, "Ben tells me you're working on the Steak Expectations campaign."

"Hoping to," she said and glanced at Ben. He grinned at her, an encouraging sign.

"You're with—?"

"Carnaby and Ross."

"An old neighbor of mine," Alan said. "I used to work for Madden and Masters, Marcus and Malone."

"I'm impressed." Known as M and M's along Madison Avenue, the agency was one of the largest and most prestigious in the ad industry. "Why'd you decide to leave?"

"I came here a couple of times on business and fell in love with the city. Cincinnati seemed like a good place to raise a family, away from the New York rat race, so I applied for a job with a stable company here."

"Let me guess," Jill said. "You work for Procter and Gamble." The company was one of Cincinnati's main claims to fame and its biggest employer, the Procter & Gamble headquarters a city landmark.

"Right," Alan said. "What about you? Has this trip prompted you to think of a change?"

Jill considered his question. A week ago her answer would have been an unequivocal no. Now she wasn't so sure. "Maybe."

"Give yourself a few more days and you may find it impossible to leave," Alan said.

"So speaks the dedicated Cincinnati booster," Trish put in.

"I understand you're a creative director," Alan continued. "Have a favorite campaign?"

"Oh, probably Galaxy Candy Bars."

"Did you do that great commercial with the athletes taking time out for a candy break?"

"Guilty," Jill said. "I wrote every word."

"Hey, that campaign is a classic," Ben said.

"Yeah, the one with the football team in the huddle talking about Galaxy was priceless," Alan said. "And speaking of football..." He jumped up to turn on the television, and that ended the conversation.

Jill smiled to herself as the game got under way. She felt as if Alan had put her through a brief job interview. *Must be his style,* she decided. As far as she knew, Procter & Gamble wasn't currently looking for in-house advertising personnel.

The game was close, but Jill found her attention wandering. She took her cue from the others, cheering whenever the Bengals scored, booing when the Jets did, but her thoughts returned to her earlier conversation with Ben.

Having heard the story of his relationship with Karen, she understood why he'd questioned her about being involved with another man. He'd suffered a disastrous blow to his ego, but he'd been strong enough to reveal his past, to open himself to her, to share his pain.

She wondered again if she could trust him enough to tell him about hers. The answer came reluctantly but honestly. She wasn't ready yet.

Would she ever be? She admitted to herself that she had no answer to that. She just wasn't sure.

WHEN THE FOOTBALL GAME ended and the four of them had toasted the Bengals' victory, Jill and Ben left. Ben dropped her off at her hotel with a kiss and a promise to see her at eight.

Now Jill paced the floor of her room. Her visit to Cincinnati would be over soon. Of course, if everything went as she hoped, she'd be back to do further work with Steak

Expectations, but what if her agency didn't get the contract? Then she might not return home for months. She should talk to her mother today.

Yet she hesitated. What would she say? How would she approach the subject of Esther's lack of support during her pregnancy?

"Come on, Jill," she said aloud. "This isn't an ad campaign. You can't script it beforehand. Just do it." Lord, even in an emotional situation, ad copy came to mind. Well, wasn't that the motto of the nineties? *Do it, Jill. Just do it.*

She picked up the telephone and punched in her parents' number. Maybe no one was home. Maybe her folks had a houseful of company. Maybe—

"Hello."

Her mother. *Darn.* "Hi," she said. "It's Jill. What's going on?"

"Not much," her mother replied. "Your father's taking a nap, Lisa and Todd took the kids to a movie, Sherry and David went out with some friends and I'm getting ready to make myself a cup of coffee."

This was her chance. Before she could change her mind, she said, "Maybe I'll come by, then, and we can visit."

"All right." Her mother sounded pleased. "We haven't had much time to talk since you've been here."

"We'll make up for that today. I'll see you in a little while." Jill put on her jacket, picked up her purse and was on her way.

Jill half hoped someone else would be there by the time she arrived. But Esther answered the door, and as Jill followed her mother into the quiet house she knew they were alone.

As usual, they went into the breakfast room. Jill sat at the table while her mother bustled about the kitchen pouring coffee and filling a plate with cookies. Jill supposed every significant conversation in her life had begun over coffee—or milk—and cookies.

"Have you found out whether your company got the contract?" Esther inquired as she joined Jill at the table.

"We should know tomorrow. I'm optimistic. Everyone at Steak Expectations seemed impressed with our presentation."

"Will getting the contract mean you'll be coming in more often?" Esther asked, stirring cream in her coffee.

"I hope so." Frequent trips would mean she could spend more time with Ben.

"I do, too." She met Jill's eyes, and smiled. "That way you could combine business with pleasure." Clearly her thoughts had followed the same path as Jill's. "Ben seems nice," she added.

Jill guessed this was her mother's oblique way of probing about her relationship with Ben. Mothers didn't interrogate grown daughters who had been living independently for years; they brought up a subject casually and hoped the daughter would take the cue. Jill took the cue. "I like him very much."

"So do I."

Her mother's unequivocal statement surprised Jill. "You do?"

"Yes. He comes across as intelligent and sincere. He has a nice sense of humor, a good job—"

Jill couldn't help smiling at the typical mother's comment.

"And," her mother continued, "he seems mature."

Unlike Mickey. "He is mature, Mom. He's thirty."
Not twenty-one.

"Yes, of course, but I wasn't talking about his age. I meant, he seems . . . responsible."

Her mother's meaning came across loud and clear. Jill bristled. "Responsible, meaning he won't get me pregnant? Don't worry, Mother. He won't. And I won't. I'm responsible, too." Good Lord, she was losing it, she thought as she heard her own words and saw the hurt look on her mother's face. Yet Jill couldn't bring herself to apologize.

"Jill, I wasn't implying that you and Ben— That you were going to get pregnant."

Jill sighed. "No, but that's what you thought. My . . . mistake is always on your mind, isn't it?"

"It's always on yours, too, I imagine."

Jill felt a lump rise in her throat. She shut her eyes. "Yes," she whispered. "Having a baby and giving her away isn't something you put behind you and forget." She opened her eyes in time to see the pain she felt reflected in her mother's eyes.

"Nor is knowing your grandchild was adopted. Even though I never saw her, I miss her every day."

Her mother's statement gave Jill pause. Never in all these years had she considered what her mother had lost. Never had she thought of her baby as her parents' grandchild, belonging to them, too. "If you felt that way, why did you insist I give her up?"

Esther was quiet for so long that Jill wondered if she was going to answer. Finally she spoke. "I felt I was doing the right thing." Her voice, usually strong, was low, uncertain. "Who ever really knows what the right thing is?"

Jill stared at her mother, the woman she'd always perceived as self-assured and confident. "I thought mothers were always right. Isn't that what you used to tell us?"

Esther gave her a wry smile. "I said that when you were children, when all I had to decide was whether you could stay up late on school nights or buy a dress that was unsuitable. Little problems, easy answers." She sighed and stirred her coffee.

Jill looked at her mother's hand. Though her nails were still beautifully manicured, the once-smooth skin on the back of her hand sagged. Jill glanced up. The sunlight coming through the window shone on her mother's face. Crow's-feet showed at the corners of her eyes. Smile lines around her mouth were now crevices. The fact that her mother was aging struck Jill suddenly, forcibly. How much had *she* contributed to the creases that were now so visible?

Esther continued, "When you have to decide what to do about your daughter's pregnancy, no mother has ready-made solutions."

"*I* should have decided."

"Jill, you were seventeen. You were a child yourself."

"She was my baby. I should have had more of a say."

"What would you have done?" Her mother's voice was gentle.

"Kept her," Jill answered promptly.

"Oh, Jill." Esther shook her head. "You weren't realistic then. You're just as unrealistic now." Before Jill had a chance to protest, she went on. "Would you have given up going to college, given up the chance for a future?"

"I gave up my baby's future."

"No, Jill. You gave her a chance for a future. You gave her a precious gift—the opportunity to be part of a com-

plete family. I know you didn't like my saying that then.
I can see you don't like hearing it now, but deep down,
you must realize it's true."

Jill said nothing. Her mother's words hurt; they'd always hurt.

"Could you have gone to college with a baby to care
for?" Esther persisted.

"I could have managed. Others have."

"I know." Her mother nodded. "But you would have
had a hard time. We could have helped financially, but
that's only one part of raising a child. Ah, Jill, don't you
know we would have been the first to tell you to keep
your baby if we'd thought it was right?"

"We, or just you, Mother?"

Esther looked away, her cheeks reddening, and Jill had
her answer. Her mother had been the one who'd pushed
for the decision and her father had agreed.

"You didn't have enough confidence in me," Jill went
on. She still resented that. "You'd be surprised how well
I can manage."

"'Can.' That's now. You're a grown woman who's
been on her own and been successful. 'Could' is another
matter. Could you have handled the situation at eighteen?"

As much as her mother's words distressed her, had always upset her, Jill had to admit they had some validity.
Perhaps that was why they'd always hurt so much. Yes,
as an eighteen-year-old who'd never been away from
home she would have had difficulty raising the baby,
but—

The question that came to mind was one she'd never
voiced . . . never dared voice. But this was a time for hon-
esty. "I could have gone to college in Cincinnati, lived at

home. You could have helped me with the baby. Why didn't you offer to do that?''

Esther said nothing. She picked up her spoon, placed it in her empty coffee mug, folded her napkin and laid it carefully on the table. Then she took the mug into the kitchen. Jill heard the sound of water, of the dishwasher opening and shutting, then she heard nothing.

She waited a moment, then rose and walked into the kitchen. Her mother stood gripping the counter, her knuckles white. ''Mother?''

Esther turned, and Jill saw tears rolling down her cheeks. Jill took a step toward her, but her mother shook her head. Jill stopped and watched the tears flow unchecked until at last her mother took a deep breath and fumbled for a Kleenex in her pocket. She wiped her eyes and blew her nose. ''I'm sorry,'' she muttered in a choked voice.

''Come back and sit down,'' Jill urged.

Esther tossed the Kleenex into the trash, then followed Jill back into the breakfast room. They sat down again, and after a moment Jill said, ''I'm sorry I've upset you, but I need an answer. Why didn't you help me, Mother?''

Esther cleared her throat. ''I just told you. I didn't want your life ruined. Even if I'd raised the baby, she would still have been yours. You'd have been branded as an unmarried mother—''

''Branded?'' Jill scoffed. ''Do you think they'd have made me wear a scarlet *A*, whoever 'they' are? Mother, we aren't living in the Dark Ages. There are plenty of unmarried mothers around.''

Esther made a gesture of dismissal. ''Oh, I know movie stars and other celebrities flaunt their illegitimate children, but I'm talking about the real world.''

Jill felt as if Esther had slapped her. "My God, Mother. Nobody uses the word 'illegitimate' anymore. And in the real world of today, unmarried women have babies. Some women even deliberately choose to conceive outside of marriage."

"Not women I know," Esther continued doggedly. She picked up the napkin that still lay at her place and crumpled it into a ball.

Trying to convince her mother otherwise was useless. She was of a different generation, and she thought and acted in accordance with her times. But Jill couldn't suppress the anger her mother's words evoked. "What would people think?" Jill said bitterly. "That's what you cared about, right?"

In a gesture that reminded Jill of Lisa, her mother raised her chin. "I won't deny it. I didn't want to see you the butt of gossip." Her tone was defensive.

Jill sensed something more. "And?"

"And I didn't want to be talked about, either."

Jill frowned. "What could anyone have said about you?"

"I don't know. That I was a bad mother, I guess. That I let you run wild."

Through a red haze of anger, Jill cried, "So you pushed me into giving up my child to save yourself?"

Esther dropped her head into her hands. "Oh, honey, no. Don't think that of me. That was such a small part of it. I did what I honestly thought was best. And I've regretted it ever since." Her voice was so low Jill had to strain to hear. After a moment she lifted her head and looked directly at Jill. "I've lived with guilt every day of my life."

Jill stared at her mother. On the heels of anger came, first, the realization that she hadn't been alone in her guilt and anguish, then sympathy for her mother's pain and finally resentment. "Why didn't you support me when I needed you?" she asked. "I was seventeen, I still needed my mother to love me no matter what had happened. Instead, all I got was disapproval. Why? And why didn't you tell me how you felt?"

"Would you have understood?"

"I think so."

Esther shook her head. "I've never been good at sharing my deeper feelings. Your father reminds me of that often," she added with a brittle laugh. "I wanted to talk to you, but I . . . I couldn't."

"You should have tried. Talking would have helped."

"And you needed my help." Tears welled again in Esther's eyes. "I failed you. I buried myself in preparations for Lisa's wedding instead of giving you what you needed."

Jill couldn't dispute the words, not even to salvage her mother's feelings. "All I sensed was your disappointment in me."

"Oh, Jill, I wasn't disappointed in you. I was sad at seeing my dreams for you fall apart. You had so much potential—to learn, to accomplish, to live a successful life. I saw all that crumbling around you."

"You didn't think of *my* dreams," Jill accused. "You disapproved of me."

"Never of *you*. Of your actions, yes, but not of you. Tell me," Esther said, "what would you do if you had the chance to live that time over again?"

Jill considered the question. How wonderful if you could push some cosmic rewind button and pause at a crossroads in your life where you could make another choice.

What would she have done? "Well, for one thing I wouldn't have been so...impulsive about my relationship with Mickey." She thought of the past two nights, of Ben's tender assurance that he would protect her. "Then I wouldn't have gotten pregnant, and I would have saved us all a lot of grief."

"Suppose you *had* gotten pregnant, though. If you had another chance, what would you do?"

"I always thought I had the answer to that. Now I'm not so sure," Jill admitted, "but I still think I would have kept my baby."

"You did the right thing for her, Jill," her mother repeated and covered Jill's hand with hers.

Jill stared at their hands for a moment, then looked up. She needed a respite from the tension, a breather. "I want some more coffee. How about you?" She went into the kitchen, refilled her mug and got a fresh one for her mother. Her conversation with Lisa the other morning came to mind. "What were your dreams for Lisa?" she asked over her shoulder.

Esther shrugged. "I always pictured her in a vine-covered cottage."

Jill set the mugs back on the table, stirred a liberal helping of sugar into hers and sipped. "The typical homemaker, up to her elbows in dishwater. Mom, that's passé."

"No, that's Lisa. At least, I used to think so."

"You know, your image of her made her feel bad."

Her mother looked so shocked and dismayed that Jill realized Esther had never been aware of the labels she'd pinned on her daughters or of the dissension those labels had caused. Well, she'd confronted her mother about the pregnancy. Now was the time for them to face more long-standing issues.

"I didn't create an image for Lisa," Esther insisted. "She made her own image. I just responded."

"Your response to her made her feel dumb."

Esther set her mug down and shook her head. "Lisa is anything but dumb. Look at all she's achieved."

"You sound like you didn't expect her to accomplish anything other than producing babies and baking pies."

"I—"

"Lisa says you saw her as an airhead—pretty but not very smart."

Her mother dropped the spoon into her mug with a clatter. "That's ridiculous!" she snapped. "Lisa's never said a word about this. If she has something to say to me, I'll listen . . . but to her."

Oh, Lord. Now I've opened a can of worms. Jill hadn't meant to create conflict between her mother and sister. Softly she said, "In a way, this is between you and Lisa, but it affected me, too."

Esther didn't answer. Stony faced, she stared out the window.

Jill sat quietly, waiting for her mother's temper to cool. When she thought it prudent to speak, she touched her mother's hand and said, "Your picture of me was different."

At that, Esther nodded. "I imagined you'd have a career *and* a family."

"Superwoman. Why?"

"You had the intelligence and the drive."

Jill took a breath. She might as well speak her piece now and get it over with, she thought. "Part of the reason Lisa and I have been at each other's throats all these years is that we've each been jealous of the way you pictured the other."

Esther sniffed. "It's always the mother's fault, isn't it? Mothers get blamed for everything that goes wrong."

"I'm not blaming you." Jill sighed. "I just want you to listen to my feelings the way I listened to yours." She leaned forward. "Lisa and I are trying hard to get past our childhood jealousy. We hadn't thought about the reason for our anger at each other until we talked the other morning. She says you saw me as the smart one who would have it all, and for years she was jealous." She grimaced. "I certainly didn't live up to your expectations."

"You still will."

Jill clenched her hands. "That's just the point. I don't want to live up to your expectations. I want to live up to my own."

Jill watched as comprehension dawned in her mother's eyes. "I...I never thought about that," Esther said. "I only wanted the best for you girls."

"I know, but I have to decide what's best, and Lisa does, too."

Esther nodded, and Jill saw that at last her mother understood. Esther stared down at her hands for a long while. Then she looked up. "Jill."

"Yes?"

"I...I'm glad we had this talk." She shook her head. "Parenting's not easy. In fact, it's the hardest job you'll ever undertake."

"I hope I'll find that out."

"You'll still have a child someday."

"But not that one." After a moment Jill said, "I want to have a baby, a child I can keep and love." A picture of herself with a rosy-cheeked infant flashed into her mind. She saw herself bending over the crib, tucking her child in, then looking up to meet the eyes of... of Ben. His baby. The idea seemed so natural, as if she'd been waiting all her life for him, for his love.

Her mother smiled. "Maybe you'll find the right person to give you marriage and children sooner than you think. Maybe you've already found him."

For the first time she felt comfortable enough with her mother to admit some of her feelings about Ben. "Could be."

"I have a feeling it could," Esther agreed and patted Jill's hand. She glanced at the clock. "I should wake your father. He's been sleeping all afternoon."

They'd finished talking for now, but the channels of communication had been opened. When her mother left, Jill wandered into the living room, picked up the Sunday issue of the Cincinnati *Enquirer* and curled up on the couch. Soon afterward, Sherry and David returned.

"Hi." Sherry flopped down on the other end of the sofa. "What are you wearing tonight?"

"A multicolored chiffon."

"Want me to do your hair? We could put it up, make you look sleek and sophisticated." She turned to David. "Wanna come watch, honey?"

He rolled his eyes. "Thanks, I'll pass."

Jill chuckled as she and her sister walked upstairs. Sherry was the hair specialist in the family, the one Jill and Lisa had counted on for help with their coiffures. "I doubt anything could make me look sophisticated, but let's try."

She showered and washed her hair, then sat at Sherry's dressing table and let her sister work her magic. Sherry pulled Jill's hair into a smooth coil and pinned it up. Lisa wandered in and flopped on her stomach on the bed and Whitney tried to copy the hairdo on her Cabbage Patch doll.

Sherry stood back to admire her handiwork. "You look stunning."

Jill picked up the hand mirror and viewed herself from all angles. "Will it stay put?"

"Sure. But let's pull out a few tendrils, and you'll look even more glamorous. Trust me," she intoned. "I am *ze expehrt*."

"Aunt Jill, you look pretty," Whitney said.

"Think so, sweetie?"

"Uh-huh. You look . . . grown-up."

Jill laughed with the others, but later in her hotel room, as she turned in front of the full-length mirror, she agreed. With her flyaway curls tamed and pinned up, she looked elegant for the first time in her life. The sleek hairstyle contrasted with the long flowing skirt and full gauzy sleeves of her dress. Its colors suited her—a rainbow of blues and purples, from powder blue to azure, lavender to plum. She twirled in a circle, enjoying the feel of chiffon brushing against her skin.

She fitted the lapis-and-crystal earrings she'd bought the other afternoon into her ears and stood back to admire the effect. *Perfect,* she decided, and flicked an earring with her finger, watching the light play over the crystal.

Tonight would be special. An evening with the man she loved. "I love you, Ben Abrams," she said aloud, savoring the words on her tongue, listening to their melody, realizing the truth of them. Love had burst over her in less than a week. So quick, but true nevertheless. And, her heart beginning to pound, she knew she was ready to tell Ben her feelings. She smiled at herself in the mirror. She'd tell him . . . tonight.

BEN STOOD BEFORE HIS bathroom mirror, razor in hand, bath towel knotted around his waist. From the living room came the music of *Phantom of the Opera*. Ben warbled along with the love song, " 'That's all I ask of you.' " So what if he was off-key? He didn't care. He felt marvelous. He was in love.

And this time it was right. Karen had been a horrendous mistake, but Jill—she was the answer to his dreams. He gave his cheek one last swipe with his razor. The heck with a long, drawn-out campaign. His feelings for Jill were strong and sure. Why wait to declare them? Why postpone asking her to marry him? He'd ask her . . . tonight.

The telephone interrupted his thoughts.

"Hi, it's Alan."

"Well, what did you think of her?" Ben asked, though he was sure he knew the answer.

"Buddy, you struck gold. The copy you showed me for the Steak Expectations campaign is first-rate, but even if I hadn't seen that, I'd have hired her on the spot once I heard she'd done the Galaxy ads."

"Fantastic!"

"She's a great copywriter, and you seem to think she's great all around. You're pretty serious about her, huh?"

"Right. Damn serious."

"Good luck."

"Thanks, pal," Ben said. "Keep your fingers crossed."

An hour later he stood outside Jill's room. He knocked, the door swung open and he stood open-mouthed, as tongue-tied as a teenager on his first date.

In the half-light she looked mysterious and alluring. The blues of her dress reminded him of the ocean, changing with the play of light through the water. The light coming from behind her cast a golden halo about her head and filtered through long, slender earrings that swung gently from her lobes.

She'd done something different with her hair—swept it up some way—and he pictured himself removing the pins, one by one, until her curls fell loose about her shoulders.

"Hello." Her smile was sultry.

He swallowed. "Hi."

She stood aside for him to enter. He took a step closer and her perfume drifted to his nostrils. Not her usual scent, but sweeter, more flowery, like summer roses.

"You look—" He couldn't think of a word adequate to describe the picture she presented tonight, so he settled for "beautiful."

"Thank you." She ran her eyes over him. "You're beautiful yourself. Born to wear black tie."

"Is that someone's ad?" he asked.

"Mine. For you." She turned. "I'll get my stole, and we can go."

Ben glanced down and noticed the florist's box in his hand. He'd been so enthralled with Jill, he'd forgotten. "Wait, I have something for you." He held out the box.

She opened it and withdrew a corsage of white rosebuds. "Oh, Ben. How lovely. Thank you." She held it to her face, brushing the soft petals across her cheek, then took a deep breath. "I'll wear it in my hair."

She went to the mirror and frowned with concentration as she pinned the corsage behind one ear. "What do you think?"

He came up behind her and kissed the side of her neck. The fragrance of rose petals mingled with the floral bouquet of her perfume. "Beautiful," he breathed and turned her in his arms.

Her mouth met his, her arms twined around his neck.
The taste of her poured into him, through him, as if she
were a part of him. "Let's stay here," he muttered.

Jill stepped out of his embrace. "Not a chance. I want
to show off my handsome escort. Besides, there's always
later."

"Or earlier," he suggested as he watched her pick up
a stole in the same filmy material as her dress.

She slipped the stole over her shoulders, picked up an
evening purse and opened the door. "Come on."

"I guess I'm outvoted." But that was all right, he
thought as he took her arm. He wanted to make love to
her, of course, but he could wait. He had the uncanny
feeling that, even when they weren't engaged in the act of
love, they were linked in some vital way. Just as their lips
had blended a moment ago, as their arms entwined now,
their psyches were joined. Pleased at the notion, he
pulled her close to him.

When they arrived on the mezzanine level, the ballroom was already filling. The buzz of voices and laughter, the tinkle of glasses, the scent of perfume permeated
the air. Ben noticed the still-empty head table and wondered if Karen would sit there.

He glanced around the room. Vases of blue and white
carnations adorned each table. At each place he saw
plastic dreidels filled with Chanukah candies. A large
menorah, with seven oversize candles, sat in the center of
the front table. To the left, members of the band were
unpacking their sheet music and tuning their instru-
ments.

He and Jill walked across the dance floor. Finally they
spotted Sherry waving and made their way to the table.
As they came nearer, an auburn-haired woman and a
dark-haired, broad-shouldered man turned. Ben didn't

know the woman, but the man he recognized immediately. Mickey Zimmerman.

Not at all pleased at the prospect of spending the evening in such close proximity to Jill's old boyfriend, Ben muttered, "A face from your past."

Jill shrugged. "Seems we're both encountering ghosts of Chanukahs past this evening."

She seemed unperturbed at Mickey's presence. *Good.* She was evidently no more uncomfortable at seeing Mickey than he would be at running into Karen. After all, he reminded himself, her involvement with Zimmerman had been years ago.

When they reached the table, Mickey rose and extended a hand. "Ben Abrams! It's been a long time."

"Zimmerman. Good to see you."

Mickey introduced his wife, who reached up to give Jill a hug. Ben remembered that Jill had mentioned Mickey was married to her cousin. In that case, they'd probably seen one another many times over the years. Still, he was relieved when Jill headed for a chair on the other side of the table, next to Sherry.

Soon after they were seated, Ben noticed that the noise level in the ballroom had increased. The tables around them were now occupied. He turned and craned his neck to look at the head table and caught sight of Karen at one end.

He hadn't seen her since the night she'd walked out on him. She looked the same—slim, blond, lovely. And deceitful.

Jill tapped him on the arm. "Checking out your own ghost?" she asked.

"Yeah."

"Still haunted?" Her tone was light, but her eyes betrayed the seriousness of the question.

"Not at all. You?"

She shook her head, and he leaned over and planted a kiss on her nose. "I'm glad," he whispered.

A squeal from the microphone got their attention. They turned as the master of ceremonies began. "Ladies and gentlemen, welcome to the annual Season of Light Ball benefiting the Shirley Cohen Adoption Agency. Shirley and Morton Cohen, well-loved Cincinnati philanthropists, donated funds to open the country's first Jewish adoption agency over thirty years ago. Since then, the Cohen Agency has grown and prospered, and today is known as the premier among such agencies. It has branches in Cleveland, Philadelphia, Washington, D.C. and Atlanta and since its inception has placed over five thousand babies, both Jewish and non-Jewish."

Enthusiastic applause and murmurs of interest sounded from the audience.

"Now I'd like to introduce our head table." The auxiliary president, the benefit chairman and agency administrators were presented. Karen was one of the last. Once—even as recently as six months ago—the sound of her name, the sight of her graciously acknowledging the introduction would have distressed Ben. Now she was simply a familiar face. Someone he'd once known, but whom he scarcely remembered.

"Now, in honor of this season of light, I'd like to call on Sandra Miller, chairman of the Cohen board, to light the Chanukah candles."

"Thank you." Mrs. Miller lifted the *shammash.* "Please join me in reciting the blessing. *Baruch atah adonai—*"

As he joined in the Hebrew words, Ben reached for Jill's hand. If tonight ended as he hoped, this would be the beginning of a lifetime of Chanukahs. And this holiday, this season of light and promise, would always be special to them.

The speaker for the evening, a popular local television personality, came next. Finally the master of ceremonies returned to the mike. "You're all invited to enjoy yourselves, partake of the buffet and dance to the music of Harry Weisman and his orchestra. And, of course, join me later when I announce the winners of our eight spectacular raffle prizes, one for each night of Chanukah."

The band swung into a lively number, and Ben asked Jill, "What are the prizes?"

"A fur coat, a ski package in Vail, a bed-and-breakfast weekend in New York—"

"I'd like that one."

She gave him an intimate smile. "*That* one's available any time. I took a chance on a better one."

"What?"

Eyes sparkling, she shook her head. "Uh-uh. My lips are sealed. But don't forget to take me up on the weekend. Want to dance?"

He nodded, and they joined the other couples crowding the floor. They danced well together, Jill anticipating his movements and following with ease. Again, he thought how well their bodies were attuned to one another.

They saw Uncle Phil, waltzing Jill's mother around the floor in a passable imitation of Arthur Murray. He saluted them as he whirled past. There was Jill's grandmother, dancing sedately with the white-haired gentleman from the synagogue and later with a bespectacled man who was talking to her earnestly. Between numbers, friends of Ben's came up to be introduced to Jill, and old acquaintances of hers hailed them, as well.

"I don't recognize a soul," she whispered. "Am I faking it well enough?"

"Like a pro." He laughed and pulled her closer. The band swung into a love song, and he drew her nearer still. The feel of her breasts against his chest, her thighs pressed to his was both ecstasy and an exercise in frustration. He wanted her. If he could let his body have its way, he'd sweep her into his arms and carry her upstairs, away from the crowd, into their private world. Yet he loved being with her here, moving to the music, showing her off to his friends. He sighed and rested his cheek against her hair, inhaling the scent of rosebuds.

When the band took a break, they wandered over to the table where Bubbi sat, this time in the company of a bald, rotund man with whom she was engaged in laughing conversation. After Bubbi introduced her companion to Jill and Ben as the owner of a kosher butcher shop, the gentleman excused himself to refill their plates.

"Bubbi, you're the belle of the ball tonight," Jill said, giving her grandmother a fond smile.

Bubbi nodded and smiled archly. "I haven't forgotten how to flirt."

"No, you certainly haven't."

"Well," her grandmother said with a shrug, "what do they say about riding a bicycle? Once you know how, it stays with you."

"Are you husband hunting?" Jill inquired.

"Husband? Pah. Maybe in my old age when I need someone to care for me, but not now."

Ben smiled at her. "I don't think you'll ever reach old age."

Her eyes twinkled. "No. God willing, I'll stay young until the day I die."

What a delightful lady, Ben thought and hoped he'd be around to see her granddaughter grow into such a vibrant old age.

Uncle Phil approached the table. "How are you, young man? Mind if I steal my niece for a spin around the floor?"

"Not at all." Ben relinquished Jill's hand and watched her uncle tuck it under his arm and lead her away.

"So," Bubbi said, giving him a level look, "should I ask you your intentions regarding my granddaughter?"

Ben laughed. "My intentions are strictly honorable."

Bubbi nodded with satisfaction. "Good. She's a flower, but a fragile one that needs to be lovingly tended."

He had sensed the fragility beneath the veneer of confident professionalism, and he wanted to know more. But before he could ask, Bubbi's companion returned with two heaping plates, and the conversation turned in other directions.

Ben watched Jill dance with her uncle and with several other partners. Then he excused himself and strolled toward the bar.

"Yes, sir?" the bartender asked.

"Scotch on the rocks."

The bartender filled a glass with ice cubes and poured a generous portion from the bottle.

"I see you haven't changed your drinking habits," said a throaty feminine voice behind him.

His hand, closing around the glass, jerked. Liquor sloshed over his sleeve. He turned. "Karen."

"Hello, Ben." Her tone was faintly amused, her eyes on his sleeve. "How are you?"

"Wet." He swiped ineffectually at the cuff and cursed himself for reacting like a bumbling idiot when she'd surprised him. "How about you?"

"I'm great."

She certainly looked great. Slim and sleek, smooth blond hair pulled back to reveal a fine-boned face, sherry-colored eyes and a mouth that could be sensuous or censorious as the mood struck her.

"How long have you been back in Cincinnati?" he asked.

"Four months."

"You apparently made a good career move. Congratulations."

"Thanks." She narrowed her eyes, undoubtedly trying to determine if he was sincere. He was. He'd always wished Karen well in her career. She was good at what she did and deserved to advance. "What about you?" she asked. "Still into steaks?"

He thought of Jill's Bubbi referring to him as "the meat man" the other evening, and smiled. "For the moment."

"I'm sure you've done well . . . or well done."

He chuckled. Her sense of humor had been one of the first things that attracted him. Only later did he learn that her rapier wit could wound as well as amuse.

"Are you seeing anyone?" she asked.

"Yes." He compared the two women. Karen was glamour, sophistication . . . and all surface; Jill was sweetness and love through and through. And that's what he wanted now, something deep and lasting.

Not that he cared, but because he sensed that Karen expected it, he asked, "What about you?"

She nodded.

As if he were an observer outside himself, Ben examined his reaction to this information. He felt nothing.

"Well," she said. "It's been nice seeing you." She stepped away, then turned. "Ben."

"Yes?"

"No hard feelings about the past, I hope."

"No," he replied without the slightest feeling of anger or bitterness, simply the desire to state a fact. "You taught me a lesson." When she raised a brow in question, he said, "I learned the importance of trust." He, too, turned and walked away.

Halfway across the ballroom he caught Jill's eye and knew she'd been watching his interchange with Karen. He quickened his steps.

As he reached her side the band began a slow, romantic ballad. He took Jill's hand, needing to hold her.

She resisted. She stared into his eyes, her expression betraying vulnerability. "How was—?"

"My conversation with Karen? Just hello and goodbye." He tightened his hand on Jill's arm and urged her toward him. "I exorcised that ghost long ago."

She took a step closer. "Are you certain?"

He pulled her nearer. "Yes."

One more step and she was in his arms. He pressed his lips to her temple. "I prefer the ghost of Chanukah present." *And future.*

He felt her shoulders relax, heard her soft laugh. "I'm not a ghost."

He kissed her hair. No, she wasn't a ghost. She was warmth and life and hope. She was love and trust. After his experience with Karen he knew that last quality was the most important, and, by God, he was going to have it in his life.

CHAPTER ELEVEN

THE MUSIC DIED AWAY, but Jill stayed in Ben's arms, her body pressed to his, her eyes closed.

She felt his lips against her ear. "I think the song's over."

"Mmm."

With a soft laugh he drew back. "If we stay like this much longer, we're going to embarrass ourselves."

Her eyelids fluttered open. She met his gaze and caught her breath. His voice had been teasing; his eyes were anything but amused. Dark, intense, filled with desire, they captured and held her.

"Later." He spoke so softly she couldn't hear, but she read the word on his lips. Her mouth went dry.

A drum roll sounded, and Jill started. She blinked and looked around her, thrust from a dream world back to reality.

"Ladies and gentlemen." The master of ceremonies' voice was dramatic. "Please join us now for our raffle drawing. In the next twenty minutes, eight fabulous prizes will be given away. Get out your ticket stubs, folks, and find out if you're one of our lucky winners."

Murmurs of excitement danced through the crowd. Chairs scraped as people hurried back to their tables. Jill tugged Ben's arm. "Let's sit down." She headed for their table, with Ben following behind her. Over her shoulder she told him, "I have twenty chances, and I'm feeling lucky."

"Twenty! Maybe you'll win more than one prize."

"No, I only bought chances on one of them."

"Which one?"

She tossed her head and grinned at him. "You'll see." At the table she dug in her purse and extracted a book of ticket stubs as the music blared again.

"Okay, folks, we're ready to begin with prize number one. A ski package for two in beautiful Vail, Colorado donated by Mountainview Condos."

"Is that *the* prize?" Ben asked, running a finger down Jill's cheek. "We could use it together. I could keep you warm."

The picture of a week at a ski resort—a week with Ben—flashed through Jill's mind. Chilly air, the rush of wind against her face as she sped down the slopes and in the evenings a crackling fire and the heat of Ben's body close to hers. But she laughed and shook her head.

She waited through the awarding of the first three prizes, her excitement growing. When the MC finally announced the fourth prize, Jill said, "Here's what I've been waiting for. Listen."

"Prize number four is one that's increased in value in just the last few hours. And tomorrow night, if the Miami Dolphins beat the Houston Oilers, it will go up even more. Ladies and gentlemen, hold on to your hats while we draw for prize number four, the hottest ticket in the room this evening—two season passes *on the fifty-yard line* for next year's Bengals games!"

"Wow!" Ben said. "If you win, you'll be in every other weekend. I've got my fingers crossed."

"Come on, come on!" Jill held her breath as the MC invited the director of the Jewish Community Center to come up and draw.

"What are your numbers?" Sherry whispered to her.

"Four forty-three to four sixty-two. Wish me luck."

The master of ceremonies cleared his throat. "The winner is four...twenty—"

"Rats!" Jill said in disgust and dropped her stubs on the table.

"No, excuse me. That's four fifty...four fifty-seven."

Jill's hand went to her mouth to stifle a squeal, but the sound came out anyway as she shot out of her chair. "I won! I actually won!" Laughing with delight, she started across the room, then scurried back to get the ticket stub she'd dropped in her excitement. She held it aloft and flew across the ballroom to claim the envelope, while applause and envious groans sounded around her.

Back at the table, she thrust the envelope into Ben's hand. "Happy Chanukah!" She threw her arms around his neck and hugged him.

"You're giving these to me?"

"Yeah. You can wave to me when the TV camera pans the stands."

"Thank you." He planted a kiss on her mouth, then murmured, "But I won't have to wave if you're there with me."

She loved the idea of spending weekends with Ben. They could sit in the stands at Riverfront Stadium, bundled up in coats and mufflers, and cheer for the Bengals. "That's right," she said.

He gave her another kiss, then looked at the tickets as if he couldn't believe he really had them. "This is great."

Jill agreed. She was thrilled with the excitement of winning, with the pleasure of giving Ben something he'd enjoy. She smiled as the people around them congratulated her on her good fortune and Ben on his unexpected present. And she anticipated next year's football season; maybe she would make those weekend visits. For the first time in ages, the future looked bright.

WHEN THE REST of the prizes had been given out, the music began again. Ben held out his hand. "A celebration waltz."

"That's not a waltz, but let's celebrate, anyway."

On the dance floor, people waylaid them.

"How'd you get so lucky?"

"How many chances did you buy?"

"Let me take those tickets off your hands, darlin'. Football's not for ladies."

Jill laughed. "I guess I'm not a lady, then. I love it. But you're too late." She gestured to Ben. "I gave them to him."

"Aw, darn!"

"Jill Levin!" A voice from behind her caught her attention. "I haven't seen you in years."

"Steven Goodman!" For once she recognized someone, and no wonder. Her childhood pal hadn't changed. He still had the same spiky red hair, the same freckled face and devilish grin. "Gosh, I'm glad to see you." She turned to Ben. "Steven was my cohort in mayhem and mischief when we were kids."

The two men exchanged greetings, then Steven winked at Jill. "It's great to see you."

"Thanks. Lisa tells me you've transferred to the side of law and order."

"Yep, I'm a district attorney. If your friend here will let me borrow you for a dance, I'll tell you all about my illustrious career."

Ben nodded and strolled back to their table. Jill and Steven danced several numbers, catching up on one another's lives, then another old friend came up and claimed her. She glanced across the ballroom and shrugged at Ben, wondering if he minded, but he grinned and saluted her with his glass. After a minute she saw him dancing with Sherry, then, as other friends and family approached her, she lost sight of him.

Out of breath after two fast numbers in a row, she was on her way back to their table when she felt a hand on her arm. She turned to meet Mickey Zimmerman's gray eyes.

"Jill."

"Hello, Mickey." She glanced at his hand. Where was the electricity his touch had once generated? Gone. She felt no more than she had when Steven Goodman or Uncle Phil had held her for a dance. Certainly nothing like the charge that zinged through her at the slightest brush of Ben's fingers on her skin.

"Dance with me," Mickey said, and when she nodded he took her hand and led her back onto the floor.

They were close to one another for the first time in years, but the distance between them felt like a chasm. Although outwardly they were just a man and a woman having a pleasant, impersonal dance, inside, Jill's emotions churned. Did he remember the past, she wondered. Did it mean anything to him?

"You look good," Mickey said.

"Thanks." Compared to when they'd parted years ago, of course she looked good. Then she'd been pale, terrified. Pregnant.

"Are you and Abrams . . . seeing each other?"

"We've been going out this past week."

"He's a nice guy. I didn't know him well in school, but everyone liked him."

They danced in silence for a few minutes, then Mickey said, "I'd like to talk to you. Can we sit down somewhere?"

She hesitated, then said, "All right." She glanced around the crowded ballroom. Whatever Mickey had to say, she didn't want to hear it in public.

"Let's find someplace private," he suggested, to her relief.

She looked directly at Mickey now and was surprised to see uncertainty in his eyes. As he steered her toward the door, her stomach muscles tightened from a mixture of fear and anger.

She scanned the ballroom for Ben but couldn't spot him. He was probably flaunting his football tickets to some envious group of Bengal fans. Anyway, this conversation wouldn't take long. All she could handle with Mickey would be a few minutes.

They left the ballroom and turned down a quiet hallway. "Over there," Mickey said, pointing to a small sitting area near an empty meeting room, screened by a bank of tall potted plants.

The music from the ballroom was muted here. They sat on a couch backed by the greenery and facing away from the corridor.

Jill felt stiff and uncomfortable. Except for the few words she and Mickey had exchanged yesterday, they hadn't spoken in over eight years. Where would they begin?

To keep her hands busy, she straightened her skirt with unnecessary care, brushed a few stray wisps of hair off her neck, then clenched her hands in her lap.

Mickey, too, seemed ill at ease. He stared down at the floor for a moment, then took a breath and said, "I've wanted to talk to you for a long time. To ask you what happened ... back then."

Jill heard the anxiety in his voice. She ran her fingers over the rose velvet couch and took a deep breath, but that didn't make what she had to say any easier. "I had the baby."

His eyes widened with shock. "Had the baby," he repeated. He was silent for a long moment. "I guess I should have known you would."

Long-held anger simmered inside her. "What did you want to hear, Mickey? That the pregnancy was just my imagination and it went away? Or that I took your advice—got rid of it, nice and neat?"

He clenched his fists. "No. God, no."

"What, then?"

"That—I don't know. God, Jill, I'm sorry." He reached for her hand, but she jerked it back.

"Don't touch me," she snapped. With an effort she kept her voice steady, but she knew her lips were trembling. "You weren't sorry then. 'Take care of it, Jill.' Wasn't that what you said? You wanted me to eliminate the error. Get rid of it, like ... like junk mail. Unsolicited material."

His face ravaged, he swore. "Dammit, I never meant for you to do that. I was thinking out loud that day, and that was the only option I could come up with right then."

Suddenly, like air rushing from a balloon, the charge of adrenaline drained away, leaving her spent. "Was it? Marriage was another option, but you didn't want that one."

"For God's sake, Jill, we'd already broken up. We weren't right for each other, and we both knew it. Besides, I was a kid. I was scared to death."

"So was I."

"If we'd gotten married—"

She sighed. "That would have been a lousy start to a marriage. Two kids, both scared stiff. No, I guess marriage wasn't the answer."

"I was terrified of getting married," Mickey said. "I'd just gotten my acceptance to grad school...."

"You had your whole life planned, didn't you? And you went ahead with those plans. You just shut our little problem out, pretended it never happened."

"No!" Mickey slammed his fist on the arm of the couch. "I didn't just shut it out."

"Didn't you?" Jill asked bitterly. "What did you do that day after you took me back to the hotel?"

Mickey ran his fingers through his hair, leaving it as ragged as it had been in his car that day long ago. "I... I had a final. I guess I answered the questions, but afterward I didn't remember. I was... in shock."

Jill heard a peal of laughter from down the hall. Were people still laughing? Had *she* been laughing a few minutes ago? Now that she'd plunged into the past, the mirth was gone. "Want to know what I did that day?" she asked.

"No... yes. What did you do?"

"Went upstairs to my room. Do you know," she continued, surprised that she actually sounded as if she were having a normal, everyday conversation, "that was the first time I'd stayed at a hotel alone? I told my folks I was staying at the dorm with a friend, but I got a room instead. And after we talked, I went upstairs and shut the door and had morning sickness all afternoon.

"I can shut my eyes and see that room," she continued. "There were pictures over the bed. People sitting at an outdoor café, laughing. I wanted to yank those pictures off the wall and stomp on them, but I didn't. I just stared at the walls until they closed in on me."

"Jill," he pleaded, but she shook her head.

Sometime during that interminable day, between bouts of nausea and storms of tears, she'd faced the fact that the pregnancy was hers alone, that only she could make the choice of continuing or ending it. Now she voiced that truth. "I couldn't stop thinking about the pregnancy, even for a little while. It stayed with me every minute. But not with you. What did you do after your final? What did you do that summer?" she went on relentlessly. "What did you think about?"

He spread his hands. "I had a summer job, I worked as many hours as I could, I stayed out late. Yeah, I tried to shut the problem out, but I couldn't. Every night I'd stay awake thinking about the baby, about you, wondering if you were all right."

"But you never called to find out."

He stared at the floor. "No, and I'm ashamed of that. I thought when I dropped you at the hotel that you'd decided to—"

"To terminate the pregnancy?"

He nodded and continued. "I asked about you, checked with some friends from Cincinnati. I tried to be discreet, not to ask too much. Someone told me you'd gone away to summer school. I thought..." His voice trailed off.

"That I'd had the abortion? Or maybe a miscarriage? No, I dropped out of sight. I couldn't walk around Cincinnati, flaunting the evidence of my mistake. As soon as I began to show, I went to Washington to stay with my aunt. To hide out."

He raised his eyes and looked at her. "I know you must have had a hard time, but I'm glad you didn't take the advice I gave you that day."

"I couldn't."

"Thank God. Those were the words of a kid, a mixed-up kid, and I regret them."

Looking into his eyes, she saw nothing but sincerity, and she believed him. "I was upset and confused, but I couldn't consider *not* having the baby. She was inside me, a life we'd made. She had a right to live."

"She?"

"Yes, a girl. I called her . . . Sarah."

His face went white. "Sarah," he repeated, his voice choked. "Sarah . . . I'd give anything to see her."

"So would I."

One of Mickey's hands was balled into a fist, the other grasped the side of the couch. "Wh-what happened to her?"

"She was adopted. The Cohen Agency handled it."

"So you don't know . . . ?" He hesitated.

"Where she is? No, I don't know where she is or how she is." She clasped her hands in her lap. "I only saw her for a minute. They let me hold her, then they took her away. I could still hear her crying when the nurse walked out of the delivery room with her and shut the door."

"Oh, God," Mickey whispered. "My . . . our baby. I . . . I want to see her."

Jill laughed harshly. "She's not yours or mine anymore, Mickey, and she's not a baby any longer. She's somebody's child, somebody's eight-year-old daughter."

He rubbed his eyes. "Of course. That was stupid."

"No, it was natural, under the circumstances." She took a deep breath. "I only hope she's happy."

"So do I," he murmured. "Did you ever think of...of keeping her?"

"Only for nine months. My folks talked me out of it, though. When you're a child, everyone tells you your parents are always right. Well, there I was, seventeen, still a child, and I'd just made the mistake of my life. And my parents kept insisting the only thing to do was give the baby away." She raised pain-filled eyes to Mickey's.

"I wish I'd been there to help you make the decision."

"You were a kid, too," Jill pointed out, and he didn't contradict her. She continued, "I listened to my parents. After I'd just been so wrong, how could I be sure what I wanted—to keep the baby—was right? After an experience like that, you can't be sure *anything* you do, anything you think, is right."

"Ah, Jill." Mickey reached for her hand, and this time she didn't pull away. They sat quietly, fingers linked. "You did the right thing in giving her away," he said finally.

"So everyone says. I've never been sure."

"Somewhere, someone blesses you every day for what you did."

Jill wiped a tear from the corner of her eye. "I guess you know." When he nodded, she asked, "What's it like on the other side? When you adopt?" She looked down at their hands. "Hearing won't be easy for me, but I have to know...to reassure myself I did the right thing."

Mickey nodded. "Adopting a baby is terrifying...beautiful. When you see that little human being for the first time and know she's going to be yours, you're overwhelmed. I suppose the feeling's not so different when you're birth parents, but at least then you've had nine months to get used to the idea. While you're waiting to adopt, the baby's in the back of your mind, but not in the same way. Then suddenly one day you get a call, and pow! You have a child!''

She saw the joy in Mickey's expression and wondered if her child's adoptive parents had felt the same jubilation when they'd received the call to come and pick her up. She hoped they had, even though the loss of her child still hurt. ''A surprise,'' she murmured.

''Yeah. We ran around like crazy, buying baby clothes, setting up a nursery, calling our families. Then we went to get her and all of a sudden there we were, the three of us. The first thing Roz said when we got home was, 'We must have been crazy, thinking we'd know what to do with a baby.' She was scared to death, I was scared to death. Then Sarah started to cry, Roz picked her up and, just like that, we were parents.''

''Parents,'' Jill murmured wistfully. ''I hope I'll be one someday.''

Mickey squeezed her hand. ''You will.''

''But not . . . hers.''

''No, and neither will I. I'm my Sarah's dad and I love her. We'll probably adopt again, and I'll love that child, too, but . . .'' He paused and then continued, his voice unsteady, ''but this baby, *our* baby, is the only child I'll ever father, and I'll never know her. That hurts.''

Jill nodded. She knew that sort of pain very well. Then she asked, ''Does Roz know . . . about my pregnancy?''

''No. I never told her because I didn't know what finally happened. And for what it's worth to you, I didn't know Roz was your cousin until after we were engaged and I came to Cincinnati to meet her relatives.''

She nodded, accepting his explanation. ''Will you tell her now?''

He didn't answer. Instead, he took a deep breath and stared at a spot on the wall. Finally he said, "I don't know. Maybe, after I've had some time to get used to the idea. You've had eight years. This is new for me." He touched Jill's cheek and gave her a sad smile. "We...*I* made a mess of things, didn't I?"

She covered his hand with hers. They had a bond between them, forged by shared passion, tempered now by shared pain. That link would never be broken. Somewhere a child gave evidence. Perhaps, through that child, their own personal tragedy had a silver lining.

Jill felt years of anger and bitterness begin to melt away. What was the point in carrying that old baggage, in maintaining that grudge against Mickey? He'd been a kid; he'd reacted as a kid. She saw that now. And now she could put the past behind her and get on with her life.

She smiled at Mickey. "Not such a mess. We had our baby."

He nodded and bent his head. The kiss they exchanged was a gentle one, a kiss between friends.

CHAPTER TWELVE

"OUR BABY."

The words struck Ben like hammer blows. He stood frozen, mesmerized, as Mickey Zimmerman lowered his head and covered Jill's lips with his. Whether the kiss was tender or passionate, he couldn't tell, and he didn't want to find out. Before Jill and Mickey parted, he turned. His heart thudding dully in his chest, his body moving like a robot's, he made his way back to the ballroom. He wanted a drink.

"Scotch," he growled at the bartender, tipped the proffered glass back and downed the liquor in a gulp, then ordered another round.

Glass in hand, he leaned against the wall. His other hand, the one in his pocket, was knotted into a fist. Anger churned in his gut, pain knifed through him, as he replayed the scene he'd just witnessed. Jill and Mickey. A kiss, soft words. A scene that had left him reeling with shock and confusion.

He'd seen Jill dancing with Mickey earlier and thought little of it. They were old friends, cousins now. Why shouldn't they share a dance? When they left the ballroom together a few minutes later, he'd shrugged it off. Maybe they needed some air, maybe they were going to talk to someone. As time passed and they didn't return, he began to wonder where they'd gone. People were beginning to drift away from the party, and, anxious to be alone with Jill, he had set out to find her.

She and Mickey weren't in the foyer, nor were they downstairs in the bar. He'd almost concluded that they'd returned to the ballroom and he'd missed them, when on impulse he decided to turn down a side hall.

That's when he spotted them, sitting close together on a love seat and so deep in conversation they were oblivious to their surroundings.

Ben approached them and opened his mouth to speak, then shut it abruptly when he saw Mickey lift his hand to Jill's cheek, saw her turn to smile into his eyes, put her hand over his.

Ben took a step nearer, then stopped. Jill said something in a low voice. He couldn't hear all she said, only the last two words. "Our baby."

Now he stood, watching and waiting. Mickey came into the ballroom first, sat beside his wife and touched her shoulder gently. Only minutes ago the man had been touching Jill, looking at her with that same tender expression.

Shortly afterward Jill entered the ballroom and glanced around. Her eyes met Ben's; she smiled and waved. He watched her come toward him, her face glowing as if she were glad to see him. She could teach Karen a thing or two about deceit.

She came up to him. "Hi," she said. "I looked for you a while ago."

"I've been right here."

She apparently didn't notice the underlying note of strain. "I think the crowd's starting to thin. I could be talked into going upstairs."

"Whatever you say."

She frowned, evidently puzzled by the remark, then said, "Let's tell my family good-night, then we can leave."

Ben said nothing; he simply followed her to the table and echoed her good-night to the group, which no longer included the Zimmermans. As they crossed the ballroom, Jill waved to several acquaintances, then when they reached the foyer, she tucked her arm in his. Ben fought to keep from flinching at her touch.

In the elevator he stood tense and silent. When they reached Jill's floor, he walked stiffly down the hall. Jill didn't seem to notice. She chattered about the benefit, the football tickets, the music, until Ben was certain he couldn't endure another word.

They reached her room. She opened her door, tossed her purse and stole on the desk, then turned to him and twined her arms about his neck. "Make love to me, Ben," she whispered.

Stiffly, methodically, he disengaged her hands. "No."

She stared at him in surprise. "What's wrong?"

"I don't share, and I won't be a substitute."

Puzzlement was replaced by annoyance. "You may think you're making sense, but this is Greek to me. Spell it out, will you?"

"I saw you with Zimmerman." He didn't even try to hide the hurt and confusion.

Her face paled, her eyes widened with shock and she stumbled back against the bed. She sank down, touching the surface with one hand as if to make sure it was solid. Then she sighed. "Is that what this is about?"

"Yeah." Standing with arms folded across his chest, he eyed her dispassionately, belying the emotions that surged within him. "Would you like to explain?"

She made a small, helpless gesture. "I— Sit down, Ben."

He chose the chair by the desk. Mistake. Her stole lay inches away. On it he could smell her perfume, that soft rose-petal fragrance. He kept his voice curt. "I'm sitting."

He saw her swallow. Then she said, "Mickey and I... there... there's nothing between us."

"Nothing? What about—" he made himself say the words "—a baby?"

He wanted her to deny there was a baby, to swear it wasn't true. Instead, she dropped her head into her hands and whispered brokenly, "Oh, God, you know. How did... how did you find out?"

"I heard you and Zimmerman talking. You said something about 'our baby.'" His voice rose. "Then you kissed him."

"Don't shout at me, Ben. Just...just listen, will you?"

He couldn't refuse her. Damn, as hurt and confused as he was, he was enough of a fool that he still loved her. That's what made the pain so gut wrenching. "All right." He sat back, steepled his fingers and waited.

"I had a baby... Mickey's baby... when I was eighteen." She said the words in a low, ragged tone as if every syllable were being torn from her soul.

Until this moment he'd prayed that he'd misinterpreted her conversation downstairs. But it was true... and she hadn't told him.

"We slept together maybe half a dozen times," Jill said. "The last time was over spring break when Mickey came to Cincinnati to visit. By the time spring vacation was over, we'd broken up. Six weeks later I found out I was...I was...pregnant. We'd been too careless to take precautions, so there I was, two weeks away from high school graduation, unmarried and pregnant.''

She stopped and took a shaky breath. Ben glanced down and saw that sometime during her speech he'd reached for her stole and that his fingers now caressed it as if it were her skin. He stared at the silky material for a moment, then tossed the stole back on the desk.

Jill continued. "Even though we'd broken up, I went to Mickey. I told my parents we had a date, and I went to Columbus and told him what had happened." She stopped and looked away, her hand playing absently with the bedspread, picking at the threads.

"Go on," Ben prodded.

"He... he didn't want anything to do with the situation."

Her words came in a rush, and Ben grasped the sides of the chair. He'd never been a violent person, but suddenly he wanted to strangle that irresponsible boy who'd left Jill to face a pregnancy alone. "What happened?" he ground out.

"I told my parents. I had the baby. Mickey never knew... until tonight. She was born on the first night of Chanukah. That's funny, isn't it?" she added with a sob in her voice. "Everything significant in my life seems to happen during Chanukah." She took a breath, squared her shoulders and went on. "I gave her up for adoption through the Cohen Agency."

"That's it?"

"That's the story. Until yesterday when he came by my folks' house with Roz, I'd never seen Mickey again. I didn't come home for their wedding—I guess you can understand why."

He had to know. "Do you... do you still care about him?"

She shook her head vehemently. "Of course not, but he'll always be part of my life. We have a child between us. We're ... we'll always be connected."

Ben was silent for a long time. Then he voiced the question that had to be asked. "Why didn't you tell me?"

She gave a strangled laugh. "Because I was scared. Because I didn't know how."

She met his gaze, and he looked away. He got up, went to the window and pulled the drapes apart to stare out. He didn't register what he saw as he gazed into the night. He only knew he couldn't deal with the pain and the pleading in Jill's eyes.

"Ben."

Her voice came from directly behind him. He turned and saw her stricken face. He wanted to grab her by the shoulders and shake her, wanted to draw her into his arms and comfort her. At this moment he didn't know what he wanted.

"Ben, talk to me."

He stalked past her. "I ... can't. I'm having a tough time taking all this in."

Jill began to laugh, her voice rising hysterically. "*You're* having a tough time. That's a joke. I'm the one having a hard time. I—" She turned away and covered her face with her hands. Choked sobs tore from her throat.

He couldn't stand to see her cry. He went to her and patted her shoulder awkwardly, not daring to take her in his arms. "Hush." He reached into his pocket for a handkerchief. "Here."

She blew her nose and took a step away from him. He reached toward her, but she shrugged him off. "No, don't." She returned to the bed, sat down again and gazed at him with red-rimmed eyes. "Tell me why this is so hard for *you*."

"The shock of overhearing it, for one thing."

"Okay, I can understand that."

"I didn't know whether this was an ongoing affair you were talking about, or—"

"Wait a minute. This is the second time you've implied that I could be having an affair with someone else. Is that what you think of me? That I'm the kind of woman who'd sleep with two men at once, or..." She paused as if a thought had suddenly struck her. "Or does this have something to do with what you think of yourself? That you can't hold a woman's interest?"

She was on target, he realized. His experience with Karen had shattered his self-esteem. Perhaps he *didn't* feel he could keep a woman's attention. "I don't know," he muttered.

Jill leaned forward. "Ben, I haven't made love with anyone... *anyone*... since Mickey. Until you. I haven't trusted anyone enough."

There'd been no one else. Hadn't he suspected that? Her trepidation, her innocence had been clear indications.

A day ago, two days ago, her words would have moved him deeply. Now he wasn't sure what he felt, only that something was lacking. And Jill had just voiced what it was. Trust. "Do you really trust me?" he demanded. "Evidently not enough to tell me about your past."

"I explained that. I was frightened." Her eyes, dry now, flashed in anger. "Want to know what of? Lack of understanding. The very thing that's happening now."

"It's hard to be sympathetic, under the circumstances."

"Are you accusing me of being deliberately deceptive?" she shot back. "I wasn't ready to tell you."

"I shared my experience with Karen. I trusted you."

"And I gave you what you needed. When you told me about Karen, I listened with compassion, not anger." She stood and paced the room, then halted in front of Ben and glared at him. "And how can you begin to compare the two situations? Do you have any idea how long it takes to get over the trauma I went through? How hard I've worked even to trust myself? Ben," she went on, more quietly, "we've known each other only a week . . ."

He could see she was trying to reason with him, but he didn't feel reasonable just now. "How long is your 'trust timetable'? *Two* weeks? A year? A lifetime?"

"Stop it," she said. Her voice trembled with anger. "Do you hear what you're saying? You're expecting something of me that *you* can't give." She turned away from him, sat down again and shut her eyes.

Ben stared at her, seeing on her face the stark evidence of the wounds he'd inflicted. Only hours ago he'd been planning to ask her to marry him. Now his dreams lay broken at his feet. He tried to explain his feelings. "If you'd told me yourself, if I'd heard it from you instead of the way I did, I think I could have been understanding."

"But we'll never know, will we?" she said. Her voice was sad. She opened her eyes and gave him a level look. "Where do we go from here, Ben?"

He couldn't answer. He felt tired, numb, confused. "I don't know. I need time to get used to this." When he saw the pain in her eyes, he spread his hands. "I'm sorry, Jill. That's all I can say."

She nodded. "Well, then, I guess all we can do now is say good-night."

"Yeah." He went to the door and opened it. "I'll call you," he said and walked out without looking at her again.

Jill listened to the click of the door closing. "I won't hold my breath," she murmured.

She stood and began undressing. She took a hanger from the closet and hung up her dress, carefully fastening each button, smoothing each wrinkle. If she let go, if she thought about what had just happened, she would shatter. Perhaps she was dreaming, she thought. Certainly, everything around her seemed unreal.

She took off her earrings and put them in her jewelry case, then unfastened the pendant Ben had given her. She cradled it in her palm. The symbol of his heart, he'd said. A sob burst from her lips, and she flung the necklace against the wall. She left it where it fell, blinked her tears away and walked to the dresser.

In front of the mirror, she removed the pins from her hair, one by one. The rosebud corsage fell into her hand. The petals were wilting, turning brown along the edges. Didn't take long for a flower to fade.

She tore a petal off and ran her finger over it. The fragrance rose up sweetly. Jill grimaced. Another flower to add to her list of never-agains. Like the gardenias from Lisa's wedding, roses would now evoke only bitter memories. She tossed the flower into the trash can and continued taking her hair down, but her hands began to tremble and refused to stop.

The tears came then. Sobs of pain, anger. At Ben, at Mickey, at herself, even at Carnaby and Ross for sending her here. How had all this happened? This was the night she'd planned to tell Ben she loved him. The last thing she'd expected was to end the evening alone.

Alone again. And all because Ben had overheard her conversation with Mickey. What if she *had* told Ben herself? Would that really have made a difference, or would he still have been as angry and hurt?

Dear God, was her mistake going to cast a pall over the rest of her life? Would she never live it down? None of this was fair. Her tears flowed faster now. Hot, bitter tears of regret and self-recrimination. She stumbled to the bed and sat there, weeping until no tears were left. Her breath still catching in her throat, she found Ben's handkerchief and dried her eyes.

She looked around the room. Anonymous. Empty. She needed to be with someone.

On impulse, she reached for the phone and punched in Bubbi's number. After five rings she heard her grandmother's sleepy voice. "Hello."

Jill glanced at the clock. Oh, Lord, it was one-thirty. She hadn't given a thought to the time. "Bubbi, it's Jill. I'm sorry, I didn't realize it was so late. I'll...I'll call you back in the morning."

"I'm awake," her grandmother said, her voice stronger now. "What's wrong?"

"Nothing...everything. Bubbi, can I come over?" She hated the tremulous note in her voice, but she couldn't help it.

"Of course, but I don't like the idea of your going out alone in the middle of the night."

"Don't worry. I'll have the valet get my car, and I'll keep the doors locked."

Quickly she pulled on a pair of pants and a sweater. As she picked up her purse, she glanced down and saw a flash of silver—the necklace Ben had given her. She took a step toward the door, stopped and turned to pick up the heart. As angry as she was at Ben, she couldn't bring herself to leave it lying on the floor. She fastened it around her neck again, slipping it inside her shirt.

Twenty minutes later, when she reached Bubbi's house, she saw a light shining in the living-room window. Even though she was sorry she'd awakened her grandmother, Jill sighed with relief. Of all the people in her life, Bubbi was the one she could talk to, the person who understood her best.

The front door opened before she was halfway up the walk. Bubbi stood in the doorway, dressed in a blue velour bathrobe, her face devoid of makeup, but her hair neatly combed. She looked worried, but that wouldn't have stopped her from fixing her hair. Jill couldn't remember ever having seen Bubbi with a hair out of place.

As Jill mounted the porch steps, she said, "Bubbi, I'm so sorry I got you up. I shouldn't have done this."

"And why not? Something is bothering you, and what's a grandmother for? To listen, that's what. Come in."

Jill went inside. As always, the house felt warm and welcoming.

"Come," Bubbi said briskly. "I've made some tea. You'll drink and you'll tell me what's wrong."

Jill followed her into the breakfast room, sat across from her and gratefully sipped the hot beverage, which Bubbi had already laced with sugar.

"So?" Bubbi said when Jill put down her cup.

"Oh, Bubbi. My life is a mess," Jill said with a sigh.

"Now, now. In the middle of the night things always look bad." Bubbi's voice was soothing.

"Ben walked out on me."

Bubbi stared at her in stunned silence. "I don't believe it. That nice boy? I sat with him at the table this evening, and when he spoke of you his eyes were full of love."

"Not anymore, I'm afraid." While her grandmother listened gravely, Jill told her what had happened that evening. "And then he said, 'I need time to get used to this,' and he left."

Bubbi sat quietly for a few moments, then said, "So you'll give him time, and he'll be back."

Though she wanted to believe Bubbi's words, Jill shook her head. "I don't think so. I didn't trust him enough to tell him, and now he doesn't trust me. You see, he had a bad experience once," and she told her grandmother the story of Karen.

Bubbi nodded. "He'll get over it in time. This boy...excuse me, this man loves you, Jill. You'll give him the time, and then you'll fight for him."

"I'm leaving Tuesday. I don't have much time."

Her grandmother chuckled at that. "What's this? They've disbanded the telephone company? They don't sell airplane tickets anymore? You'll call him, or you'll come to see him. He'll look up from his steaks one day, and you'll be there."

Jill couldn't help but join in the laughter.

"Good. You're laughing," Bubbi said. "Shall I tell you a story? When you were a little girl, you always liked my stories."

"Yes, I remember." Jill nodded. How many times had she curled up on the couch or fallen asleep to the sound of Bubbi's voice telling folktales or fairy tales or stories about her girlhood in Russia?

"Once upon a time," Bubbi began as if Jill were still a child, "there was a girl named Rachel."

"This one is about you," Jill said.

Bubbi nodded. "And about your zayde. It's a love story." She folded her hands and smiled. "My Aaron, may he rest in peace, was a handsome young man, and I was very much in love with him. And he was in love with me, too, of course."

"Of course," Jill agreed. "How could he help it?"

"He couldn't. Just like your Ben," Bubbi said. "Well, one afternoon I was sitting on the swing on my mother's front porch. And along came Sam Perchonek. Sam was crazy about my sister Rose, but he was so shy, bless his heart, and so tongue-tied, he couldn't tell her. He used to talk to me, though, hoping I would put in a good word for him with Rose, and of course, I did.

"Well, on this particular day, Sam saw me and he came and sat beside me on the swing to talk. About Rose. We were swinging and talking, talking and swinging, and all of a sudden—I don't know why—I ran my hand over the arm of the swing and got a splinter. You know how those can hurt. I couldn't get it out, so Sam, because he was a gentleman, took my hand and worked the splinter out.

"Now just at that time along came Aaron, and what did he see? Sam Perchonek and me, holding hands. Aaron was angry. His face turned red. He stood on the sidewalk and shouted at me. He wouldn't even come on the porch. 'That's it, Rachel,' he said. 'You're holding hands with this...this...' Well, in front of me he shouldn't have said such a word. 'We're through,' he said, and off he went."

"And what did you do?" Enthralled with her grandmother's tale, Jill had almost forgotten her troubles.

"Exactly what you should do. I gave him time—three days. Then I got dressed in my best clothes, took the streetcar downtown to where he was working in Katz's Dry Goods Store. I found him sweeping the floor, and what did I do? I marched right up to him and said, 'Aaron Blum, Sam was taking a splinter out of my hand. Listen to me, Aaron,' I said, 'I love you and if you had any brains, you would see it and I wouldn't have to tell you.' ''

"What happened?"

"What happened? Right away, he dropped the broom and he said, 'I love you, too, Rachel.' I said, 'Fine, so when are we getting married?' And right then, we set the date."

"And you lived happily ever after," Jill said.

"That's right. And the moral of the story is, if you love Ben Abrams, you'll fight for him. And you'll win."

"Thank you, Bubbi," Jill said and smiled. "Now I know what to do. Fight . . . and win." She glanced at the clock. "Goodness, I've kept you up half the night."

"When you get old, you don't need as much sleep," Bubbi assured her.

"I should be going."

"At three in the morning? I should say not. You'll sleep in the guest room. Come, I'll find you a nightgown. It won't fit so well, but you'll be warm."

Yawning, Jill followed Bubbi to her room, took the flannel gown and was soon curled up under the quilt she remembered from childhood weekends here. Almost immediately she fell asleep.

When Jill woke the next morning, Bubbi was already bustling around the kitchen, setting out orange juice, making coffee, warming bagels. They had breakfast together, then Jill checked the time. "I'd better get back to the hotel. My agency team will be expecting me."

Bubbi walked her to the door, and Jill hugged her grandmother. "Thank you for listening to me. And for the story."

"Remember, fight!"

Jill gave her a thumbs-up sign. "I'll remember." She started down the sidewalk, then turned. "I'll call you before I leave tomorrow," she said before she got into her car.

As she drove downtown, her dark mood lifted with the morning sunshine. She parked her car and hurried through the hotel lobby, her step light.

When she opened the door to her room, she heard the phone ringing and ran to pick it up. Maybe it was Ben. Out of breath, she said, "Hello."

"Where the heck have you been?" The tension in Hope's voice fairly leaped through the wire.

"I was at my grandmother's. I didn't think you'd be ready to meet yet. It's only ten after nine. What's up?"

"We'll talk about it when you get here. Dan and I are in my room." Before Jill could ask anything more, Hope hung up.

Jill didn't bother to change clothes or even recomb her hair. As she hurried down the hall to the elevator, she felt the clutch of nerves. Whatever was up didn't sound good.

A few minutes later she tapped nervously on Hope's door.

Hope opened it immediately. Two spots of angry red color dotted her cheeks.

"What is it?" Jill asked.

"I heard from Wellner," Hope replied.

"Bad news?"

"You could say that. We didn't get the account."

CHAPTER THIRTEEN

"WHAT!" JILL STOOD in the doorway, gaping at her colleague.

Hope pulled her inside. "You heard me. We got a call at a quarter to nine. They said 'thanks, but no, thanks.' The contract went to Tolar."

Jill couldn't believe what Hope had said. After her friend's terse phone call, she'd anticipated problems—perhaps significant changes in the concept, perhaps questions about the budget. But being passed over for the business—never. She glanced at Dan, who stood by the window.

"You heard her," he said glumly. "I'll admit, I didn't expect this. I thought I got a clear message Friday that we were home free."

Hope paced the room. "Did we misunderstand, or did they lead us on?"

Jill sank down on the nearest chair. A funny feeling took root in her stomach and began to grow. "I thought we had the account, too," she muttered. "Who called you?" she asked Hope.

"McMinn."

"What exactly did he say?"

"'We thank you for your interest in the Steak Expectations account,'" Hope mimicked McMinn's formal style, "'but after reviewing the proposals, we've decided to go with the Tolar Agency.' Those were his words. Verbatim.''

"We," Jill mused. "We. That means McMinn and—" she shot out of her chair "—Ben!"

She marched to the phone. "That low-down—never mind." She ignored Dan's shocked expression and Hope's questioning look, yanked the telephone receiver off the hook and jabbed in Wellner's number. When she heard the receptionist's cheerful voice, she snapped, "Ben Abrams."

"What's going on?" Hope mouthed, but Jill held up a hand to quiet her.

"Shh, they're putting me through." She tapped her foot until Ben's secretary answered, then said, "Mr. Abrams, please."

"I'm sorry. Mr. Abrams isn't at his desk," the secretary replied in that insipidly pleasant tone that told Jill the woman was lying. "Would you like to leave a message?"

"Tell him that— Never mind. I'll call back." Jill slammed down the receiver.

"Okay. Explain," Hope ordered.

"Ben and I had a . . . misunderstanding last night."

"And?" Hope prompted.

Dan made a tsking noise with his tongue. "Hope, can't you read between the lines? Our Jill believes the esteemed Mr. Abrams has attempted to even the score."

Jill's cheeks reddened, but she couldn't contradict Dan. His assumption was right on target.

Hope frowned. "Is he right, Jill?"

"I'm afraid so."

Dan shook his head. "Aren't you being a wee bit melodramatic?"

Hope, ever logical, agreed. "The agency's missed out on business before. For all sorts of reasons."

Dan chimed in. "I remember when we were short-listed for the Adams Peanut Oil campaign, and we thought we had it sewed up, when, poof!" He gestured broadly. "The 'sure thing' disappeared into thin air."

Hope nodded. "This is business, Jill."

Maybe that was true, but nothing her colleagues said made Jill feel any better. To her, this was intensely personal. She sat staring into space, fingering the silver, heart-shaped pendant she still wore. She was surprised it hadn't broken.

"Jill, brooding isn't doing you or the agency any good," Hope said.

Jill nodded, but continued to ponder what had happened. The more she thought, the more she believed that Ben had chosen the perfect means of repaying her for last night. What a rotten thing to do. How could he?

"Come on, Jill," Hope said. "What we need is action. First off, can you patch up your disagreement with Abrams?"

Bubbi's advice to fight for Ben no longer seemed appropriate. Did she want to fight for a man who would wreak vengeance on her company because of a private disagreement? She shook her head. "Can I straighten out the personal part? Right now, I don't know how I feel about that. I'd be willing to maintain a business relationship if it will salvage the account."

"Give it a try," Hope said. "Call him back, and this time leave a message."

"Okay."

This time the secretary informed her that Mr. Abrams was in a meeting, another standard brush-off. She left her name and the number of Hope's room and asked that he call her back as soon as possible.

"Nine twenty-five. Now we wait," Hope said.

AT NINE-THIRTY BEN dragged into his office. Susan looked up, glanced pointedly at her watch, then frowned. "You look like you tied one on last night."

"Thanks a lot. I might as well have," he mumbled. His head weighed a ton, his eyes burned from lack of sleep and his arms and legs felt numb. He'd driven home from the Hyatt on automatic pilot, his mind inundated with conflicting thoughts and emotions. Anger, pain, longing. Halfway home he'd almost turned around and headed back to the hotel. But he couldn't. As he'd told Jill, he needed time to get used to the idea that she'd given birth to Zimmerman's child. Unfortunately, a night of turning the idea over and over in his mind hadn't helped one iota. And he hadn't been able to shut off his thoughts and go to sleep. Even trying to knock himself out with push-ups hadn't helped.

"Coffee?" Susan asked.

"Yeah, thanks."

She poured a steaming cup, black, and followed him into his office. "You have a stack of messages on your desk and a memo from Mr. McMinn."

He reached for the coffee cup, eased into his chair and shoved the phone messages aside in favor of the memo. He took a gulp of coffee, scanned the sheet of paper, then read it again.

"Damn!"

He slammed the cup on his desk, sloshing coffee over the memo, and stalked out of his office. "I'll be with McMinn," he snarled at Susan.

Fueled by fury, he charged down the hall. As he passed McMinn's secretary and headed for the inner door, the woman half rose from her chair. "I'm sorry, Mr. Abrams," she said, "Mr. McMinn is on long distance. He can't be disturbed. He—"

She stood, wringing her hands ineffectually, as Ben passed her and shoved McMinn's door open. The older man looked up, clearly annoyed at the disturbance, and attempted to wave Ben out. But Ben planted himself in the doorway, legs apart, hands clenched at his sides.

He held McMinn's eyes until his boss said, with a grimace, "I'll get back to you later," and put down the receiver. He glowered at Ben. "This is highly irregular. What do you w—?"

"You know damn well what I want." Ben took half a dozen steps toward the desk and saw McMinn flinch. "You overrode my decision on the Steak Expectations account, and I want an explanation."

McMinn shrugged, in an obvious effort to gain the advantage. "I chose to override because, in view of your relationship with Ms. Levin, I felt your decision was an emotional one."

"Emotional, hell! Carnaby and Ross had the best proposal by a long shot. I know it, you know it and everyone else who saw their presentation knows it. You had no right—" he leaned over the desk menacingly, and McMinn moved his chair back "—*no right,* dammit, to reverse my decision."

"Of course I had the right. I'm your superior in this organization, and I'm the final word. Besides, I've had far more experience in these situations than you have." His tone condescending, McMinn continued. "Carnaby and Ross had an excellent presentation, I agree, but their concept was...mediocre at best."

"Mediocre!" Ben growled. The fact that McMinn was indeed his superior made no difference to him. Diplomacy deserted him and he made no effort to censor his words. "If that's what you think, your judgment isn't worth—"

McMinn's face reddened. "That's enough! The reason for my decision should be obvious, but since you seem to have difficulty understanding, I'll explain. Sit down and listen. Perhaps this will be instructive for you...in the future." The tone of his last phrase indicated that Ben had better start considering a future somewhere other than the Wellner Corporation.

Ben didn't give a damn. He sat, folded his arms across his chest and waited.

"An advertising campaign must focus on the product." McMinn spoke slowly, as if he were presenting a lesson to an elementary school student. "Now, since food is a restaurant's product, an effective campaign must play that up. While Carnaby and Ross had a clever idea, their campaign bypassed the food in favor of the customer. Such a campaign is unsound. The Tolar Agency put the emphasis where it belongs—on the meat. 'Well done' tells the potential customer what to expect from a meal at Steak Expectations—good food." He waited a minute, then said, "Do you understand?"

"Yeah, I understand that you chose an inferior campaign. What I don't understand is why."

McMinn pushed his chair back and stood. "I've given you a clear and simple explanation. If you can't comprehend it, then I suggest you reread some of your college advertising texts." He rearranged a stack of papers so that they were aligned with the edge of the desk, then added, "The decision has been made and communicated to Tolar, Carnaby and Ross, and HG and B. I suggest you accept it because nothing you say or do can change matters now.'' He glanced at the door. ''I'm sure you have work to do.''

Ben rose. He felt like punching McMinn in his haughty face, but he stopped himself. He turned and left McMinn's office, contenting himself with slamming the door behind him. He did the same with the door to his own office, stalked to the window and stared out.

This was the second time in twenty-four hours he'd wanted to slug someone, the second time his trust had been violated. At least he wasn't shocked at McMinn's deceit; Jill's was a different matter. Though he'd known her only a week, he'd been certain she was straightforward and sincere. ''Damn!'' he swore. He couldn't think of Jill now. He needed to deal with the crisis at hand.

Ben stood without moving for a long while, waiting for his anger to abate so he could think logically. At last he began trying to make sense out of what had happened this morning.

Carnaby and Ross had clearly submitted an outstanding proposal. Why, then, would McMinn bypass them in favor of Tolar? His boss's arguments didn't make sense. Tolar's campaign, focus on the meat notwithstanding, was inferior to Carnaby and Ross's. Hell, it hadn't even been as good as HG and B's, the third agency in the running. Yet McMinn, he recalled, had been touting Tolar even before Carnaby and Ross had given their presentation.

Ben smelled a rat here. Trouble was, he couldn't figure out what kind.

He heard the door open and turned to see Susan behind him. ''Whew,'' she remarked. ''Smoke's coming out of your ears. McMinn give you a tough time?''

"I'm afraid I gave him an even tougher one. Not very smart of me. No finesse."

Susan grinned. "Old Pruneface is hard to finesse."

"Pruneface?"

"Yeah." She giggled. "That's what the office staff calls Mr. McMinn."

Ben joined in her laughter, enjoying the momentary release of tension. He had to admit the moniker was an apt one.

"Ben, I'm sorry McMinn decided on Tolar. Everyone around here was betting on Carnaby and Ross."

"Me, too," Ben said with a sigh. He walked back to his desk and sat down, rubbing his temple. Susan undoubtedly knew who'd gotten the account because she'd read his memo from McMinn. But he wouldn't be surprised if, with her antennae turned to anything of interest in the corporation, she'd known even before the memo crossed his desk. He raised his head. "Do you think you could find out why McMinn picked Tolar?"

She checked her watch. "Maybe, if I take my coffee break now."

"Okay, go ahead." As she started out the door, he added, "Ask the switchboard to hold my calls."

As he waited, his thoughts swung back to Jill. How had she taken the news that Carnaby and Ross had lost the business? She must have been stunned. Ben had as good as told her that her agency was the front-runner. Did she think he'd lied, used that as a ploy to get her into bed? God, he hoped not. Did she assume he'd taken revenge on her for last night? He'd better call and straighten that out.

He tried her room and got no answer, waited five minutes and called again. He didn't want to leave a message. Another ten minutes passed while he paced the floor. He picked up the telephone a third time and hesitated. What would he say? As yet, he had no answer as to why Carnaby and Ross hadn't gotten the account. All he could tell her at this point was, "I'm sorry." And would she believe him? After what had happened last night, he needed to make his explanation in person. He put the phone down.

A tap sounded on the door, and Susan entered.

"Well?" he asked.

"I went for coffee early so I could catch Cora. That's when she goes," she began.

"Cora?"

"You know—Mr. McMinn's secretary. She's not so fond of Mr. McMinn but she likes to be in control. She was upset that you barged into her boss's office."

"Tough," Ben muttered.

"She felt that made her look bad, and besides, she said you had no right. You know she's just like he is about protocol. Well, after she finished berating me about you—as if I could tell you what to do—she told me in confidence that Mr. McMinn has been under a great deal of pressure lately."

"His wife is ill," Ben said.

"Yes, and the medical expenses are mounting. The chemo made her sick, and he's had to hire someone to take care of her during the day. Plus, they added a room to their house and did some other remodeling last year and that cost more than they expected. To pay for all this, he had to sell some stock at a loss, so he's not in the best shape financially."

"Sorry to hear all that, but I doubt my visit to him added substantially to his troubles."

"But it did," Susan said. "You questioned his decision on the ad campaign."

"He told Cora that?" Ben was surprised that Mc-Minn would admit to his secretary that someone had questioned his authority.

"He didn't have to tell her. You weren't exactly whispering when you were in his office," Susan pointed out.

"True. But why was he so disturbed?"

"Cora thinks he's afraid you'll go over his head."

"Yeah, that would upset ol' Pruneface. And it's not such a bad idea," Ben said, considering his options.

"Going over his head wouldn't be his only concern," Susan went on. "What's important to him is that *Tolar keep that account.*"

"I knew all along McMinn favored Tolar. Why?"

"Three reasons. First, McMinn and George Tolar are old friends. They went to college together."

So much for keeping personal relationships out of the office, Ben thought. Of course, this wasn't as personal as his association with Jill, but it sure as hell wasn't just a business connection. "Go on."

"Second, Mr. McMinn's position here is shaky."

Ben nodded. "That's been clear for a while."

"Okay, reason number three is the biggie. After Tolar made their presentation, Cora overheard Mr. Tolar offer Mr. McMinn a vice presidency at his agency plus a substantial signing bonus in return for—"

"Let me guess," Ben said through clenched teeth. "In return for the Steak Expectations account!" He spat out a furious oath. "That bastard!" Too agitated to sit, he got up and paced the length of his office, then turned. "Susan, are you positive all this is true?"

"Absolutely." She crossed her heart. "When Cora's upset, she likes to talk. And I'm a good listener." She stood. "Well, I have some work to do."

"Thanks, Susan," Ben said. "If the CIA ever has an opening, I'll give you a good reference."

She gave him a snappy salute and left his office.

Ben continued pacing. His anger with McMinn peaked, then ebbed, tempered with pity. The man was a hypocrite, constantly preaching proprieties, and then opting for the expedient. In this case, with a sick wife, financial problems and a precarious position at work, Ben supposed what McMinn had done was understandable. *Understandable but totally unacceptable, not to mention unethical.* He'd done the company an injustice by choosing an inferior campaign, and he'd cheated Carnaby and Ross out of a contract that should have been theirs.

Next question. Could anything be done to repair the damage? Ben supposed he could make an appointment with the Wellner CEO, expose the whole ugly mess, ruin McMinn's career. Or maybe the CEO wouldn't believe Ben's story. Maybe McMinn had covered himself. Maybe the CEO himself loved the Tolar campaign.

Damn, he needed to get away from the office and think about his situation at Wellner...and about Jill. He understood that McMinn had done what he thought he had to do. Why, Ben wondered, couldn't he cut Jill an equal amount of slack? She'd kept her secret because she was afraid of his reaction, and he'd done everything possible to prove her right.

Still, he couldn't equate Jill and McMinn. She'd just entered into the kind of intimate relationship she insisted she'd avoided for years. Shouldn't she have been honest and open?

Raking his fingers through his hair, he glanced at the untidy pile of messages and papers on his desk. To hell with them. He needed space.

He yanked his coat from the rack in the corner and opened his door. Susan looked up from her computer. "I'm going out," he told her. "I'm not sure when I'll be back."

She nodded in perfect understanding. "I'll cover for you. Just be sure to check in later."

JILL LOOKED AT THE CLOCK. The hour that had passed since her last call to Ben seemed like five. As the time had dragged on, Dan had given up doodling on an art pad and was now engrossed in a magazine. Hope had alternated between pacing and thumbing through the hotel's tourist information. Finally she'd shrugged, taken a sheaf of papers from her briefcase and begun working on another of her accounts.

Jill had spent the entire hour staring moodily out the window, her chin in her hands, thinking. Would Ben really switch agencies because of her? Surely he was too professional for that, but perhaps her picture of the imperturbable businessman was a fallacy. After all, she'd known him only a few days. Perhaps she didn't know him at all.

When would he call? She checked the clock again. Only three minutes had gone by since she'd last looked. "I'm going to call him again," she announced and reached for the phone.

This time her effort was rewarded with, "Mr. Abrams is out of the office."

"Where can I reach him?"

She noticed a slight hesitation before the woman said, "He just left and he had several places to go. I don't know his exact schedule. He should be calling in, though. May I give him a message?"

Making an effort to keep the frustration out of her voice, Jill repeated her earlier message and hung up. "Damn!" she muttered.

She waited until just before noon, then tried again. She wasn't surprised that this time Ben's secretary recognized her voice. "I'm sorry, Ms. Levin. He hasn't called in and I don't think he'll be back in the office any time soon. I'll have him call you first thing tomorrow."

Jill didn't bother telling her that tomorrow would be too late. The Carnaby and Ross team would be catching an eight a.m. plane to New York.

Hope looked up as Jill put the phone down. "Drop it, Jill. Calling him isn't going to change things."

"Yeah," Dan agreed. "Be philosophical. You win some, you lose some. It's tough to lose your first time out, but you'll have other chances." He rose, stretched and ambled to the door. "Anyone for lunch?" Neither Hope nor Jill took him up on his invitation, so with a wave over his shoulder, he left.

"Dan's right, you know," Hope said.

Jill leaned against the headboard. "I suppose so, but damn, this hurts."

"Why do I have the feeling that the hurt has nothing to do with Carnaby and Ross?"

Jill's laugh was dry. "Because you're perceptive, or because I'm transparent. You're right. I feel bad about the account, but I feel worse because of what happened between Ben and me." She fingered the pendant he'd given her. "Darn, Hope. Everything was going so well, and then we had this stupid misunderstanding, and I guess it's over between us."

"Are you going to leave it at that? Just take this lying down?"

"Lord, you sound like my grandmother."

"Wise beyond my years, huh? Thanks a lot," Hope said with a fake bow. "Seriously, what are you going to do?"

"Darned if I know." Jill sighed. "I guess the next step is to leave a message on his home answering machine."

When the recording came on and she heard his deep voice, the voice she'd heard whispering her name in the throes of passion, she had to fight back tears. Swallowing hard, she said, "Ben, this is Jill. I'm leaving early tomorrow morning, but I'd like to talk to you before I go. Please call me."

But she didn't have much hope.

BEN DROVE AIMLESSLY, giving himself time to calm down. Thoughts crowded his mind, emotions surged within him. The account, his job, his relationship with Jill—everything in his life seemed to have erupted like a massive volcano within the past few hours. What did he do now?

He realized that sometime during his mindless wandering, he'd turned toward the riverfront. Now he made a deliberate decision to follow that instinctive inclination. He'd always been drawn to water, found riverside views both relaxing and inspiring.

He turned into Sawyer Point, parked and headed for the path along the river. Despite snow on the ground and the chill breeze from the water, Ben enjoyed being outdoors. He walked slowly, appreciating the view of the broad Ohio, the Kentucky shore across the water, a silver jet flying westward past Mount Adams against a cloudless blue sky. He took a deep breath of cool, moist air. His nerves began to settle, his jumbled thoughts to calm.

Methodically he considered his options. His anger at McMinn was still strong, the man's personal problems notwithstanding. He supposed he could bury his feelings, set things right with McMinn and go on as before. Did he want to? *No,* he told himself emphatically. The idea of crawling into McMinn's office, his tail between his legs, with some false apology for his harsh words this morning was abhorrent to him. Okay, that was out. What else could he do?

If the scuttlebutt from Susan was accurate, and it usually was, then McMinn might soon be on his way out. Ben could be in line for his boss's position. Was that what he wanted? More money, more responsibility, more prestige went with the job. All were appealing, but he couldn't honestly say he wanted to gain them by sitting in McMinn's chair... and that possibility was still hypothetical.

That brought him to the third and most attractive prospect—opening his own agency with Alan Jeffreys. He'd been dissatisfied with his work at Wellner for some time. At first he'd felt a vague unease, then as his conflicts with McMinn had increased, unease had become displeasure. And today his antagonism toward his boss had boiled over.

He'd been longing for the opportunity to do things his own way, the challenge to try his own wings. Here was his chance. Why not take it? Grab for the brass ring?

He had the means. Alan had already looked into financing their start-up and had assured Ben that funds were available. Ben had enough money saved to tide him over the first year or so while the agency was getting established. All that remained now was a yes to Alan and a letter of resignation to Wellner.

Ben paused and leaned against a tree. He stood for a long time, lost in thought. "Decision time," he said, repeating Alan's words of last week. He took a deep breath and pushed himself away from the trunk. "Okay, Abrams. Now or never. Go for it."

He turned back the way he had come, his stride purposeful, assured. When he reached his car, he checked the time. Alan should be back from lunch. At the thought of lunch, Ben heard his stomach growl. He'd celebrate his decision with a burger at the Coach and Four, call Alan from there.

He felt good about the conclusion he'd come to. He only wished he felt as positive about his relationship with Jill. He had to bring that to a conclusion, too. He couldn't just cut his losses and run, leave things up in the air, or could he?

Uncertain what to do about Jill, he drove across to the Kentucky side of the river and headed for an old house that had been converted to a small restaurant. He ordered, then pulled a quarter from his pocket and went to the pay phone he'd spotted in an alcove near the back. Fortunately, he was put through to Alan immediately. "Alan, it's Ben."

"Hey, buddy, what's going on?"

For a moment Ben felt as if he were standing on a high diving board, teetering on the edge. He took the plunge. "I'm drafting a resignation letter to Wellner. When do you want to get started?"

An instant of disbelief, then excitement zinged across the phone lines. "My God, is that a yes?"

"Damn right."

"What happened?" Alan asked. "I thought you were still being cautious."

Ben gave him a brief rundown on the events of the day, then asked, "Can we get together before you leave for Denver?"

"Sure. Tomorrow night. Come for dinner."

"I'll be there. Meanwhile, I'm going to turn in my resignation. Thirty days."

"Sounds good to me."

Sounded good to Ben, too. In fact, the idea sounded terrific. He hung up the phone and went back to the table, where his hamburger was waiting. It was the best burger he'd had in years.

JILL DUMPED HER SUITCASE on the bed and began to pack. Last night and this morning had left her feeling battered and numb, but she couldn't sit around like a zombie forever. She'd had enough of waiting for Ben to return her call. Half an hour ago she'd decided to end her telephone vigil, check out of the hotel and spend the rest of the afternoon with her family.

So what if he didn't call, she thought as she yanked a skirt off the hanger and tossed it into the bag. Hope and Dan were right. Nothing could be done to change the decision about the account. If the Steak Expectations executives didn't know a good ad campaign when they saw one, too bad for them, she decided. If they chose an inferior agency with a lousy idea, then they'd just have to suffer the consequences.

As for her, she'd have another pitch to make one day soon. Her promotion wasn't lost, just postponed.

She slammed the suitcase shut and dragged it to the door. The bag was heavy, and she should call for a bellhop, but rage gave her strength and she decided to carry it down herself.

She glanced at the telephone once more before she left the room, then shook her head. She'd made more than enough calls to Ben.

A few minutes later she left the hotel garage and headed out of the downtown area. Instead of going directly to her parents' house, though, she decided to take a last drive through the city.

Automatically she turned toward Mount Adams Park. She'd always been attracted to hills, to the feeling of height, the panoramic views. She'd missed them in New York, where the only comparable views were from the tops of skyscrapers.

When she reached her destination, she pulled to the side of the road, buttoned her coat and got out of the car. The city lay below her with the river alongside, shimmering in the afternoon sunlight.

Only a few days ago she'd dreaded her trip to Cincinnati; now she hated the thought of leaving. She'd become reacquainted with her family this week, and she intended to maintain that connection. She would come home again soon, perhaps in the spring during Passover.

She'd see her family then, but not Ben. That hurt, would continue to hurt for a long time. But she had to face reality. And now, while she stood in the calming presence of the hills, was the time. Here, where the height distanced her from the city below, perhaps she could achieve some detachment from the events of the past day.

Ben's inability to deal with her past—that was *his* problem. She could do nothing but allow him to come to terms with it. She didn't see the situation as he did. He viewed it as lack of trust; she thought of it as lack of time. They'd known each other such a short while. Their relationship hadn't grown slowly but exploded overnight.

Though he had confided in her about Karen, Jill knew she'd have needed much more time before she could have faced telling Ben about her own past. How much time, she wasn't certain. Maybe months, maybe even years. What had happened instead was unfortunate but couldn't be undone.

And the Steak Expectations account. That was hard to take. Bubbi had told her to fight for Ben. If he was the kind of man who would vent his anger at her by sabotaging her agency, then she didn't want to fight for him.

"I don't need him," she told herself and vowed right here, right now to put him behind her.

That was easier said than done. The memory of this week would remain with her, a slow-healing wound, raw and aching. She wondered how long it would take the ache to fade...or if it ever would. She blinked back a tear, telling herself the wind had caused it. Then she turned and walked slowly back to her car. Once inside, she headed home.

She dreaded telling her family that not only had her agency failed to capture the Steak Expectations account, but she and Ben had ended the relationship that had seemed so promising a scant twenty-four hours ago.

Moments later she sat in the den with her sisters, her mother and her grandmother around her. Suddenly, sharing her bad news didn't seem so difficult. She took a breath and simply told them about the day's events. Instantly her family rallied around her.

"What a rat! He doesn't know what he's giving up," Sherry said with such fierce loyalty that Jill had to laugh.

Lisa agreed. "And I liked the guy. Obviously, I was taken in by looks and charm. He's a jerk."

"What's a jerk, Mommy?" Whitney piped up from the corner where she had been playing so quietly with her miniature dollhouse that they'd forgotten she was in the room.

"Little pitchers—" Sherry murmured.

"—Have big ears," Lisa finished. "Nothing, honey. It's just an expression."

"What's a 'spression?"

"A funny way of saying something."

"Is Aunt Jill's friend Ben a jerk?"

Lisa was saved from answering when Kevin tore into the room, skidded to a halt in response to his mother's warning frown and said to Whitney, "Wanna play Star Wars with me and Jared?"

Clearly flattered to be asked, Whitney jumped up. Then she gave her brother a measuring look and said, "Can I be the princess?"

Kevin hesitated. "Why don't you be a space pirate?"

Whitney sat down. "Uh-uh."

Faced with the loss of an essential player, Kevin gave in. "Okay, you can be the princess...the first time." Whitney got up again. "Then you can..." Their voices trailed off as they left.

"She's no pushover," Lisa said, smiling fondly after her children. "But back to the jerk—"

"Have you talked to him, Jill?" her mother asked.

When Jill shook her head, Sherry asked, "Do you want to? Seems to me he has two strikes against him. First he blew up about the baby and then he changed his mind about the ad campaign."

"I would like to talk to him," Jill said, "and I've tried. I've left a dozen messages, but he hasn't called back. Maybe I'll try him again tonight. I'd like some closure on this."

Bubbi, who hadn't said much until now, looked at her thoughtfully. "So what have you learned from this, Jill?"

Jill considered. What had she learned? *That men aren't to be trusted? That they always betray you?* That was one conclusion she could have drawn. But, no, she didn't think that was what she'd carry away with her, not this time.

She looked at Bubbi. "That I'm a survivor," she said slowly. "That I took a risk ánd lost, but—" Her voice surer now, she continued, "But that I can love, and someday I will again."

Bubbi nodded, evidently satisfied with Jill's response. "Someday, God willing, the right person will come knocking at your door."

Jill smiled through a veil of tears. "And I'll be right there to open it," she promised.

BEN GOT OUT of the elevator and strode down the hall toward his office.

Susan looked up in surprise when he passed her desk. "I didn't expect you back. Your phone's been ringing off the wall."

Ben held up a hand. "Hold off on the messages for a few minutes. I need to take care of a couple of things."

Actually, he had only two items on his agenda, and the first was to write the letter of resignation. He sat at his desk, reached for a legal pad and drafted a brief letter. He said nothing about his disagreement with McMinn, only that he was leaving to pursue other interests. Then he took care of the next item of business, a letter to the CEO protesting the decision to award the Steak Expectations contract to Tolar. He omitted any reference to Mc-

Minn's double-dealing. If the Wellner executives wanted to investigate further, they'd find out for themselves.

When he finished, he rose and, feeling as if he had crossed his personal Rubicon, he went out and handed Susan the letters. "Type these up for me, would you?"

"Sure." She glanced at the first sheet and her eyes widened. "Ben!"

"Yeah, I'm leaving."

"You're sure?"

He nodded emphatically. "I've had it with McMinn, Susan, up to here. Even if he goes, I don't want to be here anymore."

"What are you going to do?"

"I've got some ideas."

"Well, whatever they are, I wish you the best of luck."

"Thanks," he told her. "I'll sign both of these as soon as you have them ready."

He went back into his office and sat at his desk. A pile of messages lay in front of him. He'd better get to them before he left for the day. After all, he still worked for Wellner. He rifled through the slips, looking for any that were urgent.

"Jill Levin. Jill Levin." Good God, he still hadn't called Jill. What must she be thinking? Quickly he checked the phone number and punched it in.

"Hello."

Not Jill. Must be—"Hope, this is Ben Abrams. May I speak to Jill?"

A pause, just long enough to let him know Hope's feelings, then a cool, "You reached my room. She isn't here."

"Okay, I'll call her room."

"She checked out a couple of hours ago."

He felt his heart plummet. "Checked out? Where is she? Has she gone back to New York?" At Hope's silence, he said, "Look, I have to talk to her. I have a lot of things to explain . . . to all of you, but I need to talk to Jill first. Can you tell me where she is?"

Hope's sigh was audible. "She's spending the night with her family. We're leaving in the morning."

Relief coursed through him. "Thanks," he said. "Thanks a lot."

He reached for the telephone directory, then changed his mind. As he'd told himself earlier, the phone wasn't the place to resolve things with Jill.

He got up just as Susan tapped on his door and opened it. "Here's your resignation letter. Three copies."

He signed two, directed her to route one to McMinn and one to the president of the Steak Expectations division, then tossed the other in his briefcase. Silently she handed him the letter to the CEO, and he signed that, too, then said, "Gotta go. I'll see you tomorrow."

A few minutes later, as he drove through downtown Cincinnati, he tried to decide what he would say to Jill. First, he owed her an apology for not contacting her earlier, then an explanation.

Would she listen to his account of what McMinn had done? Or would she be as illogically angry as . . . as *he'd* been when he'd overheard her talking with Mickey last night? He certainly hadn't listened to *her* explanation about the affair with Zimmerman or her reasons for not confiding her past. Maybe she would have told him eventually, but Ben knew he hadn't given her the benefit of the doubt.

He knew something else, too. He'd let Karen control his expectations about relationships. In fact, as Jill had pointed out last night, he'd let Karen dictate his feelings about himself.

What a rotten mess he'd made. He prayed Jill would be more understanding than he'd been. God, how he prayed she would. He loved her. He wanted her in his life, and if he had to fight to get her back, then he would. "Whatever it takes, I'll do," he vowed.

What could he do to show to her he was serious about a future between them? He considered and discarded plans. Nothing he could think of seemed sufficient to demonstrate his feelings. Nothing except—

With a sudden grin, his first of the day, he stepped on the brake. Ignoring the obscene gesture of the driver behind him, he made a U-turn into a shopping center. His brakes squealed as he came to an abrupt stop. He was out of the car in an instant, slamming the door behind him, and jogging across the parking lot.

JILL SAT CURLED UP on her parents' living-room couch, leafing through a magazine. Her mother and Sherry were in the kitchen. Lisa, who was returning to Omaha tomorrow, was upstairs packing. Kevin, as usual, was in the family room engrossed in cartoons.

Across the room her father leaned back in his favorite armchair reading the evening paper. Bubbi sat on the other end of the couch, knitting a blanket for Whitney's doll as Whitney looked on. Bubbi's fingers flew, her knitting needles clicked. The sound was familiar, soothing, a sound Jill had listened to throughout her childhood.

The scene was tranquil, and though her wounds were still fresh, she felt some of that peace seeping into her.

The doorbell startled her.

"Must be Paul Foley," her father said, putting his paper aside.

"Don't get up, Dad. I'll answer it," Jill said, already crossing the room.

"Tell Paul the pipe wrench he wanted to borrow is in the garage," her father called.

"Okay." She pulled the door open. "Mr. Foley, the—" She stopped, dumbfounded, staring at Ben. What had Bubbi just said about the right man knocking at her door? Her heart began to thud.

"Jill, can I talk to you?"

"Is that Paul?" came her father's voice from the living room.

"No, Dad. It's for me," she called over her shoulder. "Come in," she told Ben.

He glanced past her into the living room and shook his head. "I'd rather talk to you in private. Why don't we go for a ride?"

Jill opened the coat closet and got out her jacket. "Okay." She turned and stepped back into the living room. "Ben is here. We're going out for a while."

Bubbi looked up, eyes twinkling, and Jill knew that she, too, remembered the remark she'd made earlier.

Outside, Jill pulled her jacket tight around her. The sun was almost gone, and the evening promised to be cold. Yet when Ben motioned toward his car, she shook her head. "Let's talk here." She motioned to the two chairs on the porch. They sat facing one another. Jill waited.

Ben took a deep breath. "I owe you an explanation for this morning and for last night."

"Yes, I think you do."

"Let's start with today," he said. "That one's easier."

"All right."

"Jill," he said, leaning forward earnestly, "after your presentation on Friday, I had no doubt that Carnaby and Ross had the slickest ad campaign I'd seen in a long time."

"Then why—"

"Let me finish," he said. "I made my decision, left a memo for Frank and went home believing you—Carnaby and Ross—had the contract. When I got to the office this morning, I learned that Frank had reversed that decision and given the account to Tolar."

"But the decision was yours. Couldn't you call him on it? Or go over his head?"

"Don't you think I wanted to? But Frank had already gotten in touch with Tolar. And the chain of command at Steak Expectations gives him that authority. I can't do a darn thing except tell you I'm sorry."

Jill tried to smile. "I guess in this business you win some, you lose some," she said, quoting Dan. "But I won't pretend missing out on the contract doesn't hurt."

"Believe me, Jill, I'm hurting, too. Because I found out McMinn had a personal agenda in this." Briefly he explained what he'd learned from Susan.

Although she felt better knowing McMinn was responsible, that Ben hadn't turned on her after all, Jill was stunned at his story. "But that's...that's unethical," she sputtered. "A conflict of interest."

"You're right. I'm as mad as you are. So I've done the only thing I can. I've registered a complaint with the CEO and I've resigned."

For a moment Jill thought she'd misunderstood. He'd resigned! Good Lord, that was a serious step. An irrevocable decision. "But...but what will you do?"

"Go into business." At her look of utter disbelief, he smiled. "Alan Jeffreys and I have been talking for some time about starting our own ad agency, but I've been vacillating. I guess I've been waiting for something to push me over the edge. Well, this was it. I turned in my resignation this afternoon."

"Ben, I don't know what to say."

"For starters, you could wish me good luck," he said, smiling at her.

"You know I do."

"And you could come with us."

Jill frowned, again wondering if she'd heard him correctly. "I . . . I don't understand."

"We'll need a top-notch creative director. I can't think of anyone who'd fill the bill better than you. After Alan met you the other day, he agreed."

Speechless, Jill got up and walked to the edge of the porch. Her hand moving restlessly on the rail, she stared out into the yard, watching the fading sunset.

Of course she was flattered that Ben and Alan would offer her the position. She knew she could do an outstanding job. She also knew that a comparable opportunity was unlikely to come along any time soon.

But a job offer wasn't what she wanted from Ben. She wanted . . . much more. He'd come over here to make her a business offer, hadn't said anything about a relationship beyond a professional one. And that would never be enough for her. No, she thought, blinking back a tear, she'd just gotten her hopes up, only to have them dashed in her face.

How could she possibly take the job? How could she work with Ben? Seeing him every day, all the while wondering how he spent his nights, would be pure agony.

She turned, hoping she could keep her voice steady when she gave him her answer. "Ben, thank you. I appreciate the compliment, but I'd better decline."

She saw the disappointment in his eyes. "Why?" he asked.

"Please, Ben." She turned away again. "It just wouldn't work, that's all."

She sensed him come up behind her. "I think we could work very well together if you'd give us a chance." His words were soft, seductive.

Jill knew she had to be honest. "I couldn't, not after . . . after all that's happened between us."

She felt his hands drop gently to her shoulders. "Turn around," he said. "Please."

Slowly she turned and looked into his eyes. Dark, filled with longing, they held promises she was afraid to believe.

"You're thinking of last night," he said softly.

She shivered. "Yes." He took her cold hands in his and rubbed them gently, warming them with his touch. He tried to pull her closer but she held back.

"I acted like a fool last night," he said. "I almost gave up the most important person in the world to me. I love you, Jill."

He tightened his hold on her hands, but still she resisted. "In spite of . . . of the baby?"

"The baby itself was never the issue for me. I was upset because you didn't tell me." He hesitated for a moment, his expression open and vulnerable. "What I said last night was a knee-jerk reaction. I'd just spoken to Karen. Seeing her again reminded me of that old wound. Then when I saw you with Mickey, I went off like a bomb."

Jill smiled. "The first night you came over, Sherry said you reminded her of a load of dynamite."

His brows shot up. "I'll have to talk to her about that later. But back to last night—I was unfair to you. Here you've listened to my explanations about McMinn and about Karen, but I didn't do the same for you. What a bastard! Can you...can you think about forgiving me?"

"I already have."

With a groan, he pulled her against him and now she went willingly into his arms. His lips came down to claim hers, possessively, triumphantly. "I didn't think I'd ever hold you again," he whispered.

"I didn't, either." Glorying in the power of his kiss, she returned it with all the passion he'd awakened in her. To hear his voice, to feel him against her, to touch him again was heaven. When they broke apart she told him what was in her heart. "I love you, Ben."

"Enough to marry me?"

An electric charge of excitement and love shot through her. "Yes."

"Enough to work with me?"

"Even that." She laughed.

He looked into her eyes, his own dark and serious. "I want to have children someday."

"So do I."

"I know they won't take the place of the child you gave up—"

"No, but they won't have to. They'll have their own places in our hearts," Jill said softly.

Ben nodded. He lifted her off her feet and hugged her tight. "You've given me the best Chanukah gift I've ever had." Then he set her back down. "I have something for you, too," he told her, reaching into his jacket pocket. "I'd planned to ask you to marry me last night, but my craziness got in the way. If you'd said yes, I imagined us celebrating the new account and shopping for a ring to-day. Since that didn't materialize, I did the best I could."

He handed her something round. Jill frowned. The sun had gone down completely, and in the darkness of the covered porch she couldn't make out what the object was. It looked like a plastic egg.

She held it up to her eyes. A plastic bubble from a grocery store vending machine, with a ring inside. She began to laugh.

"Don't laugh." Ben pretended to be offended. "It's your 'gagement ring."

Still chuckling, Jill broke open the container and held out her hand so Ben could slip the ring on her finger. "I love the ring. I love *you*." She kissed him again.

He drew back and grinned at her. "Shall we tell your family our news?"

"They'll be thrilled."

When they reached the front door, she pushed the bell three times. "That'll get their attention."

She opened the door just as her father hurried into the entry hall. "Jill, why are you ringing the bell? Is something wrong?"

"No, something's right." Tugging Ben by his arm, she strode into the living room. Her mother and Sherry arrived from the kitchen. From upstairs came Lisa's voice. "What's going on down there?"

"Come down," Jill called. "I have an announcement." When Lisa appeared, Jill held up her hand to show off the ring and said, "Ben and I are getting married."

Squeals of excitement, shouts of congratulations filled the room. Ben's arm was pumped by everyone in the family; Jill was embraced and kissed.

Her mother's eyes misted as she put her arms around Jill. "No more living out my dreams. You have *your* dream now," she said.

Whitney held her arms up for a hug, then examined Jill's ring with interest. "It's a ruby like mine," she said, pleased. "Are you and Ben 'gaged like Miss Marcia? Will you get married, too?" When Jill nodded, Whitney gave her a puzzled frown. "But Mommy said Ben was a j—"

"Whitney!" Lisa grabbed her daughter's hand. "Why don't we go get Kevin and tell him it's time to light the candles?"

Ben raised a brow, but Jill laughed and shook her head. Someday...someday far in the future she'd tell Ben what Whitney had started to say and why. But not now.

When Lisa returned with the children, they all gathered around while Joel Levin recited the blessing and lit the Chanukah candles.

The last night. All eight candles stood glowing in their holders. Jill moved closer to Ben, loving the feel of his arm around her, the knowledge that he was hers. One of the first things they'd purchase as man and wife, she decided, would be a menorah, a symbol of all the Chanukahs they would share for the rest of their lives. This Chanukah, their first, had truly been a festival of light. Jill felt that glow reflected in her heart.

"Can we have our presents now?" Kevin asked.

"In a minute," Joel answered. He left the room and returned a few moments later carrying a tray of filled glasses—wine for the adults, grape juice for the children. "Now," he said, raising his glass, "a toast to Ben and Jill. *L'chaim!*" The others, even Whitney and Kevin, echoed his words.

Jill and Ben turned to one another. *"L'chaim,"* Ben said softly and took a sip of wine.

Jill nodded and repeated the words with all the love in her heart—for Ben, for the life they would build together, for the lives they would create. *"L'chaim,"* she said. "To life!"

ROMANCE IS A YEARLONG EVENT!

Celebrate the most romantic day of the year with MY VALENTINE! (February)

CRYSTAL CREEK
When you come for a visit Texas-style, you won't want to leave! (March)

Celebrate the joy, excitement and adjustment that comes with being JUST MARRIED! (April)

Go back in time and discover the West as it was meant to be . . . UNTAMED— Maverick Hearts! (July)

LINGERING SHADOWS
New York Times bestselling author Penny Jordan brings you her latest blockbuster. Don't miss it! (August)

BACK BY POPULAR DEMAND!!!
Calloway Corners, involving stories of four sisters coping with family, business and romance! (September)

FRIENDS, FAMILIES, LOVERS
Join us for these heartwarming love stories that evoke memories of family and friends. (October)

Capture the magic and romance of Christmas past with HARLEQUIN HISTORICAL CHRISTMAS STORIES! (November)

WATCH FOR FURTHER DETAILS IN ALL HARLEQUIN BOOKS!

HAPPY VALENTINE'S DAY

James Rafferty had only forty-eight hours, and he wanted to make the most of them.... Helen Emerson had never had a Valentine's Day like this before!

Celebrate this special day for lovers, with a very special book from American Romance!

#473 ONE MORE VALENTINE
by Anne Stuart

Next month, Anne Stuart and American Romance have a delightful Valentine's Day surprise in store just for you. All the passion, drama—even a touch of mystery—you expect from this award-winning author.

Don't miss American Romance
#473 ONE MORE VALENTINE!

Also look for Anne Stuart's short story, "Saints Alive," in Harlequin's MY VALENTINE 1993 collection.

Jared: He'd had the courage to fight in Vietnam. But did he have the courage to fight for the woman he loved?

THE SOLDIER OF FORTUNE
By Kelly Street
Temptation #421, December

All men are not created equal. Some are rough around the edges. Tough-minded but tenderhearted. Incredibly sexy. The tempting fulfillment of every woman's fantasy.

When it's time to fight for what they believe in, to win that special woman, our Rebels and Rogues are heroes at heart. Twelve Rebels and Rogues, one each month in 1992, only from Harlequin Temptation.

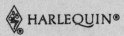

1993

The most romantic day of the year is here! Escape into the exquisite world of love with MY VALENTINE 1993. What better way to celebrate Valentine's Day than with this very romantic, sensuous collection of four original short stories, written by some of Harlequin's most popular authors.

**ANNE STUART
JUDITH ARNOLD
ANNE McALLISTER
LINDA RANDALL WISDOM**

**THIS VALENTINE'S DAY, DISCOVER ROMANCE
WITH MY VALENTINE 1993**

Available in February wherever Harlequin Books are sold.   VAL93

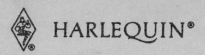 **HARLEQUIN®**

THE TAGGARTS OF TEXAS!

Harlequin's Ruth Jean Dale brings you
THE TAGGARTS OF TEXAS!

Those Taggart men—strong, sexy and hard to resist...

You've met Jesse James Taggart in FIREWORKS!
Harlequin Romance #3205 (July 1992)

And Trey Smith—he's THE RED-BLOODED YANKEE!
Harlequin Temptation #413 (October 1992)

Now meet Daniel Boone Taggart in SHOWDOWN!
Harlequin Romance #3242 (January 1993)

And finally the Taggarts who started it all—in LEGEND!
Harlequin Historical #168 (April 1993)

Read all the Taggart romances!
Meet all the Taggart men!

Available wherever Harlequin Books are sold.